Bellemere

A Novel

by

Walter Allen

Synchronicity
press

InSync Communications LLC and Synchronicity Press
2445 River Tree Circle
Sanford, Florida 32771
http://www.insynchronicity.com

ISBN: 0-9673439-5-X

First Synchronicity Press Edition
10 9 8 7 6 5 4 3 2

Synchronicity Press books are available at special discounts when purchased in bulk for use in seminars, as premiums or in sales promotions. Special editions or book excerpts can also be created to specification. For details, contact InSync Communications LLC at the address above.

Cover Design by Jonathan Pennell
Book Design/Typesetting by Stephanie Murphy

Printed in the United States of America

Dedication

Bellemere is dedicated to my wife, Bettie.
Without her inspiration, patience, and assistance,
the book would not have been completed.

Special Acknowledgments

Major Frank Manuel, 1st Infantry Division, U. S. Army, retired; a combat veteran of World War II, who fought the battles I wrote about.

Kay Edwards Hall and Betsy Holloway, who so superbly edited my manuscript.

Acknowledgments

Nancy Abberger, Frank Allen, Bonnie Allen, Bill Allen, Red Carruthers, William C. Cooper, Ph.D., Wayne Cooper, Jack Fox, Leon Handley, Pete Hartsaw, Major General Ronald O. Harrison, Jesse Holbrook, Jack Hearn, Doris Manuel, Bill McCree, Professor Tom Mack, Ken McCall, Louise and Jack Nants, Win Pendleton, Clarence Peterson, Roger E. Phillips, M.D., Roger V. Phillips, Tom Quinby, James C. Robinson, Wallace R. Roy, Ph.D., Thomas I. Scott, M.D., Iris Scott, Darrell Shea, M.D., Ann Shea, Dick and Cree Sherman, Carl Sutphin, Henry Swanson, Robert E. Umphrey, Ph.D., and Sara Van Arsdale.

Bellemere

A Novel

1

Peachtree Creek
July 20, 1864

Silas Taylor owned no slaves, never wanted any. Dirt farmers in Bibb County picked their own cotton, slaughtered their own hogs, and mended their own fences, but there he stood, at the center of a mile-wide front of Confederate infantry, facing General George H. Thomas's United States Army rumbling across wooden bridges at Peachtree Creek. With Atlanta at his back, Silas realized his army was outnumbered by Yankees committed to killing every Rebel and freeing every slave in Georgia. He believed that defending the "Hub of the South" was not a stand in defense of slavery; it was a matter of survival. The Federals were there to destroy him and his army's primary storehouse of food and ammunition. Without Atlanta, the war was lost.

Silas gazed across a grassy field gradually rising to a crest a half-mile away. Beyond lay the coming battleground, unknown and unwanted. If he were home, cotton would be knee-high and Pa would be working him half to death, but he'd be eating good food, and nobody would be shooting at him. He looked down at his bruised bare feet, remembering the first boots Pa had bought him rawhide, matching Pa's weathered face. A half-smile crossed his lips, then quickly vanished as bugles blared; it was the same call he had heard at Chickamauga, Lookout Mountain, and Missionary Ridge. I'm here 'cause everybody else is here, he thought. Nobody gonna cut and run—nobody. He licked his lips and swallowed.

In a gravelly voice, tall and horse-faced Sergeant Tom Willis commanded, "Fix bayonets! Prepare to move out."

Silas's fingers froze as he struggled to affix the bayonet to his rifle. "Ain't that just like General Hood," he mumbled. "We gonna attack the bluebellies." So far he had survived each battle with only minor wounds; but deep inside, he felt his luck would not hold.

Willis frowned as he watched Silas struggle and said, "Get hold of yourself, man."

The paralysis in Silas's fingers departed as the bayonet snapped into place. He squared his broad shoulders and with the back of his hand wiped sweat from his black whiskers. "Don't worry none about me, I'm ready." A doe scampered across the field, disappearing in the trees beyond the clearing — chased, thought Silas, by some hound of hell, emptying the field, preparing a graveyard in Georgia clay.

Red battle flags whipped in the hot wind as the Confederates moved forward toward Peachtree Creek. When Silas reached the crest of the field, he saw formations of bluecoats in long lines below and mounted Union officers wearing black plumed hats dashing about. With a deafening roar, Federal batteries opened fire, tearing holes in the advancing rebel line. There were no barricades or trenches, no places of protection. Silas feared something would break inside his skull. The pace quickened as the Rebel yell went up; then, like a tidal wave against a cliff, ranks collided and screams filled the air.

At the edge of the battlefield, along a tree line of tall pines, a column of Confederate cavalry galloped undetected, flanking the Federals. With sabers flashing in the sun they attacked, slashing and maiming. A Rebel trooper tore an American flag from a color bearer's hands, then shot him in the chest with his revolver. Holding high his trophy, he galloped away with others back to the Rebel line.

Now, Confederate batteries opened, raking Union ranks in withering fire. The field became a slaughter house as men and horses fell, soaking the earth with blood. At the center of the field, a Federal soldier knocked Willis to the ground with his rifle butt. Silas turned and rammed his bayonet through the Yankee's back. He withdrew, wheeled and fired, hitting another soldier in the face. The fallen man's head became a broken melon.

Near a thick stand of rhododendron, Sergeant Willis cried out, "Over here! Over here!" Silas and eight others knelt and fired at a squad of charging Yankees. When the bullet hit, it felt like a horse kick in the chest. Silas fell. Gasping, blood soaked, and dizzy from the stench of gun smoke, he crawled a few yards and collapsed. When Willis lifted him and carried him to the rear, Silas's lips moved, but he could not make a sound. "Don't try to talk," said Willis.

The battle raged until darkness fell over Peachtree Creek. The Confederate plan to divide the Union army had failed. In the distance, over tree tops, a yellow moon rose over three thousand bodies. The only sound was water falling over rocks in the creek.

Stretcher bearers moved Silas to a white canvas tent; there, by the light of a flickering lamp, Silas screamed as a half-bald surgeon with deep-set eyes and hollow cheeks probed deeply in his chest. Blood spurted as the doctor removed the bullet, sewed up the cavity, wiped his hands on his long, bloodstained coat, dressed the wound and hurried off to another bleeding soldier. The night seemed endless. With each breath, Silas felt as though a wooden stake jabbed in and out of his chest, stabbing his life away. He thought of Fowler, Morris, and Jackson, all killed at Lookout Mountain. Soon it would be over. He, too, would die. Semiconscious, he was wrapped in a quilt and transferred to a makeshift hospital in Atlanta. There nurses worked through the night, bandaging, feeding, and reassuring wounded soldiers lying in the lobby and in the hallways of the old wooden structure.

Silas moaned as soldiers placed him in a narrow space between two dying men. Stripped to the waist, he lay wallowing in blood- soaked bandages, crying "water — water."

Nurse Mary Cummings heard his cry. She cradled him in her arms and whispered, "It's all right. It's all right." She placed a canteen to his lips and watched him gulp the water.

His eyes opened slowly. He did not notice her mousy hair, framing a broad nose, thin lips, and a square jaw. He saw an angel. He smiled and fell into a deep sleep.

At dawn, Silas opened his eyes. It was no illusion: his "Angel" stood before him.

"Wake up! Wake up!" she cried. "You've been asleep too long."

Silas stared, for a moment; then he turned to look at wounded men lying beside him. Green flies flew near his face and the sweet-sour odor of gangrene filled his nostrils.

"Open wide," she said. "It's oatmeal, all we have."

He shuddered. "Can't. Where am I?"

"No time for questions — eat."

As she fed him, he mumbled, "Stay with me."

She shook her head. "Too many wounded."

"Just a little while."

A faint smile appeared on her face.

"What's your name?" he asked.

"Mary. Mary Cummings."

September 1, 1864. The bombardment of Atlanta finally lifted and like the quiet eye of a great storm, silence fell over the city. But shortly before midnight, a series of cataclysmic explosions echoed through the streets, shaking the hospital; then the clatter of horses and the rumble of rolling wagons began and continued throughout the night. Silas knew what it meant, his army had destroyed their powder and withdrawn, leaving no protection for those who remained.

When dawn came, Silas saw fear in the faces of wounded men huddling helplessly on the floor. He sat with his back to the wall, knowing he must leave. Mary would help, he knew it. He had felt her warmth when she fed him, when she dressed his wound, and especially when he called her "Angel."

Mary's hands trembled as she offered stale bread to Silas and whispered in his ear. "Our army has destroyed everything and left Atlanta."

Silas nodded. "Yeah. The bluebellies will come and burn everything to the ground." His dark eyes locked on Mary's. "Take whatever medication you can hide in your bag and offer it to anyone with a horse and wagon. You and I must leave now."

"W-where will we go?"

"Anywhere! Go now, before it's too late."

Mary filled her bag with amber bottles of morphia and dashed to the street which was filled with people frantically packing possessions in wagons; others ran aimlessly in every direction. An elderly man told Mary the only escape route was the road to LaGrange. She offered morphia to drivers as she ran from wagon to wagon, but no one listened. Near the south barricade to the city she climbed on a buggy driven by a black woman, but was whipped until she fell to the street.

"Get in the wagon." The unmistakable voice of her father boomed above the roar of rolling wagons. There in the dusty, clay street, holding the reins to his excited bay stallion, stood a giant whose face was ringed by copper hair.

"Daddy," she cried.

"Get in, girl. Get in."

"Daddy," she said, her skirt and hair blowing about in swirling wind, "there's a soldier. Help me with him. "

"Why, in heaven's name, one soldier?"

"I want to save him."

He stared for a moment, then nodded. "Get in — hurry."

As they drew near the hospital, bandaged and limping soldiers helped each other down steps leading to the street. "Go get him," said Mr. Cummings. "I can't leave the wagon."

Mary hurried to his bedroll; it was empty. "Silas," she shouted. Frantically she searched for him, then she found him crawling toward the exit. "Climb on my back," she cried.

Grimacing in pain, he shook his head. "Can't do it."

She rolled him in a quilt and dragged him to the street; there her father placed him in the wagon. They fell in line with wagons filled with old men and women, young mothers with children, and black nannies, all headed south. As they moved beyond the barricades, the odor of death filled the air. Broken wagons, furniture, and clothing, stained with red clay dust, were strewn along the road. When rain swept out of the west and pelted Silas's face, he remembered a rainy September day back home in Bibb County. Morris and Jackson had been there too. They had run home from school in the downpour, splashing, yelling, and laughing as they went. Bibb County ... fishing in the creek ... eating watermelon ... pulling Amanda's pigtails.

Silas smiled as the rain splashed on his skin. Mary reached for a coat to cover him, but he held her arm. "It feels so good," he said. Ten miles out, the clouds cleared away. Silas stared at the red glow in the darkening sky over Atlanta, wondering what had happened to his army, and how much longer the war could last.

At sunrise, William Cummings drove the wagon through a forest of dogwood, elm, and maple. Long shafts of light peered through branches, recreating a scene Silas remembered: light, through trees, bathing Ma's headstone at the little cemetery near the Baptist church. Pa had regularly whipped him, but Ma had rubbed ointment on his red marks. At her gravesite, Pa had stood rigidly beside him saying: "The Lord giveth and the Lord taketh away."

Mary took Silas's hand. "What you mumbling about?" He shook his head.

They entered Troup County and continued to the village of Hogansville. High on a hill overlooking a field of shoulder-high corn, stood Cumming's cabin. As Silas inhaled the smell of oakwood smoke drifting down the valley, mud-colored hounds yelped, jumped the rail fence, and raced down the clay road to meet the wagon.

When Mr. Cummings pulled up to the porch, Mary's mother ran from the cabin and threw her arms around her daughter. "You're safe! Thank God he found you, baby."

Cummings placed his hand on his wife's shoulder. "Surprise, Mama — wounded soldier boy."

Her eyes opened wide. "Who is he?"

Mary wrung her hands as she faced her mother. "His name is Silas."

Mrs. Cummings paused, then nodded. "Bring him inside."

At one end of the cabin's largest room was a massive stone fireplace, larger than any Silas had seen. Black pots and pans hung from the chimney or sat near the hearth. A grandfather clock with chains and weights of bright brass rested in the corner of the pine flooring. A small fire flickered in the hearth, and the aroma of baking bread wafted past Silas's nose. For the first time since Peachtree Creek, he was really hungry.

"Put him on the sofa," said Bertha Cummings.

Mary redressed his wound, then cooked bacon, eggs, and poured hot coffee for Silas. When he had eaten, she placed a blanket over him. He reached out and touched her arm, then closed his eyes and slept.

Bertha drew herself up to the full height of her five foot-two frame and asked, "Who's going to tell me about him?"

Mr. Cummings shrugged as he ate bacon.

Mary stared at the fire. "Can't explain it. Out of two hundred wounded men, he was special." She smiled and rubbed her arms. "He called me Angel."

Bertha's eyelids narrowed. "If the Yankees come and find him, they'll kill him and burn us out."

Mary lowered her head. "I know."

"You know and yet you brought him here?"

Mary placed her fingers to her lips.

Bertha's voice softened. "Well, if they come, we'll hide him in the cellar."

Weeks had gone by. Silas's strength had partially returned. He began milking "Molly," the only cow left on the Cummingses' place after the Yankees had slaughtered and roasted the other three. William Cummings had hidden Molly in the deep woods beyond the creek. "Now," he said, "it's up to her to supply the milk."

On Friday, Silas had gathered brown eggs from the hen house, fed table scraps to the hounds, and hauled water from the well. That morning he had bartered corn for coffee, salt, and sugar in LaGrange, brought it back, and tied up the gray mule. He sat on the big oak stump near the well and began to think. Could go back to the army, but the war's about over. Could go back home to Bibb County, but why? Folks dead — Yankees took everything. Could just leave and look for work, but where? He stood to leave when a fat brown squirrel ran up the stone wall of the well, sat on the edge of the bucket, drank water, then jumped down to the ground and fed on kernels of corn Bertha had placed in a wooden bowl. Mary's a good woman, he thought, and she saved my life. Marriage is the only thing that makes sense. He winked at the fat squirrel and then walked to the cabin as the autumn wind blew brown leaves about his feet.

After lunch, Silas sat near the fireplace on a burlap covered sofa and placed his arm around Mary's shoulder. "Never thought I'd be asking somebody to marry me, but that's what I'm doing. What do you think?"

She looked down as she spoke. "Hope you're not just trying to repay me."

"You and your mama and daddy been mighty good to me, but I'm asking you cause you're a fine woman, a woman that'll make me a good wife."

Mary raised her head and smiled. "Let's get married, Silas. You know I love you."

Bertha held the wedding under the big oak, near the creek, not far from the Cummingses' family graveyard. Uncle Jack and Aunt Mamie sat in chairs William brought down from the house; everyone else stood. Mary wore her mother's white wool dress, button-down shoes, and a white felt bonnet. Silas had put on the new shirt, black wool coat, pants, and high top shoes William had given him. When William fumbled with his gold pocket watch and scratched his beard, Bertha patted his hand. "Simmer down. Preacher will be here in good time."

Just before noon the silver-haired old preacher, with sideburns that met at the point of his chin, rode up on a tired-looking mule, slowly dismounted, and pulled a worn Bible from his saddle bag. Everyone took their places and waited while the preacher's arthritic fingers slowly turned pages. Silas looked at the bubbling creek, remembering the moment the bullet hit ... the night he almost died in Mary's arms ... the wagon trip out of Atlanta ... the rain....

"Do you?" Asked the preacher.

Silas turned and saw a white-clad angel standing beside him.

"Yes," he nodded. "Yes I do."

"Then I pronounce you man and wife."

*W*hen the war ended in the spring, thousands of Georgians walked home — gaunt soldiers returning to towns of rubble, burnt-out homes, and scorched fields, proud, unarmed men in gray rags, their cause defeated. Almost every family had lost either a father, son, or husband, their bodies molding in unmarked graves.

In Hogansville, Silas and William had labored all summer to grow enough corn and wheat to barter for beef, sugar, salt, and coffee. They cleared a plot of land at the crest of a ridge for the Taylors' cabin, cut pine logs for walls and flooring, and sawed oak for ceiling beams and doors. They took rocks from the creek to build the chimney and cut cedar shingles for the roof. The view from the porch of the cabin was the cornfield, and beyond that the Cummingses' place, nearly surrounded by oak trees. Silas drove the last nail in the pine railing of his porch, stood back and looked at his new home, then turned to William. "Thanks to you, we finished it just in time. Baby could come any day."

William rubbed his red whiskers. "Yeah, listen, Bertha and I saved enough to help with pots, pans, dishes, and the like."

Silas shook his head. "You didn't need to do that."

"Well, you and Mary are all we got."

Silas stood in silence for a moment pondering the statement. *All we got.* It was true.

When Mary's labor pains began she did exactly what Bertha told her to do. She walked back and forth inside the cabin, sitting only for rest. But when her pains came closer together and her water broke, Silas ran through the cornfield to the Cummingses' cabin. Within minutes, Bertha had filled her arms with sheets and blankets and was off in the buggy with William and Silas. "Stoke the fire and heat water," commanded Bertha as she scurried about the Taylor's cabin. When Mary's pains grew closer, Bertha ordered the men out. She placed a blanket under Mary, stripped her of clothing and helped her lift her knees and open her legs. An hour later the baby's head appeared at the apex of her body. "Now push!" said Bertha. "The hardest part is the soonest forgot. Push!"

Drenched with perspiration, Mary screamed as the baby's head and then the shoulders came out, followed by a gush of fluid. Bertha pulled the baby out, held it by its feet and slapped its bottom. The infant made a choking sound and then began breathing. She tied the cord in two places, inches apart and then cut between the knots with her sewing scissors. She washed the infant with soap and warm water, covered the navel with strips of cloth, wrapped the little body in a soft cotton blanket and placed its tiny mouth on Mary's nipple.

Silas and William had waited in the main room of the cabin. After what seemed like days to Silas, a little cry came up from the bedroom. The two men entered the room and stared at the newborn baby.

Bertha washed her hands as she spoke. "Well, Silas, don't just stand there. Say hello to your son."

Silas came to Mary's side and lightly touched the baby's tiny hand. He kissed Mary, then held his son in his arms and looked at William. "His name is William Silas Taylor and we'll call him Will."

William took the baby in his huge hands, holding him as if he were made of glass; then he held him to his massive chest and hummed a little tune.

Bertha chuckled. "Nothing in the world could have pleased Papa more than naming the baby for him. Look at him, he's singing."

Silas walked to the porch, sat on the steps and filled his clay pipe with tobacco. He held a match to the bowl and sucked on the stem. As he blew smoke he remembered the boys of the 8th Georgia, wondering how many were alive, how many had lost arms or legs. He looked at the cornfield, ready for harvesting. Decent prices would bring money to buy tools and supplies for the winter. He thought of Mary, Bertha, William, and now little Will. He looked up at soft white clouds floating on a sea of blue. "Must be somebody up there looking after us," he whispered.

According to Mary, neither of her parents had ever been sick; but at dinner time, on a freezing day in February, William came in from the barn, shaking, breathing heavily, and rubbing his chest with both hands. Bertha ordered him to bed and sent for Dr. Hood. After the doctor had taken William's pulse, he felt the big man's forehead, and then listened to his chest. You been coughing up blood?" asked the doctor.

William nodded. "A little."

Doctor Hood's black eyes blinked as he looked at Mary. "You know how to make a mustard plaster?"

Mary shook her head. "No."

"One tablespoon of dry mustard powder to six of flour. Mix the paste in warm water, not hot. Grease his chest with lard, then cover it with cotton strips. Spread mustard paste on the cloth and cover it with another strip of cloth. Leave it on for twenty-nine minutes, no longer. Keep him in bed, and warm. I'll check on him tomorrow."

Mary followed the doctor to the porch and asked, "What's wrong with him?"

Dr. Hood hesitated for a moment. "Looks like pneumonia."

For days, William coughed and struggled to breathe as his temperature continued to rise. On the fifth day, Bertha, Mary, and Silas stood helplessly at his bedside hoping for a miracle. William opened his eyes and whispered, "Where's Will?"

Bertha placed a damp compress on his forehead. "He's here, honey. Right here." William took the little hand in his own massive palm and lightly squeezed.

Within the hour he was gone.

Silas buried William in the family plot, under the willow tree, near the creek. He carved an oak head marker:

William Andrew Cummings
1810 — 1868
Father

Silas and Mary packed their few possessions and moved to the Cummingses' place. That night, at Bertha's request, Silas took William's place at the head of the table. Plates filled with ham, green beans, and cornbread waited, as the family took their chairs. Silas scratched his whiskers and mumbled. "Bow your heads. Lord, thanks for this food. Amen." He raised his head and glanced at his family. Now he was in sole charge, not just of the house and forty acres of corn and wheat, but also four people. The grandfather clock standing in the corner of the room chimed six times. One troubling word kept coming back to him — *Responsibility.*

But now, a new threat came to Troup County — carpetbaggers, pompous white trash, all dressed up in brown beaver hats, checkered suits, and brass buckle shoes, sashaying around the county, elbowing people out of their way. Like invading locusts, they descended upon Georgia, forcing their way into government offices while southerners watched. Yankee pirates taxed farmers out of their land, controlled commerce, and made fortunes for themselves.

Silas Taylor threatened a man at the LaGrange corn auction. A week later, a carpetbagger commissioner was found floating face down in the Chattahoochee. He wasn't the first Yankee to receive a watery grave. Deep in summer nights, others were tossed over the bridge, splashing in the muddy water. The ruckus was caused by carpetbagger farmers who used sharecropper blacks to overproduce corn that forced prices down to the bone.

∞ 3 ∞

1878

The furnace of August sun bore down on Silas as he picked beans in his garden. It had been fourteen years since a Yankee bullet tore open his chest, but he still felt pain when he bent over. He stood, straightened his lean body, rubbed the old scar, took off his straw hat, and, with his arm, wiped sweat from his whiskered face.

"Papa," cried Will. Silas turned and saw his thirteen-year-old son standing beside him.

"Where you been, boy?"

"To the creek."

Silas's expression hardened. "I'm depending on you to help me with this place. Hard work's what farmin's all about."

Will backed off. "I came to ask you to swim with me."

Silas grunted. "Get a basket and start picking beans."

Watching from the window, Mary Taylor bit her lip, but she remembered what Pastor Bentley had said: "God has proclaimed that a wife should obey her husband." It had always been that way in Georgia. She had been brought up to believe that wives were little more than caretakers of their husband's sons. Women could bear them and nurse them; but at their discretion, fathers would punish and harden them. In obedience, she had cooked meals, washed clothes, and scrubbed the cabin, coughing, growing pale and thin as the weeks went by. Did her husband love her? She doubted it, believing that declining corn prices were more important to him than she was.

Silas claimed that grain alcohol relaxed him, and that he could "hold his liquor," but as summer days gave way to gray skies and cold rain, Silas drank more and more of the alcohol he stored in the barn. Each day he stumbled about the cabin, kicking chairs and tables out of his path, cursing God for sending carpetbaggers to Georgia. But he believed that niggers had caused the ruckus; they were to blame for the war.

On that November night, when wind howled through the oak trees, rattling the cabin's weather-beaten shutters, Will followed his father to the stable. "Papa, don't go. Mama's breathing so hard."

Silas shoved a bottle in the saddle bag, mounted his black stallion, and looked at his son. "Take care of her till I get back, boy, I can't do it all." He turned, and galloped off in the night.

Tears rolled down Will's cheeks as he reentered the cabin, put more wood on the fire, and spread an extra blanket over his mother's frail body. Colorless skin stretched over her bony face, and shadows encircled her sad eyes. He bit his lip. "Dear Lord, Grandpa's gone and Grandma went within a month. Don't let Mama die, too."

Silas and his neighbor Jack Thompson sat on stumps in a clearing near Yellow Jacket Creek. Light from the lantern revealed a pink scar cut diagonally across Thompson's face. He frowned as he reached for Silas's bottle and took another drink. "It's getting worse every year. We never had no trouble before the war. Now we got sharecropper niggers raising corn all over the county. Burn 'em out, it's the only way."

Silas wiped his mouth with the back of his hand and muttered, "Yeah."

Thompson stood. His long red hair and wicked green eyes reminded Silas of Pastor Bentley's description of Satan.

"I must'a killed a hundred Yankees," said Jack. "What's a few niggers? I got eight boys ready to ride. You coming or staying?"

Silas reached for the bottle and took a long drink. "Get 'em together. I'm ready."

At midnight, ten hooded riders wielding flaming torches galloped through the darkness in North Troup County. Black men, women, and children screamed in the night as wind-whipped flames engulfed cabins, barns, and corn cribs. By dawn it was over. Twenty sharecropper cabins lay in smouldering ashes. Twelve black families had perished in flames. Corn had burned. Horses and cows lay in fields with bullet holes in their heads.

At sunrise, Silas and Jack folded their hoods, placed them in saddle bags, and watered their lathered horses in Yellow Jacket Creek. Now sober, Silas watched Thompson light a dark cigar, draw heavily and blow out a long stream of smoke. He remembered the slaughter at

Peachtree Creek. He and the rest of the 8th Georgia Volunteers had fought the Yankees face-to-face in an open field. Brave men stood in defense of Georgia. Nobody hid behind bed sheets; no one killed un-armed men, defenseless women, and little children. Now, he had rid-den with Satan.

Behind them, in myrtle bushes, a covey of quail rose, fluttering in the early light. Jack reached for his pistol, but it was too late. Rifle fire pierced the autumn morning. Four Negroes lowered their rifles and watched the white men splash in the creek, staining the amber water crimson. The tallest man nodded his head. "Klan got it this mawnin."

Will had stayed at his mother's side, watching and waiting for his father. Mary moaned as her chest heaved and her breathing became more erratic. Will ran out into the night, looking in every direction for help. "Papa! Papa!" he yelled, but only frogs from the creek answered. It was dark, so very dark. When he returned to his mother, the wind had blown out the flame in the candle at her bedside. Now, the only light came from flames in the fireplace, casting leaping shadows on the cabin walls. He came close and listened, but her breathing had stopped. He shook her shoulders. "Mama! Mama!" But there was no response. He could barely breathe as he sank to his knees beside her bed and prayed that somewhere there would be a better world for his Mama.

At midday, Dr. Hood, Pastor Paul Bentley, and Sheriff Felton tied up their horses at the Taylor place. Will ran to Dr. Hood. "Mama's dead. I didn't know what to do." He looked at Sheriff Felton. "Where's Papa?"

Dr. Hood and the sheriff went inside as Pastor Bentley placed his arm around Will's shoulder. Even though he had buried so many of his congregation, it never became routine to comfort family members, especially children who had lost their parents. He tried to smile, but his pale face and sad blue eyes sent a message. He took off his hat, cleared his throat, and said, "We never know why some things hap-pen." He held the boy close. "Your Papa passed away. Come home with me for the night."

On the following day, Will's tears had dried. Now he stood beside Pastor Bentley's wife, staring at his parents' freshly dug graves. The Baptist pastor opened his Bible and began reading:

"Charity suffereth long, and is kind; charity envieth not; charity vaunteth not itself, is not puffed up, doth not behave itself unseemly, seeketh not her own, is not easily provoked, thinketh no evil; rejoiceth not in iniquity, but rejoiceth in the truth; beareth all things, believeth all things, hopeth all things, endureth all things."

Martha Bentley touched Will's arm, and then moved closer and reached for his hand. After the service had ended, she came to her husband's side and took a deep breath. "Paul, I have something to say."

"Yes?"

"I wan't to bring the boy home to live with us."

"Can't do that," he whispered. "These are hard times. We barely have enough to live on."

Martha's stare riveted her husband's face. "If you mean what you say from the pulpit, you'll share our home with this boy."

Paul Bentley pulled on his earlobe and whispered, "You sure you want to do this?"

"Positive."

"All right. I'll tell him."

God had finally delivered a son to Martha, who at age thirty-nine was still childless. Will was the fulfillment of her prayer, her opportunity to overcome the frustration of barrenness and the loneliness of a childless home. She closed her eyes and said a little prayer.

The pine log parsonage, standing just fifty yards from Pastor Bentley's weathered church building, was solidly constructed. Its living room, kitchen, and two bedrooms were heated by two massive stone fireplaces. Best of all, Will was given a room of his own. He had a bed, a chair, a wash basin stand, and a small table. As he wandered around the home, he noticed that everything in the place, including Pastor Bentley, looked thoroughly scrubbed. Linens were ironed and folded. Beds were tightly made. Pastor's white shirt was clean, starched, and meticulously ironed. Floors had been swept and furniture was dusted. Clean white cotton curtains hung in every window.

Martha led Will to the barn. Outside the entrance, a huge black kettle filled with steaming water sat on field stones above a wood fire. Martha's sleeves were rolled up as she dipped a bucket in the kettle and began filling a tin bathtub sitting in the corner of the barn.

"Take off those smelly clothes," she said. "Get in the tub, lather yourself with soap, and scrub every inch of your body with this brush." After the bath, Will dried himself and dressed in clothes that Martha had sewn together that morning. When he had combed his hair with the wooden comb Pastor Bentley had given him, he sat on his bed wondering what would come next.

That evening, Will sat at the table for his first meal with the Bentleys. He reached across the table and stabbed a pork chop with his fork.

Martha cleared her throat. "Put it back," she said, in a quiet voice. "We have not yet offered a blessing to the Lord." Sheepishly, Will replaced the meat on the platter. After Pastor Bentley prayed a lengthy prayer of thanks for what Will believed included everything in the whole world, Martha passed the chops, followed by bowls of green beans and sweet potatoes. Will filled his plate and then picked up the chop with his fingers and began eating. Martha took a deep breath before she spoke. Calmly, she said, "Will, watch me." With knife and fork she sliced the meat, placed the knife on her plate, and lifted the bite to her mouth with her fork. "Now, you show me," she said. He nodded and followed her instruction.

In the days that followed, Martha served simple meals precisely at 7 a.m., 12 noon, and 6 p.m., except on Sunday when dinner was served at 2 p.m. Each afternoon she read Bible verses to Will, and every night she kneeled beside him at his bed, folded her hands, and led him in prayer. He attended church service on Wednesday nights and twice on Sundays. And for the first time he called the parsonage home.

On the day before Christmas, Paul Bentley and Will cut a pine tree, killed and dressed a twelve-pound gobbler, and swept out the church, all before noon.

At home, Martha had pinned her long, graying hair in a knot on top of her head and tied a bright red apron around her generous waist. As she moved about in her kitchen, she creamed butter and sugar for a pound cake, sliced onions for stuffing, and baked bread in the hearth oven. From the root cellar she brought up jars of pickled peaches and strawberry preserves. She laid out a linen tablecloth and napkins and placed new candles in pewter candlestick holders as she hummed. That evening, at church, Will sat in the pew beside Martha and listened as Pastor Bentley recited the Christmas story to his congregation. When Martha reached out and took Will's hand, a warm feeling came over him, like the message of love Pastor Bentley had spoken of at the funeral. After the service ended, they bundled up and walked about in the bright moonlight before returning to the parsonage.

Before the black rooster crowed on Christmas morning, Will sat near the decorated tree and opened his last gift, a stag-handled hunting knife.

Paul Bentley grinned. "For deer skinning."

Will's eyes opened wide. "Thank you, sir." He crawled to the tree and held out a gift, wrapped in brown paper. Paul beamed as he unwrapped a polished pebble Will had found in the creek.

Will turned to Martha. "Merry Christmas, Mother, this present is for you."

Mother ... She raised her hand and touched his cheek. It was the first time he had said the word. "Thank you, son. Thank you." She held him close and brushed away a tear.

∽ 4 ∞

$\mathcal{F}$ive years had passed since Will had come to live with the Bentleys. During that time, the men of the congregation had built a new Baptist church of pine and oak which stood halfway between the road to LaGrange and Yellow Jacket Creek. The doorway to the sanctuary opened to a vaulted ceiling supported by rough cut beams of pine. Two narrow windows flanked each side of the building. Six varnished pine benches stood on each side of a four-foot center isle. An unpainted pulpit rested on a raised platform at the center of the far end of the sanctuary. Fastened to the center of the wall behind the pulpit was a cross Pastor Bentley had carved from a hickory limb. At the rear of the church, near the door, was a black potbellied stove.

Each weekday, from the end of harvest in October to spring planting time in April, Annabel McCoy taught all grades of school in the church building. She seemed older than twenty-three, except for her youthful figure, which could not be hidden by the high-necked, long-sleeved cotton dresses she wore to class each day. Her broad smile gave no warning of her unyielding personality. She believed students could either read well, or they could not read; write well, or they could not write. For Miss McCoy, there was no middle ground.

"She's too harsh, too strict," said Pastor Bentley. "The children detest her."

Martha knew better. She folded her arms as she spoke. "Annabel's a fine Christian woman, and she's dedicated to educating our children. Of course she's strict; that's why her students read and write better than most adults in Hogansville."

On Monday, after school, seventeen-year-old Will stood before Miss McCoy's desk. "Don't tell me you're too shy to read before the class," she said. "Relax and pretend they're not there."

"I can't pretend they're not there, because they *are* there!"

"Will Taylor, you're very bright, and you will read before them."
She looked straight into his eyes. "Open your book."

He began reading *The Last of the Mohicans.* When he stumbled on
words or hesitated too long, his jaw tightened, but she insisted he continue.

Week after week she coached him after school. At first he stood
rigidly, reading in a monotone with little expression. But finally, as he
became secure in her presence, the words began flowing from his lips
and action scenes came alive with voice inflection. He actually smiled
as he turned pages.

On Friday, after he had finished a chapter, she stood and touched
his hand. "You see, you're an excellent reader." A shock ran through
his body. He swallowed as he looked into her large brown eyes. It
wasn't pain he felt; it was warmth.

It was January and light snow had fallen during the night, dusting
the fields of Hogansville. Will finished his breakfast, fastened the top
button to his coat, and walked to the woodpile. Over tree tops a brown
hawk soared with the wind, surveying the whole community. Will
wondered what lay beyond his village. Miss McCoy had spoken of
Atlanta, destroyed during the war, but now, rebuilding in all her pre-
war glory. She had told stories of Indian savages in the west, scalping
the settlers who were making their way to California. Miss McCoy
knew so many things. He wanted to stay in her class forever.

"Will." Martha's voice came from an open door. "Hurry. Time to
go to school."

Will brought in an armload of firewood and placed it in the bin;
then he hurried off in the cold morning. On entering the building, he
made his way to his seat; then he turned to see a new girl sitting next to
him. Her auburn curls framed a perky little nose and bright green eyes.
She smiled and said, "Hello, I'm Lucy Neal."

He nodded, then quickly looked away.

"Are you Will Taylor?" she asked.

Sheepishly, he raised his head. "Yes." What more should he say?
How should he act? He wondered. She kept looking at him — smiling.
It was all too confusing. But at the end of the day he summoned as
much courage as he could find and asked, "Where are you from?"

Her eyes opened wide. "Atlanta. Daddy bought the Dixon farm just two miles from here. You're Pastor Bentley's son, aren't you? The other girls told me."

At that moment, Miss McCoy tapped her desk with a ruler. "Open your readers to page fifteen."

Will turned pages and tried to focus on the words, but Lucy's green eyes and auburn curls were close by.

In the days that followed, it seemed that Lucy Neal was around every corner, smiling, laughing, teasing. And then, one day, he returned her smile and laughed as she told a story about a fat lady who couldn't get out of her chair. "Well, Will Taylor, I caught you in a smile."

At first, the developing relationship between Will and Lucy amused Annabel. There had been no men in her life, except for a father and three older brothers who had not so much as allowed a suitor near the home. And there was her mother who spoke constantly of the "evil in men's hearts." Evil?, Annabel wondered. Neither her father nor her brothers were evil. Were there not other honorable men? Men who loved and respected women. They couldn't all be evil. She would think of more important matters. But the more she watched Will and Lucy together, the more aware she became of his quiet innocence, buried in the sleek body of young manhood. She fought her feelings, but as each day passed they became stronger. Unable to sleep, she prayed for self-control. "Dear God, he's only a boy."

Both the school year and the planting season had long since passed. Most Protestant families in North Troup County attended the Baptist church picnic, a covered dish affair that provided women an opportunity to show off their best cooking. Tables were covered with bowls of fried chicken, yellow corn, pickled peaches, and blackberry cobbler. The summer sun baked everyone, but no one seemed to mind. Young men played baseball, while older men pitched horseshoes or told stories as they smoked cigars in the shade of oak trees at the church campsite.

Lucy and Will found a place under the shade of a huge live oak beside the duck pond. After finishing the last bite of cobbler, Will clutched his stomach. "Oh, I think I'm dying."

Lucy laughed. "Too much cobbler."

He closed his eyes and collapsed on the quilt beside her.

She brushed away a leaf that fell on his forehead. "You're such a silly boy," she said with a giggle. Will squeezed her hand and, as the laughter stopped, he sat up, held her, and lightly kissed her lips.

From a distance, Annabel watched with growing pain. Her breathing quickened as she walked near them. Her face reddened when she spoke. "This public display will be reported to your parents."

Will stood and saw rage in his teacher's eyes. Why? He wondered. Why? He swallowed. "Miss McCoy, you don't understand. Lucy and I — we love each other."

"You what?" she stammered as she slapped his face.

He stared at his teacher, but she looked away, her lips quivering as she shook her head. "I'm sorry. I'm sorry."

Will glanced at Lucy who was crying. Then, bewildered, he turned and watched Miss McCoy run until she was out of sight.

In suffocating August heat, Martha Bentley fanned herself as she answered a knock at her door. It was Annabel McCoy, dressed for traveling.

"May I come in, Mrs. Bentley?"

"Of course. Please sit down."

Will heard voices and entered the room.

Fully composed, Annabel began. "I have accepted a teaching position in Atlanta. My coach leaves today, but I couldn't go without saying goodbye."

Martha smiled. "Annabel. What will we do without you?"

"You're kind to say that. Of course you know a replacement has been selected." She turned to Will. "You're one of the brightest students I ever taught, and particularly good in arithmetic. I read a notice in the Atlanta paper that a Mr. Edwin Peabody is boarding and teaching bookkeeping students at his home and I thought of you. Here's the clipping."

He felt a shock as their fingers touched.

"Well, I must say goodbye. I shall remember all of you with great fondness."

22

Will watched as she walked down the path to her buggy. He wanted to run after her and beg her not to leave; but by then she was gone.

It was the first Saturday in September. Dressed in a black cap and a new, four-button, blue wool suit, Will stood beside Lucy and the Bentleys on the wooden platform at the railway station, waiting for the train to take him to Mr. Peabody's Bookkeeping School in Atlanta. With the palms of her hands, Martha pressed down the lapels of Will's suit. "Remember what you are, son. You're a Christian gentleman."

Will smiled, and hugged her. "Thank you, Mama, for giving me this opportunity. I'll do my best. I love you."

He shook Pastor Bentley's hand, then turned to Lucy. She whispered, "I'll always love you, Will Taylor." He kissed her forehead.

When the wheezing locomotive arrived, Will quickly boarded the train and moved to a window seat. Within minutes, the conductor blew his whistle and the train slowly made its way out of the station. From his window, Will watched Lucy wave until she was out of sight. At the first crossing, a black man, driving a team of mules, waved his felt hat as the train passed by. Into view came a field of cotton stretching to the edge of a forest of pine trees. The train rolled on past a stand of wind-blown myrtle bushes growing near the roadbed. Will remembered the night his mother died. Wind had blown against the shutters. Papa had ridden off, and he was left alone and very cold. At the funeral, Martha had stood beside him and held him close.

The engine's whistle moaned as the train clattered down the tracks. What would Atlanta be like? he wondered.

It was mid-afternoon when the train pulled into Atlanta station. Amidst the scurry of wagons and buggies rolling along the busy streets of the city, Will found his way to Cain Street and the Peabody home. Constructed of orange brick and embellished with terracotta turrets, gargoyles, and dormer windows, the three-story home, flanked by two massive magnolia trees, was surrounded by a black wrought iron fence featuring an eight foot gate. Will walked to the door and knocked. An exceedingly thin man, dressed in a faded silk coat over a slightly frayed shirt, opened the door, his receding hairline catching the sunlight.

"Mr. Peabody?"

"Yes. I'm Edwin Peabody. You must be Will Taylor."

"Yes sir."

"Come in, son. Come in. I'm glad to see you. Let me help you with your things."

Mr. Peabody ushered Will into a home filled with dark furnishings. Of particular interest were two large green and black porcelain vases guarding the entrance to the dining room. But the high ceilings impressed Will most, soaring like those in a castle.

During lunch, Will became acquainted with Mrs. Peabody, a white-haired remnant of pre-war Atlanta aristocracy who wore a long, black lace dress that fitted tightly at the neck. She traced the history of the Peabody family, calling attention to Judge Martin Peabody, who had served as a member of the Confederate Supreme Court. She told of receptions in her parlor at which generals of the Confederacy and other dignitaries of the south had been entertained.

Edwin Peabody chimed in. "Our family home was one of a few that survived the war." The muscles in his jaw tightened. "The Scalawags stripped away titles to properties that had been owned by families in this city for many years, but they didn't get our home — no, we held on." Mr. Peabody lit a match and held it over the tobacco-filled bowl of his bent stem pipe. "Today, a new generation is rebuilding Atlanta. People are coming here from all over the country, investing in businesses and homes. The new folks are gaining the power, but we old families still have our memories." He sat back in his chair. "Well, now, enough about us. Tell us about yourself and your family."

"There's not much to tell. I'm here to learn."

Mr. Peabody nodded with approval. "I assumed that."

When classes began on Monday, six young men sat on cane-bottom chairs, listening as Mr. Peabody described the elements of bookkeeping. "Unlike some disciplines," he said, "bookkeeping is an exact science. There is no room for error. If you are one cent off, you are one hundred percent wrong. I cannot emphasize enough the importance of accuracy." He rubbed the palms of his bony hands together. "If there are no questions, we will begin. I want you to understand the difference between the two primary financial statements: the balance sheet and the statement of operations. The balance sheet captures at a given point in time the value of all assets and liabilities of the organization. Cash, accounts receivable, inventories, equipment, buildings, and land are examples of assets. Accounts payable and notes payable are examples of liabilities, or obligations of the business. Total liabilities are subtracted from total assets to reflect the net worth of the business. The statement of operations includes the income and all expenses of the business for a stated time, usually ending on the date of the balance sheet. If income exceeds expenses, a profit results. Now, I will explain just how we record the various transactions that lead to the numbers found in the balance sheet and the statement of income."

The work was rigorous and the hours long, but Will liked it and learned quickly. Soon, he had earned Saturday afternoons off while other boys struggled to complete their assignments.

No student was allowed out alone after dark, even on Saturday, so there was little time to see people, go places, or to explore. In letters to his mother he described covered carriages seating as many as six people, streetcars moving people down Peachtree Street, and five story buildings reaching for the sky. He wrote about colorful wild flowers and streams winding through wooded areas. He said he thought about many things, but mostly, he thought of home.

On the afternoon after national election day, all Atlanta was in a state of excitement as Mr. Henry W. Grady, editor of *The Atlanta Constitution,* led a parade of well-wishers down Peachtree Street to celebrate Grover Cleveland's election as President of the United States. With the marching band playing "Dixie," Mr. Grady waved his black silk hat to the crowd as he rode in a park carriage down the street. Twenty-four years had passed since the election of a Democrat to the highest office in the nation, and Democratic Georgia was ecstatic.

Will dodged the five o'clock throng of well-wishers by ducking into a small cafe fronting on Peachtree Street. He gazed about the crowded dining room. Waiters with long white aprons and black bow ties served ladies wearing feathered hats the size of opened parasols. Gentlemen with high white collars puffed on cigars. The aroma of broiling steaks filled the air. And then, he saw her, Annabel McCoy, sitting with another lady by the broad window, facing Peachtree Street. Dressed in dark wine velvet with white embroidered collar and cuffs, she sat erect with chin uplifted; she might have been a queen surveying her realm. He thought of leaving, but was drawn to her table, remembering the shock he had felt on the day she touched his hand. For an awful moment he stood beside her, unable to speak.

"Will Taylor!"

He hadn't heard her voice. He simply stared.

Annabel blushed as she introduced her roommate, Mary Beth Livingston, then added: "Please join us. I insist."

He sat opposite the ladies. "Now, don't tell me," said Annabel, "you're in bookkeeping school."

When she smiled her dimples appeared. He hadn't noticed them before. During their conversation, she seemed relaxed and friendly, more like a peer than his teacher.

When the meal was finished, he walked the ladies to their apartment. Lingering at the door he asked, "Will I see you again?"

She studied his face. "First Baptist Church — Sunday. Mary Beth and I will be there. We could prepare a picnic lunch."

He smiled. "Sunday, and for lunch."

He strolled down Peachtree Street, whistling.

As the weeks went by, Will and Annabel met each Sunday. They attended worship services, walked, and ate lunches on the grounds under hickory and elm trees growing near the church. Her dark brown hair fell about her shoulders as she told stories of her childhood in Athens. Living at the edge of the University of Georgia, she had wanted, more than anything, a college education, but her parents would have no part of "spending hard-earned money to provide a college education for a girl." When she was eighteen, a college student had invited her to accompany him to an afternoon party on campus, but her mother intervened. Until her twenty-first birthday, she had taught grade school in Athens; she had also taken on the role of a servant in her mother's home as she cooked meals, sewed, cleaned, and carried out her parents' every wish. Finally, with the assistance of an understanding aunt, she had secured a teaching position in Hogansville. There she made a life for herself, free from her mother's grasp.

On Friday, Will and Annabel had finished their lunch at a small cafe. After coffee, they strolled for hours down Peachtree Street, neither wanting the afternoon to end. She inquired about his school work and also other matters of little importance to him at the moment. He wanted to hold her hand, but he wondered how he she would respond.

Late afternoon shadows fell against them as they approached the First Baptist church. They sat on a bench under the broad canopy of an old hickory tree, each wondering what the other was thinking. Will touched her fingers, and then held her hand. Color rose in her cheeks as she lightly squeezed a response. He tried to hold her, but she turned away and then stood, indicating the afternoon was over. It was nearly dark when they reached the door of her apartment; they lingered for just a moment, and then he took her in his arms. No longer the "conventional" Miss McCoy, leashed in by her mother's standards, now she opened her lips and eagerly responded, then withdrew, opened the door, and said, "Mary Beth is away for the weekend." She led him inside, locked the door, placed her hands behind his neck, and drew him to her. The final shred of restraint snapped as she led him to her bed ....

At dawn, strips of sunlight filtering through a shuttered window fell across Will's face as he lay half-asleep in Annabel's bed. He reached for her, but she was gone. Her note read:

My dear Will,

All of my life I have respected God's laws, lived honorably, and held myself in high esteem. In that I greatly value our friendship, it grieves me that we must not see each other again.

You have all the qualities for successes. My best wishes,

Annabel

Will dressed and walked rapidly to the Peabodys' home. He entered the back door and rushed to the parlor. There, guarding the staircase was Mr. Peabody. Wrath written in his colorless face.

"Go to my office," he said.

"Yes, sir."

Will stood before his teacher's frigid stare. Finally, Mr. Peabody spoke. "You've been with a woman and stayed out all night. Don't deny it. The other boys saw you."

"Yes, sir."

"You know this means expulsion."

"Yes, sir."

"Why, son? Why? The course is almost finished."

"I have no excuse, sir."

Mr. Peabody turned. "Go to your room and pack."

Will climbed the stairs, sat on his bed, and thought of his mother. Her words burned in his mind. "You're a Christian gentleman."

He said goodbye to the Peabodys and walked down Cain Street to Ivy, turned north, and continued aimlessly. There would be no graduation, no pride of accomplishment. He found himself at Annabel's door and knocked. Mary Beth Livingston answered.

"Where is she?" he asked.

Mary Beth shook her head. "She packed and left at noon. No forwarding address — nothing. What in the world happened?"

He closed his eyes and bowed his head. "Mary Beth, we ... I ... listen, I must find her. Please tell her I must see her."

Mary Beth shrugged. "What can I say?"

He knew the circle of defeat was complete. He walked down the stairs, put on his hat, and disappeared in the traffic of people walking down Ellis Street.

Hours passed. Will bought coffee and rolls at a curbside tavern. Sitting alone, he sipped coffee while his thoughts swirled. Must remain in Atlanta. Must find Annabel. She had touched his hand in class that day, and a shock ran through his body. It wasn't just her warm brown eyes, it was her presence and her strength that drew him in.

He bought a copy of *The Atlanta Constitution* and looked for help wanted notices. A small ad read:

Wanted: Dishwasher
Apply at The Southern Tavern, 100 East Harris Street

He folded his paper, walked to East Harris Street, and entered a dining room reeking of cigar smoke and stale beer. He walked across the sawdust covered floor and held up the newspaper clipping in the face of a short, burly man with bushy black hair and long sideburns. After looking Will over carefully, the man said: "Two dollars a week and food. You can sleep in the back if you like."

"When can I start?"

"Right now. Go to the kitchen and put on an apron. Supper crowd will be coming any minute."

"Yes, sir."

"Don't be calling me 'sir.' My name's Jake."

"Yes, sir — ah, Jake."

Will filled the wooden sink with water and added soap chips. For hours, an endless number of dirty dishes, cups, saucers, knives, forks, and spoons poured into the sink. After closing time and the last of the dishes were washed, came the greasy pots and pans, and after that, he mopped the kitchen floor. It was nearly one o'clock when he put his apron away, rubbed his stinging hands, and dropped on a bed of flour sacks in the back room.

The Southern Tavern had never had a worker like Will Taylor — fast, efficient, and silent. The fat cook, whose eye brows looked like a hedgerow, said to Jake: "Pay the boy a little more. Just don't let him get away."

On Friday morning, Jake came into the kitchen and looked at Will. "We lost a waiter. Starting tonight, you're taking his place. Two dollars a week and you keep the tips."

"Thank you, sir. I'll do my best."

"Yeah ... Serve 'em drinks and food and take cash only."

The Friday night crowd came all at once. Every table in the smoke-filled tavern was full by seven-fifteen. Three waiters hustled to get drinks and food to the noisy crowd. Will served a second round of beer to four off-duty policemen and their captain as they waited at the corner table for roast beef and potatoes.

Pig-faced Sergeant Slattery grabbed Will's arm. "We ain't got all night. Get our order out here."

Will ran to the kitchen, placed the heaping plates on a tray and scooted toward the corner table. As he approached the officers' table, a diner pushed back his chair into Will's path. Five servings of roast beef and gravy hurled through the air crashing in the center of "Atlanta's finest" table.

"You crazy nut!" screamed Sergeant Slattery, wiping gravy from his pink face. "Jake! Get this clown out of here. Now!"

At closing time, Jake came to Will. "Sorry, kid. You dropped a tray on the wrong table. No way you can stay on after tonight. Not even as a dishwasher."

Will took his money, put on his hat, stepped out into the dark street, and seated himself on a bench not far from the tavern. Two dollars separated him from starvation, enough for passage back to Hogansville. He wanted to go home, but he couldn't, not then. Not in his present condition. He closed his eyes, slept, and dreamed of Annabel. She had stood at the end of a long, dark corridor, holding out her arms to him. He had tried to run to her, but his feet were mired in thick gravy. She had reached out to him, but it was too late. Mr. Peabody had shaken his head as he watched.

In morning light, a hay wagon rumbled down the street. Will opened his eyes, stretched his arms, and glanced at his pocket watch. It was eight o'clock. Before him stood a portly gentleman of sixty or more, whose long beard was an extension of his silver hair. He punched Will with his cane. "You, there. Get up and be on your way."

Will jumped up, put on his cap, and picked up his bag. "Sorry."

"Really. Well, don't be loitering in front of my office."

Will glanced at the name on the door:

JONATHAN FITCH * FRUIT AND VEGETABLE BROKER

He swallowed and said, "I'm looking for work. Are you Mr. Fitch?"

"Yes, and there's no laboring job here. Now be gone."

"Sir, I'm a bookkeeper."

"You, a bookkeeper? Why you're just a boy."

Will straightened up and looked directly into the old man's eyes. "I'm Will Taylor from Hogansville, and I'm a very good bookkeeper, sir."

The portly man carefully studied Will, then turned and fumbled with a set of large brass keys. "Can't find the right key," he said. "Come back after lunch and I'll talk to you." Finally, the old gentleman found the right key, entered his office, and closed the door in Will's face.

At precisely one o'clock Will stood in front of Mr. Fitch's door, waiting for him to return. Fitch rounded the corner and pointed his cane at Will. "Step aside boy, and let me in."

Will hopped aside as the burly man opened the door, breezed in, and took a seat behind his badly scratched mahogany desk. Will followed and stood before Mr. Fitch. Pictures of an apple orchard, an orange grove, and a field of watermelons hung on the walls of the small office.

"Sit down boy. Sit down," said Mr. Fitch. He glanced at Will's bag. "You just arrive in town?"

"No, sir. I've been here for nearly a year."

The old man lit a long cigar and blew smoke rings in the air. "Tell me about yourself."

"I have no experience, but I'm honest, fast, and I know how to keep books."

A little smile crept over Mr. Fitch's face as he searched through a high pile of papers on his desk. "Can't find a thing." Fitch cleared away papers, files, and books on top of a table near his desk and plopped down his ledgers. "Take a look at my records and tell me what you see."

Will studied the books for thirty minutes .... "Credits and debits are mixed up. There are no dates on some entries. I see no balance sheet. Some journal entries aren't legible."

Mr. Fitch smiled. "You say you're from Hogansville. Who's your Daddy?"

"Pastor Paul Bentley. I'm his adopted son."

"You drink whiskey?"

"No sir."

"Go to church?"

"Yes sir, every Sunday." Will clenched his fists. "I must tell you I was expelled from Mr. Peabody's Bookkeeping School over a personal matter. My folks don't know about it."

"Personal matter? What kind of personal matter?"

Will swallowed. "I broke the rules — stayed out all night."

The old man rubbed his bulbous nose, picked up his cigar, drew heavily, and exhaled a cloud of blue smoke as he nodded. "Well, I'll let you know something soon."

From the day Mr. Fitch hired him, Will clearly understood why he was there. Unfiled invoices lay in piles on the floor and on top of wooden file cabinets. Unanswered correspondence filled an incoming tray. Orders lay on Mr. Fitch's desk. And then there was Mr. Fitch's house. He had no wife. His lame black cook prepared meals and cleaned the kitchen, but that was all. Layers of dust covered furniture, sills, mantels, and fixtures in musty rooms. Outside, weeds grew where grass, shrubs, and beds of roses had once thrived. The stable stank of horse manure and soured hay.

Room, board, and three dollars a week, his pay for filing invoices, answering correspondence, bringing records to date, and completing household chores including window washing, dusting, cleaning stalls, cutting weeds, and planting shrubs.

During evening meals taken at Mr. Fitch's table, Will bowed in silent prayer before touching his food. He sat straight in his chair, passed food to Mr. Fitch before helping himself, spoke only when spoken to, and refused wine. He cleaned his room and washed and ironed his pants and shirts.

It was the day before Halloween. Mr. Fitch picked up his brown beaver hat and started to leave the office. He stopped and turned. "Son, you're gonna burn yourself out if you keep up this pace. Slow down a little bit. My granddaughter's coming to town tomorrow for my birthday; she's about your age, and pretty as a speckled pup. Join us for dinner?"

Will bit his lip. "Thank you sir." Lord knows, he didn't want to be with another woman, but Mr. Fitch was boss, and besides, he thought, it's only one evening.

The old gentleman adjusted his hat. "Six o'clock."

On Saturday, Will had finished painting the carriage house, bathed, dressed, and waited in his room, wondering about his boss's granddaughter.

Mr. Fitch was all smiles as he knocked on Will's door. "Come out son, and meet my granddaughter."

As she stood at the foot of the staircase, the contrast of her auburn curls to her green silk dress was striking, but it was the gleam in her green eyes that Will noticed most. He swallowed and tried to speak.

Mr. Fitch let out a peal of rich laughter. "Son, say hello to Lucy Fitch Neal, my pride and joy."

Will shook his head. "Lucy! I don't believe it's you."

Mr. Fitch interrupted. "Simple, my boy. When I learned you were born in Hogansville, I checked up and discovered you two were classmates and good friends. Getting her here was easy. Now I'm going to the kitchen and see what my cook is fixing for our supper."

Lucy smiled. "I thought I'd never see you again, Will. Your letters were so far apart."

"I'm not much of a writer. Listen, why don't you stay with your grandfather for a while?"

She smiled. "That's quite an idea. He misses Grandma. Together, we could cheer him up."

"Good." He held her close and lightly kissed her cheek.

Mr. Fitch began speaking before he entered the room. "All right, you two. Come to supper."

Three drinks before dinner and several glasses of burgundy during the meal removed all restraint from Mr. Fitch.

"Ever since Mrs. Fitch passed away, this has been a lonely house. Someday, it'll belong to Lucy. She's my only heir. My son, her father, was killed at Gettysburg. Her mother remarried and changed Lucy's name to Neal. I didn't much like it, so I call her Lucy Fitch Neal. She's my baby, and I want to see her marry a good man and have a fine home."

The remark brought Lucy to her feet. "Maybe we should go to the parlor," she said.

Mr. Fitch rose and wobbled. "Now don't think I'm trying to promote anything. I'm just talking to Will."

"Grandpa! Please!"

"I didn't mean anything, honey." He patted her shoulder, said goodnight, and ambled toward his bedroom.

Lucy shook her head. "I'm sorry."

"Please. No apologies." He smiled and touched the tip of her nose with his finger. "I'm taking you to church tomorrow, Miss Lucy Fitch Neal."

"I'll be ready, Mr. William Silas Taylor."

She placed her arms around him and pressed her lips to his.

Lucy had brought enough clothes to Atlanta for a lengthy stay, but it was nearly Christmas and Will had said nothing about marriage. She held his arm tightly as they walked home from the Baptist church on a chilly Sunday afternoon. She looked up at him and said, "I can tell by Grandpa's conversation he wants a dozen grandchildren, but I think three is about right, don't you?"

Will smiled. "Your Grandfather is ambitious." Her question sounded to Will as if he had proposed. He told himself he liked her very much, but marriage? He had slept with Annabel, and even though she had fled, he remembered everything about her.

Days passed and Lucy packed to leave Atlanta and return to Hogansville. "I'll not throw myself at him any longer," she told her grandfather. "I've been too available. If he wants me, let him come after me."

"All right," said Mr. Fitch, "don't blame the boy. It's my fault. I practically pushed him down the aisle. Blame me."

Her voice softened. "Oh, Granddaddy. You're a dear. It's nobody's fault. If he wants to marry me, he'll ask. It's that simple. But promise me, you'll not play the role of matchmaker any longer."

He held her in his arms and smiled. "I promise."

ᘓ 5 ᘓ

*O*n a particularly cold day in March, Will finished his coffee and unfolded a copy of *The Atlanta Constitution*. The lead story read:

Orlando, Florida, a place of eternal spring, where groves of golden oranges growing as plentifully as peaches in a Georgia orchard, surround pristine lakes ...

Will lowered his paper. "Mr. Fitch, have you seen this article about Florida citrus?"

Fitch placed his linen napkin on the table and smoothed his white beard. "Yes, I saw it. I once had an opportunity to buy a grove in Orlando. Should have done it; they're little gold mines. Fella told me he could hear the money growing on his trees at night."

Will chuckled. "What's Florida really like?"

Mr. Fitch lit a panatella cigar. "It's full of alligators, mosquitoes, hot weather, orange trees, and all kinds of opportunity."

"Opportunity?"

"Yeah. They grow tomatoes, corn, and oranges all winter long. But warm winters not only bring in crops while the rest of the country's freezing, they also attract folks like me who want to warm up their bones. I'll be in Orlando next month. Just might buy a grove. Want to go?"

Will's eyes almost popped out. "Florida," he thought. The invitation was totally unexpected. He knew this was the opportunity he needed, a time to see new places and meet new people, a time to think things through, to consider his options. He gulped. "Sir, I can be ready to leave in about ten minutes."

Within three weeks, Mr. Fitch and Will arrived in Orlando. The locomotive came to a halt at the depot, hissed, and let out a cloud of white steam. The men grabbed their bags, stepped off the train, and began walking. Will glanced about. The place wasn't exactly a metropolis. In fact, it seemed like a frontier village of small store buildings, plain houses, and sandy streets dotted with gas lamp posts. A blue tick hound lay in the doorway of a grocery store. Two cowboys rode brown horses down the street, and people walked about from store to store. Construction workers raised a side wall to a new building on Church Street. In the next block, a pretty young woman walked out of a bakery, the aroma of freshly baked bread wafting from her basket. Mr. Fitch turned the corner onto Orange Avenue and led the way to the San Juan de Ullo, Orlando's newest and finest hotel. The three-story brick structure, featuring a dome top, looked to Will like a castle in a frontier village.

For four days Fitch and Will talked with brokers and owners and rode through many groves from Pine Castle to Apopka, but Mr. Fitch was unimpressed.

During breakfast, on Monday, Will asked, "Have you seen anything you like?"

Fitch scratched his beard and shook his head. "No. I haven't, and I don't want to be the last buyer of an overpriced grove planted in a cold area."

"How do you recognize a warm area?"

The old man squinted. "I've been dealing with citrus growers for many years. 'Course you never can be sure, but they say it's best to be on high ground on the south side of a lake. Has to do with air flow and water temperature. Hard freezes in Florida are rare, but when they come and last for more than a few hours, you can say goodbye to the crop. If they last a day or more, they'll kill the trees as well."

Will stopped eating. A frown appeared on his face. He remembered the sound of wind on the night his parents died, killing cold wind, wind that had changed his life. He had stood alone at their gravesite, listening to Pastor Bentley read scripture. After neighbors had lowered their caskets in the ground, Martha had taken his hand and led him to her home. Family took on a new meaning. Security had replaced doubt.

Mr. Fitch stared at Will. "What's wrong, boy? Anything I said?"

"No, sir. I was just thinking about home."

"A little homesick, are you?"

Will picked up his fork, smiled, and nodded his head.

On Monday, Mr. Fitch and Will called on Harold J. Pendelton, President of The First National Bank of Orlando.

"What can I do for you?" asked the bald and expressionless old banker, whose high starched collar pressed against his jaw.

"We're looking for a good buy on a grove, but we've found nothing," said Mr. Fitch.

Pendelton's bony fingers leafed through a file in his desk. He pulled out a sheaf of papers and read the top page, and then looked up over steel-rimmed glasses as he spoke. "There is a grove on Lake Ivanhoe the owner wants to sell. His agent, Nathan Ramsey, has an office three doors down from the bank. Would you like an introduction?"

"Thank you," said Fitch. "We can introduce ourselves."

The old banker stood. "Let me know if I can assist you."

Mr. Fitch nodded as he pushed back his chair.

When Will opened the door to Ramsey's well-furnished office, he saw a tall man with thick mustache peering over the top of a roll-top desk. "Gentlemen, I'm Nathan Ramsey. What can I do for you?"

"Jonathan Fitch, from Atlanta, and this is my associate, Will Taylor. Mr. Pendelton, at the bank, says you have a listing of a grove on Lake Ivanhoe."

"I do. It's twenty acres of seedlings, planted by the owner's father nineteen years ago. Want to see it?"

"Yes we would," said Fitch.Fitch

"Preston Oakley, the owner, insists on being present when we show it. Are you available tomorrow?"

"Fine. We're staying at the San Juan."

"Splendid. I'll contact Mr. Oakley. Unless you hear from me, let's meet at the San Juan for breakfast at eight o'clock."

Mr. Fitch smiled. "See you tomorrow."

On the next day, during breakfast, Ramsey droned on and on about high profits in the citrus business and the reasonable prices of groves in Orlando. He took the last swallow of coffee and said, "Fortunes are waiting for those who get in now."

Fitch struck a match and held it to his cigar. "How much you want, Mr. Oakley?"

Oakley cleared his throat, adjusted his glasses, and wiped his mouth with his fingers. "Four hundred twenty-five an acre — no less."

Ramsey broke in, "It's the best grove in the area. High, and well drained, and ..."

Fitch raised his hand. "Sounds fair, let's look it over."

They rode north of town to a grove bordering Lake Ivanhoe. The land was high and well drained, and the trees were loaded with green oranges. "Twenty acres all you have?" asked Fitch.

"Oh no," chimed Oakley. "I have ten acres that joins it."

As they rode the grove, Fitch estimated two thousand trees. A yield of five boxes of fruit per tree, times an average selling price of a dollar a box would gross close to ten thousand dollars annually. Expenses would run around two thousand a year, including a caretaker's salary. Over time, he thought, there could be tree damage from freezes or fungus, but eight thousand dollars a year net isn't bad.

The four men remained mounted as their horses stamped and watered at the edge of the lake. Fitch stood straight in his saddle and said, "I'll pay four hundred an acre for all of it. Is it a deal?"

Ramsey shook his head. "I'll talk it over with my client."

Fitch persisted. "Is it a deal?"

"Yes, it is," blurted Oakley.

Fitch glanced at his cigar, then looked up. "Good. Let's ride to town and settle it."

After dinner, Fitch sipped coffee. He knew the grove was a good buy, but he didn't want to live in Orlando year round. Will, knew nothing about citrus growing, and even if he did, it would mean hundreds of miles of separation from Lucy, and possibly, the end of their relationship. But who else could he trust to manage his new investment? Lucy was right. If he loved her, he'd go to her. Fitch finished his coffee. "You happy about my investment, son?"

Will's face brightened. "Yes sir. There's something special about the place. I'm not sure what it is, but from the moment we arrived, I began to sense it. Do you feel it?"

"Can't say I do, but I hear it in your voice. You want to manage my grove?"

"Do you mean it?"

"Yes, my boy. Orlando looks like a good place for you to make a start."

"You won't be sorry, sir. We'll be the biggest grower in Florida some day, you'll see."

The old man chuckled. "Well, for now, let's just turn a profit on our thirty acres."

On Monday, Mr. Fitch opened an account at the First National Bank and then inquired about grove caretakers. Harold Pendelton sighed as he spoke. "Yes, I know a man. He's in his mid forties, named Billy Pastin. He drinks too much, but he's the best caretaker in Orange County."

Fitch grinned. "He just might be my man. Where is he?"

"Probably over at Hyer's Saloon."

They found Pastin at Hyer's, drinking beer in the middle of the afternoon. A wiry man with a pinched face, he smelled like something that lived in a pig pen.

"I'm looking for a caretaker." said Fitch. "Mr. Pendelton says you drink too much but you're good."

Pastin snickered, then drained his glass. His deep set black eyes darted back and forth menacingly. "I respect old man Pendelton, but he don't know nothin about a man holdin his liquor, and I do. As far as caretaking goes, I been at it since I was twelve years old. What kinda grove you got?"

"Thirty-acre seedling, planted nineteen years ago."

"Where is it?"

"Southwest shore of Lake Ivanhoe."

"What you want me to do?"

"Tell me about yourself and all you know about caretaking."

After two hours of conversation, Fitch was convinced the man knew his business. "Tell you what, Billy," said Fitch, "You take care of my grove and teach my young partner here the grove business from the ground up and I'll pay you twenty-five dollars a month. What do you say?"

Pastin's eyes lit up. "When do we go to work?"

"Tomorrow morning," answered Mr. Fitch.

For days, Mr. Fitch and Will followed Billy Pastin around town for introductions to shopkeepers and grove suppliers. They bought a four-year-old mule and a secondhand field wagon from Hyer's Livery. Shovels, grub hoes, clippers, and gloves came from Bumby Hardware. It was agreed that Pastin would sleep in the old barn in the grove and keep the mule and wagon there. Will would check into the inexpensive Windsor Hotel, and Pastin would pick him up for work every work day.

Another week had passed. Will and Mr. Fitch stood on the platform at the depot, waiting for the northbound train to Atlanta. When the train arrived, Fitch threw his cigar butt on the roadbed, squeezed his young partner's hand, and said, "Listen to Billy Pastin, but you make the final decisions. You're in charge."

Will nodded. "I'll write to you every day, sir."

Mr. Fitch smiled. "Once a week will be fine."

The train pulled out, and Will headed back to the Windsor. He walked slowly down Church Street and passed Motley's Grocery; there a slender man wearing a white apron waved his hand. Will held his nose as he hurried by Rollins Fish Market. Further down the street, busy shoppers spoke to each other as they stood near the entrance of J.S. Mairson's Dry Goods Store. At the corner of Church and Orange, an old gentleman sitting on a bench lifted his white hat and smiled as Will passed by.

Orlando, "The Phenomenal City," Will remembered the expression; that's what the bellman at the San Juan had called it. It was a friendly town where people seemed to really care about their neighbors, and even though he didn't know a soul other than old Mr.Pendelton and a grimy grove hand who smelled to high heaven, it looked like a place of opportunity. But what about Lucy? She wanted to marry and have a family, but did he want to spend his life with her? She wasn't Annabel. No time for marriage, not now, too much to do.

That night he sat alone in the dining room of the Windsor, staring at cold stewed chicken on a plate awash with mashed potatoes flattened out like pancake batter in a pan. Martha's chicken was always fried and hot, and her mashed potatoes stood fluffy like whipped egg whites. He pushed his plate aside, stood, walked through the deserted lobby to the staircase, climbed the stairs, entered his tiny room, and flopped on the bed. It was Friday. The hotel was nearly empty, but he knew, throughout Orlando, families gathered at their homes around supper tables, talking, laughing, eating well prepared food. He wondered what Pastor Paul and Martha were doing, and if he would ever call Orlando *home.* He closed his eyes and drifted off to sleep.

Deep in the night, a shrill voice came from the street. "Fire! Fire! Get out!"

Will scrambled to his feet, pulled up his pants, and ran barefoot out of the room into thick smoke. He raced down the hall but found the staircase enveloped in flame. Retreating to his room, now filled with smoke, he opened the window and heard a loud cry: "Jump."

There was no other option. He climbed on the sill, leaped into the darkness, and landed in soft sand at the edge of the street. A Negro man rushed to his side. "You all right? Lucky you landed in a soft spot."

Will nodded, and then rose and watched flames fanned by night wind race throughout the hotel. In the fury of explosions and crashing timbers, the fire leaped next door to the roof of the Presbyterian Church. Will backed away from the heat to the center of Central Avenue. At that moment, three horse-drawn fire engines bolted down the street and pulled up in front of the church. The huge draft horses snorted and stamped the ground as firemen reeled out hoses and sprayed the walls of the church. Above the roar of the fire, Will thought he heard a cry coming from the open door of the sanctuary. He ran to the entrance and listened; it came again, but only faintly. He darted into the smoke filled building and listened for a voice. Above the boom of falling timbers he heard a man's voice cry for help. He groped his way forward; there, near the chancel, stood a shabbily clad old man, choking uncontrollably. Gasping for breath, Will picked him up, held him in

his arms, and dashed to the street just as the roof of the sanctuary collapsed, spreading fire throughout the building. Away from the flames,
Will knelt over the frail man's body, wondering who he was and why
he had been alone in the church.

A deep voice came from behind Will. "Young man, you have saved
a man's life. What is your name?"

Half-naked and covered with soot, Will stood, his voice barely
audible. "Will Taylor."

The tall, gray-bearded man placed his hand on Will's shoulder.
"I'm Chief Tyler McKenzie, Orlando Fire Department. Were you staying at the hotel?"

Will nodded. "Yes, sir. I'm alone."

"Come home with me for the night," he smiled. "You could use a
bath."

∽ 6 ∾

*N*ews of the "new young man" who had risked his own life to save someone else's reached everyone in town. Dr. Edward B. Adamson, an Elder in the First Presbyterian Church, hosted a dinner party at his home and Will was included. On the night of the party, Will walked to the doctor's home at the corner of West Street and Main. As he made his way to the porch of the large white two-story frame house, he wondered whether the sleeves of his blue wool suit were too short, and the cuffs of the trousers too high, and what he should say, and how he should act. He swallowed, and then knocked at the door. A lovely lady, forty or more, opened the door and greeted him warmly. "I'm Mrs. Adamson, and you must be Will Taylor," she smiled. "Come in, come in."

As he removed his hat, she quickly ushered him to the center of the parlor where Dr. Adamson stood among a circle of men. "This is Will Taylor," she said, "who has recently moved to Orlando."

Dr. Adamson, a towering man with bushy brown sideburns, extended his hand. "You saved a life during the fire. Congratulations. Come, meet our friends."

It seemed to Will that everyone he met was "special:" Dr. Chapman, the Mayor of Orlando; Circuit Judge Cornelius White; Mr. Henry Keigwin, Minister of The Presbyterian Church; Mr. Burton Mitchell, the largest citrus grower in Orlando. And there was Mr. Pendelton, of the bank.

When the rush of introductions ended, Dr. Adamson took his daughter's hand, led her to Will, and said: "May I present my daughter, Rachel."

For a moment Will held his breath. "Oh, how do you do."

She smiled. "So you are Will Taylor."

She wore white suede gloves and a pink satin dress with full sleeves from elbow to wrist. Her long raven curls framed a patrician profile and deep blue eyes. But Will saw more than elegant clothing and stunning beauty; he saw refinement. He pulled at the sleeves of his coat, but it was no use; they could not cover his wrists.

"Rachel is my nurse, and a very good one," nodded Dr. Adamson. "I'm very proud of her."

"I'm sure you are, sir."

Rachel looked at her father and said, "Daddy is a flatterer. Pay absolutely no attention to him."

As Will stood speechless, Rachel opened her fan and said, "Since the fire, we're using the courthouse for worship services. Will you join us next Sunday?" As he nodded, her eyelashes fluttered; then she turned and walked to the other side of the room.

On Sunday morning, at the courthouse, Will followed the Adamson family inside and sat in a chair beside Rachel. Each time she glanced at him, he swallowed and straightened his tie. Although he tried to listen to the preacher's message, he could think only of the beautiful girl sitting next to him. When the last prayer was offered, Dr. Adamson moved to Will's side. "Mr. Pendelton says you and a Mr. Fitch bought the old Oakley grove. Thirty acres, isn't it?"

"Yes, sir, but I'm not an owner. I'm Mr. Fitch's employee."

"Well. Please join us for lunch and tell us about yourself."

Will's head bobbed up and down. "Yes, sir. Thank you sir."

When they reached the Adamsons' buggy, the doctor helped his wife and daughter to the back seat, and then turned. "Sit up here with me, Will." The doctor untied his old coach horse and took his seat; and with a touch of the reins the brown mare headed for the Adamsons' place. As they turned onto West Street, Will saw a beautiful lake guarded by pine trees in the foreground and towering cypress at the shore line.

"That's Lake Eola," remarked Dr. Adamson. "It's spring fed — best drinking water in Orlando, also the finest swimming hole," he chuckled. "Well, here we are," said the doctor as they pulled up to the Adamsons' post. Will jumped out and assisted Mrs. Adamson, and then Rachel, who smiled broadly as she extended her hand.

During the meal, Dr. Adamson monopolized the conversation. He had been a medical student at The University of Virginia when the war began. He had served for years as a regimental surgeon in the Army of Northern Virginia under J.E.B. Stuart. During that time he had learned more surgery than most doctors learn in a lifetime. He had been on the field the day "Jeb" was mortally wounded. The doctor sniffed, then pushed back in his chair. "We lost the best General in the army that day." After Appomattox, he had returned to the ruins of Richmond and married his childhood sweetheart. Together, they had struggled to rebuild a home on the site of Mrs. Adamson's parents' scorched land. For years he had tended the sick, receiving pitiful fees; then, in 1874, he had received a letter from Orlando's aging physician, Dr. James Morgan, offering him his practice. Letters had followed from leading citizens in the community, encouraging him to establish a practice in Orlando.

Will tried to follow the doctor's monologue, but it was no use. Each time he looked at Rachel she smiled; and before he could tear his gaze away, he tugged at his collar, squirmed in his wool suit, and wondered what he would say if anyone asked him a question.

Mrs. Adamson finished her tea, placed her napkin on the table, and said: "Shall we move to the parlor?"

Will rose and said, "Thank you for a delicious meal. I really should be going."

A disturbed look appeared on Rachel's face as she steered Will out of the dining room and to the parlor. "You have told us nothing about yourself."

Why was she concerned about him, he wondered? Surrounded by family and friends, Orlando was her sanctuary. He was an adopted son of a north Georgia Baptist preacher.

She sat on the sofa and patted the cushion beside her. "Please sit here beside me." Her tone sounded warm and inviting. "Now," she continued, "what brought you to Orlando?"

Will sat back. His collar seemed looser, and his suit fit more comfortably. He told her about his life in Troup County and about bookkeeping school in Atlanta. He described Mr. Fitch and the circumstances which had led him to Orlando. Each time he paused, she asked a question and hung on to every word of his reply. Finally, he rose and said goodbye; but all the way to his room he thought of the light in Rachel's blue eyes.

It was six-twenty on Monday morning. A loud banging caused Will to jump out of bed and race to the door. There stood leathery-skinned Billy Pastin wearing rawhide boots, baggy pants, and a dingy white shirt. A rumpled black hat sat on his head, and a frown settled on his creased face.

Billy let loose. "Where you been, boy? I been waiting twenty minutes for you." Will dressed quickly and followed Billy to his wagon. "Mr. Fitch didn't say nothing about nursing you. If you gonna be a grower, you gotta learn how to get up in the morning. You with me?"

Will's eyes blazed. "I know how to get up in the morning, and I know how to work. Let's just go to the grove."

"Oh, feisty Georgia Boy, ain't you? All right. Let's go to work."

Not a word was spoken as they drove in early morning light down Orange Avenue to Lake Ivanhoe. Billy entered the grove and pulled up beside a towering pile of fresh manure that reeked like putrid ammonia. The overpowering stench caused Will to turn his head.

"What's the matter, boy?" said Billy. "Ain't you ever been around manure? Well, from now on you'll get used to it. You need to know a grove is just like a person; it needs food, and food to a grove is manure. You and me gonna feed the grove; then we gonna haul water, trees get mighty thirsty. Hard work's what caretaking's all about, boy."

All day, perspiration rolled down Will's body as the sun bore down relentlessly. They shoveled manure into the wagon, hauled it, and then shoveled it onto the grove. Several times they loaded a tank on the wagon, filled it with lake water, and released it between long rows of trees.

"Better get you a big straw hat and a long sleeve white shirt," said Billy. "Florida sun has no mercy on Georgia boys."

Just before the sun dropped below the trees beyond the shoreline, Billy washed his hands and boots in the lake and said, "C'mon, let's go."

Will's arms and legs ached as he stepped down from the wagon in front of Ruby's Boarding House, his new location.

Billy smirked. "I'll be here at six in the maw'nin, Georgia Boy. You be ready."

"Yeah," replied Will, "six o'clock."

Billy drove off laughing.

The shirt-soaking, hand-blistering work of shoveling smelly manure ten hours a day took the glamour out of the citrus business for Will, but he reminded himself that he was twenty years younger than Pastin, and he was determined to prove that he was as good a man as Billy.

At quitting time on Friday, Pastin made an announcement. "Hey, Georgia Boy, I'm gonna be down in Kissimmee for a couple of days. Take care of things, will you?"

Will nodded. "Yeah. See you later." Only ten acres of the grove had been fertilized, and the stench of manure had permeated Will's skin. He wondered if he was ever going to be clean enough to be with Rachel again.

On Saturday, Will scrubbed every inch of his body with a stiff brush, put on his best clothes, and headed out. He turned the corner at West Street and followed the path to the Adamsons' gate. Rachel would come to him, he thought, and he would say something clever. She would laugh and smile and ... but then he saw her, sitting in the swing with a young man in uniform.

"Will," beamed Rachel, "come over and meet my friend Stanley Edwards. He's a cadet at Virginia Military Institute."

Towering over Will, the deeply tanned cadet with a finely chiseled face gripped Will's hand. There was an athletic hardness about his body, a repelling look in his gray eyes.

Rachel broke the silence. "Stanley and I grew up together and have always been good friends. He and his family live right down the street. It's so nice to have him home on leave."

Stanley held Rachel's hand. "I must be going. See you at six thirty, Punkin."

Punkin! thought Will. Punkin! How close are they? This muscle-bound, cocksure boy with stripes up and down his sleeves can't call her that. He felt as if Stanley Edwards had robbed him of a treasure.

Rachel interrupted his thoughts. "Will, sit beside me. Whatever have you been doing these past two weeks?"

He stood there feeling like a little boy in short pants, sensing she always knew exactly what to say, and precisely how to defuse a situation.

"Well, just hard work."

"Please," she said, "have lunch with us after church tomorrow."

"Thank you."

"Now, tell me every single thing about the grove."

He wanted to tell her how hard he had been working in the grove, and how much he looked forward to being with her, but he couldn't. His mind was filled with a vision of Stanley Edwards galloping around on a black stallion while Rachel threw garlands in his path.

After church service, Will had walked alone to the Adamsons' house, sat uncomfortably across the table from Rachel, answered Dr. Adamson's questions about the grove, finished his after dinner coffee, and smiled at Mrs. Adamson. "Thank you for a delicious lunch."

Mrs. Adamson rose and everyone followed her to the parlor.

Still standing, Will glanced at Dr. Adamson. "I really should be on my way."

As he moved toward the door, Rachel took his hat from a shelf in the foyer and held it behind her back. "Let's walk by the lake," she said.

They were nearly halfway around Lake Eola before he spoke. "Hope I didn't interrupt anything yesterday."

Rachel giggled. "Of course not. Stanley is like a big brother. He's the person I've always run to with my little problems, you know."

Oh, yes, he knew. It was like pouring turpentine on an open wound. He could see the dashing cadet holding her in his powerful arms while she shared her innermost thoughts. Rachel and Stanley, deeply rooted in the community, connected by common interests. His mind raced. What could he possibly say now without sounding like a fool?

Billy Pastin was nowhere to be found on Monday morning. Will continued working in the grove, knowing Billy should have returned by this time. Kissimmee, he mused, what could be there to delay him? What if he never came back? What would Mr. Fitch do?

At the end of the week, Will rented a quarter horse at Hyer's Livery Stable and headed for Kissimmee. Summer rains had flooded portions of the sand road that cut through seventeen miles of rattlesnake infested palmetto bush. Perspiration sprang from the roots of his hair, around his neck, and between his shoulders during the long, hot ride; but finally he arrived. Several chickens roamed the dusty street as he rode through town wondering where to begin his search for Billy. He pulled up in front of Johnson's saloon, watered his horse at the trough, tied her up, walked up the stairs, pushed open the swinging door, and entered a smelly room. Women dressed in short black skirts and black stockings stood near tables of poker-playing cowboys. Behind a rough-cut pine bar, a flabby, bald, middle-aged man poured drinks. "Do you know Billy Pastin?" said Will.

The bar-tender carefully studied Will's face. "Yeah, everybody knows Billy. He got drunk again and busted up chairs and tables at the Black Turkey last week. He's in jail."

At the Kissimmee jail, Will and the sheriff stood before a one-cell tank occupied by Billy, a half-naked Negro man, and a sleeping Indian who had vomited on the floor during the night. "How much you want to get him out?" said Will.

The sheriff pushed back his hat. "Fifty dollars. Don't let him come back to town no more."

Will wondered what Mr. Fitch would say if he spent that kind of money to bail Billy out of jail. If he bailed him, Mr. Fitch might shoot him; if he didn't bail him, Fitch might still shoot him.

By the time Will returned with the money, it was late afternoon. He handed over the cash to the sheriff; and Billy, looking like a wild animal set free, stalked out of the jail, mounted, and rode off. A strong wind from the west, blowing lightning-streaked clouds, broke into a sudden summer storm, but by the time they arrived in Orlando, both the storm and Billy's arrogant mood had passed. Drops of rainwater dripped from the rim of Billy's drenched black hat as he spoke. "I'll pick you up Monday morning at six, Georgia Boy, and ah, thanks."

Two days after his return from Kissimmee, words leaped from the page of a letter Will received from Mr. Fitch. *"Lucy and I will arrive on the fifteenth. Please meet us at the depot."*

Will swallowed. Showdown time. He knew it would come. Mr. Fitch was fair-minded, but Lucy was his flesh and blood. Now, he would learn if his job rested on his relationship with her. "Always tell the truth." Pastor Bentley's words. It was simple. He would tell Lucy about Rachel. No point in stringing it out. No hem-hawing around. Just tell her. But, how did Rachel feel? Lord knows, she might be in love with Stanley Edwards. He dropped the letter on his bed and headed for the grove.

On the fifteenth, when the train pulled in from Atlanta, Will waited at the depot. He shook Mr. Fitch's hand and lightly kissed Lucy's cheek.

"Lucy. Mr. Fitch," he said, "Good to see you. There's so much to tell. Let's go to the hotel."

During supper, Will gave details of the fire that had destroyed his personal belongings. His deep tan glowed as he explained every aspect of spraying, fertilizing, and irrigating the grove.

Mr. Fitch broke in. "You and I will talk tomorrow. I'm worn out. Why don't you take Lucy for a walk."

As they strolled down Orange Avenue, he wondered how to begin. "Lucy, I'm so involved with the grove. Sorry I haven't written."

"Two letters in three months?"

"Lucy. I ..."

She put her hand on his arm. "Will, I love you, but I'm not pushing. If you want time, I can wait."

"Oh, I know, it's not that." His temples pounded.

She stopped walking. A gas street lamp reflected light on her pretty face. "What is it?" she said.

He lowered his head. "There's someone else."

She quickly withdrew. "Someone else?"

"Yes. I'm sorry."

Fighting back tears, she shook her head. "Please, say no more. I feel like such a fool."

"Lucy. I never intended to ...." She turned away and hurried back to the San Juan.

Mr. Fitch cleared his throat as he picked at his breakfast. He placed his fork on his plate and looked squarely at Will. "I can't believe you threw my little girl over — just like that. I thought you two were perfect for each other. What happened, son?"

"I feel awful about it, sir." He looked directly into Mr. Fitch's eyes. "I'm in love with another girl — it's that simple."

The old man sighed and shook his head. "You know, of course, you're throwing away the grove. It would have been yours and Lucy's after I'm gone."

"Yes sir."

"Well, that's all there is to say about it. Will you continue managing my grove?"

"Yes, sir. I would like to."

"All right. It's settled."

꒯ *7* ꒭

The fragrant blossoms of February became ripe oranges in De cember. All year, Will and Billy fertilized, pruned, and sprayed the grove, with the care a mother would give her infant. Soon, the fruit would be harvested, at least five boxes to the tree, according to Billy. Will felt sure that Mr. Fitch would be pleased.

At noon, on the Monday before Christmas, Will sipped coffee and nibbled on cheese as he sat in the shade of a huge camphor tree growing near the south boundary of the grove. Now he understood the economic fabric of Orlando, everyone connected, and all dependent upon God to produce oranges from earth and sky. But what if God became angry? What then? Can't think about that, he told himself, too many other things. He felt that Billy and any colored man could care for the grove and wondered how long it would take Mr. Fitch to come to that conclusion. He thought of Rachel. He had been with her every week for months; they had walked and talked, traveled to Winter Park in Dr. Adamson's buggy, attended plays at the opera house, and sat together in worship services every Sunday. She was not only beautiful, but also intelligent and poised. He believed she liked him, maybe more than a little, but what could he do about it? A girl like Rachel deserved a man of means, someone who had made his way, but not Stanley Edwards, who would be coming home for Christmas in a few days.

Pastin walked up and poured out the last of his cold coffee. "Let's go, Georgia Boy, plenty more work to do before dark."

Billy Pastin, pondered Will, not much on social skills, but more horse sense and grove know-how than any man in the town. If he could just keep him out of jail, Mr. Fitch's grove would be the best producer in the county.

Friends of the family arrived on Saturday for the Adamsons' annual Christmas party. A holly wreath hung on the front door, remind-

53

ing everyone that the holiday season had begun. During the day, cool December winds had swept through Orlando, bringing out winter jackets for the men and wool shawls for the ladies. Dressed in his new black suit, Will smiled confidently as Mrs. Adamson greeted him in her foyer. "Come right in. Rachel will be out in a few minutes. She and Stanley Edwards are carving turkey in the kitchen."

Stanley Edwards, thought Will. Why doesn't Cadet Stanley Edwards go off to war in China? A feeling of rejection settled over him. He began thinking. Certainly, nothing has been said ... I haven't asked ... she hasn't indicated ... oh, for heavens sake, have a good time. He glanced about the room. Burning logs crackled in the fireplace, and a Christmas tree decorated with bright garlands and little white candles stood in the corner. In the dining room, silver candelabra holding glowing tapers graced a linen covered table. A crystal punch bowl rested at the center of a side table.

Rachel came up behind him. As he turned, he saw warmth in her expression, but beside her stood Stanley with his cold eyes and brass buttons.

"Will, please sit with Stanley and me."

Stanley and me, thought Will. How about Stanley sitting with Rachel and me? He filled his plate and painfully seated himself beside her. Stanley sat on her left, and the men ate in silence as she held court, but in the middle of a sentence, Dr. Adamson broke in: "Well, Stanley, I see you earned your stripes — First Captain, just like your father." The doctor placed his arm around Stanley's shoulder. "Your dad was the finest battalion commander in the 1st Virginia. He'd be mighty proud of you, son."

Son, thought Will. So what am I? A little fella to have around until First Captain Edwards comes home? He placed his plate on a side table, backed away, and found Mr. Pendelton at the far end of the parlor.

When guests began departing, Will saw Rachel and Stanley sitting in the porch swing, holding hands. She giggled at something he had said, a hint of affection in her voice. The picture was clear. She would wait for Stanley and they would be married as soon as he graduated from VMI. Will found his hat and said goodbye to the Adamsons, his throat tightening as he hurried off in the night.

Four weeks passed; Will said nothing to Billy about Rachel during their ten hour work days in the grove. He did not attend worship services on Sunday, and he avoided the other places Rachel normally frequented.

At noon, Will stood at the counter of Bumby Hardware Store waiting, for change. He placed his new axe handle under his arm, turned and walked toward the entrance; there, in the middle of the aisle, stood Rachel. He tipped his hat and started around her as she spoke.

"Where have you been, Will?" she asked in a strained voice.

He stopped and watched her normally soft expression become livid. He tipped his hat and nodded. "Nice to see you. Please excuse me."

She stood her ground. "Will you kindly tell me why you are avoiding me?"

"You seem very well occupied."

"You're acting like a little boy," she said with anger in her voice. She spun around and left the store.

Will stomped out behind her, threw his axe handle to the floor of the wagon, and slapped the reins to the mule, his head throbbing all the way to the grove. When he returned to his room that night he found a message under his door.

Dear Will,

You are invited to join us at eleven o'clock on Saturday morning at the corner of Church and Main for the ground breaking ceremony of our new sanctuary.

Edward Adamson

Will dropped the note on his bed table, walked to the window, and looked out ... ground breaking ... new sanctuary ... beautiful setting for Rachel and Stanley's wedding. Must keep Virginia blood lines pure.

On Saturday, half the town was present for the groundbreaking. Will stood behind Dr. Adamson as Reverend Patton thanked the doctor and other members of the church for their support of the building fund; then the preacher held out his arm and prayed a long prayer. As he continued, Will opened his eyes and quickly looked at Rachel. When she smiled he turned his head away, but blood rushed through veins in his neck. The prayer finally ended, and he moved to her side, breathed deeply, and said, "May I walk you home?"

Rachel placed her arm around his arm. "Of course, you may."

He looked straight ahead. "I want to know about you and Stanley."

She stopped abruptly and looked up at him. "Will Taylor, you silly goose. You're asking me to come right out and tell you that I love you."

Will's face reddened. "I didn't know." He shook his head and smiled. "I almost went crazy when I saw you and Stanley in the swing."

"I said that Stanley is just a good friend. Now, walk me home and I'll fix lunch."

After lunch they sat in the porch swing, and for hours he talked about the grove, Billy Pastin, and Paul and Martha Bentley. When twilight came, a golden moon rose beyond the lake, peering between branches of an oak, filtering soft patterns of light on Rachel's face. As he continued talking, her gaze shifted from his eyes to his lips. "Tell me what you're thinking," she asked.

She's so lovely, he thought, but he really didn't know what to say. Certainly, it couldn't be, "Will you marry me?" An absurd idea, but what could he say? All he could think of was his meager salary backed up by twenty dollars in his savings account. He swallowed and said, "I have little to offer."

She shook her head. "It doesn't matter."

He held her in his arms. "I love you, Rachel. Marry me."

"Yes," she whispered.

He held her and kissed her lips, and then he pulled away. "I must speak to your father."

Rachel found her parents in their bedroom. "Daddy," she said, "Will has something important to say to you."

The doctor glared. "Can't it wait until tomorrow?"

Sensing what was happening, Mrs. Adamson broke in, "Edward. Please dress and go downstairs."

The doctor moaned as he rammed his arms in his robe. "Will someone tell me what's going on?"

Rachel was euphoric. "He's going to ask for my hand, Daddy."

"What! He's only a boy," snorted the doctor.

Mrs. Adamson frowned. "Yes, and a very fine boy. You were just a boy when you proposed to me."

Downstairs, Will sat in the parlor on the edge of a straight back chair. Dr. Adamson ambled down the stairs, entered the parlor, plopped down in his leather chair, and waited. It wasn't late, but the doctor looked tired. Will knew it was an awkward time to ask for Rachel's hand, but this was the time. He could hardly speak, but somehow the words rushed out. "Sir, I want to marry Rachel." There was silence for what seemed to Will like a lifetime.

Dr. Adamson pulled a white handkerchief from his pocket, blew his nose, then carefully refolded the handkerchief and placed it in the pocket of his robe. "I would think a married man would want a steady job. Do you intend to support a family solely on grove salary?"

Will bit his lip. "Sir, there's a great future in citrus. I don't intend to work for others for the rest of my life. Some day I intend to have my own grove and make a good living for my family."

The doctor rested his jaw in the palm of his hand, then smiled, and extended his hand. "You have my permission, and our blessing, son."

Will jumped to his feet. "Thank you, sir. Thank you."

Mrs. Adamson and Rachel glided into the parlor and hugged Will, then the ladies sat on the sofa and began a dialogue. Excluded from the conversation, Doctor Adamson and Will sat and listened as the ladies planned the wedding. An hour later, the doctor excused himself and went to bed. Will rose, picked up his hat, quietly slipped out of the house, and walked back to Ruby's boardinghouse.

The announcement of an April wedding created great excitement in town. Immediately, ladies began planning parties, and Mrs. Adamson became immersed in a thousand details in preparation for her daughter's wedding. As the invitation list grew, Dr. Adamson uttered an opinion: "It's all out of proportion." But of course, he was only an observer in a swirl of bridal activity.

Mrs. Adamson decided that Mrs. Alma Jernigan of Winter Park would make the bridal dress. "She's the only fine seamstress in Central Florida, in my way of thinking." The gown would be made of white corded silk, trimmed with white satin. Rachel had wanted half-sleeves and a low neckline, but Mrs. Adamson announced firmly: "You are not going to a dance but to a religious ceremony. The dress must fit snugly at the neck and the sleeves must cover the wrists."

Gifts flooded the Adamson home. The grandest present was from the Adamsons themselves, a three-year-old bay mare named Princess, and a black buggy with gold trim. Billy Pastin couldn't keep his eyes off the mare. "Finest horse flesh I ever saw," he said, as he rubbed her neck. "Adamsons must really think you're something, Will."

From Richmond came Anna Rand, Mrs. Adamson's niece and Rachel's maid of honor. When she stepped off the train at the depot, every eye focused on her broad felt hat featuring a cluster of white egret feathers blowing in the breeze. Pastor Paul and Martha Bentley came on the same train, and Will took all of them to the San Juan in his brand new buggy.

On the day before the wedding, the Bentleys hosted the rehearsal dinner in the dining room of the San Juan. Pastor Bentley looked thinner and much older to Will. Martha was heavier, and her hair was almost white; but her loving smile was still there. As the dinner began, Pastor held high his glass. "I propose a toast. Our son has been a blessing to us, but he, too, is blessed to be united with such a fine family. May you, Rachel, have many sons and daughters, and may you and Will live out your lives in obedience to our Lord. To the bride."

Will rose from his chair, went to his parents' side, and said, "If it were not for you, I would not be in this place marrying a wonderful girl." He leaned over, kissed Martha's cheek. "Thank you for rescuing my life."

The spring rain had stopped just after lunch on the day of the wedding. At Ruby's boardinghouse, Will struggled to get Pastin into the ten dollar suit ordered from Tampa. Billy frowned as he tugged at his stiff collar. "Good Lord, this thing is like a noose. You're the only person on earth I'd choke myself for."

Will chuckled. "This is worse than giving a bath to a wildcat, but sooner or later it had to come. Now, for once in your life be patient, and be still while I put this necktie on you."

At three o'clock, Will and Billy headed Princess for the San Juan to take the Bentleys to the Adamsons' house. When they passed Hyer's

Saloon, an old crony wearing faded overalls over dirty long under-wear, shouted, "Hey, Billy, you birds going to a funeral?"

Pastin scowled and looked straight ahead as all the boys in front of Hyer's slapped their thighs and howled.

"Don't look at them scarecrows," said Billy. "Not a pinch of brains in the bunch."

The Adamsons' home was a sea of gladioli, white carnations, green ferns, and potted palms. Relatives and friends made a walkway for the bride and Dr. Adamson from the oak stairway to the parlor. At the piano, Mrs. Tyler McKenzie played a medley of hymns; and after that, the window panes vibrated as Miss Agnes Moore sang "Oh Promise Me."

At four o'clock, Mrs. McKenzie began playing the Overture to The Bridal Chorus. Pastor Bentley and Will marched to an altar placed before the fireplace. The maid of honor followed, wearing a pink, floor-length, silk dress trimmed with white lace and garlands of white vio-lets in her hair. She carried a bouquet of pink rosebuds and took her place in front of Reverend Patton. Mrs. Adamson blotted tears as strains of the Bridal Chorus continued. Will took a deep breath as he watched his veiled bride and her father walk slowly toward him.

Dr. Adamson placed his daughter's hand in Will's. She vowed to love, honor, and obey her husband, in sickness and in health, in times of plenty, and in times of want. Prayers were offered and Will slid a gold wedding band on his bride's finger. Reverend Patton pronounced the benediction, and Will opened his eyes, wondering whether he had been dreaming. He held Rachel's arm, and greeted a rush of well-wish-ers.

A three-layered white wedding cake adorned with two small ce-ramic doves stood on a tea table in Mrs. Adamson's parlor. Will sliced the cake, placed a morsel in Rachel's mouth and whispered, "I love you." Her tender expression reflected her response.

The reception ended. In a hail of rice, Billy Pastin loaded the new-lyweds into Will's buggy and made a getaway to the San Juan. Will strolled nonchalantly to the registration desk, gave his name and signed the register. *William S. Taylor*. With a wink and a smile the aging clerk remarked: "That's Mr. and Mrs., isn't it?"

"Yes, it is," blushed Will. He quickly added Mr. and Mrs., signaled the bellman, took Rachel by the arm, and climbed the stairs as the hotel staff muffled their laughter. In their room Will found a bottle of champagne recessed in a wine cooler. The card read:

> *To Georgia Boy and his bride, Don't stay in bed too long. There's work to be done in the grove ... Billy*

Will glanced at Rachel and smiled. "Never thought that Cracker would become my good friend, but he is. He's my best friend."

Nervously, he opened the bottle, poured wine, offered a glass to his bride, then sat on the edge of the bed, and laughed. "I suppose you thought I was just a country boy from the hills of Georgia."

Rachel removed her bonnet and her jacket. Her long black curls fell loosely about her shoulders. She giggled as she tilted her head. "Yes, and I knew you couldn't resist me."

"Why, you conceited little girl."

He grinned, placed his glass on the table, gently kissed her cheek and then her lips, as they fell onto the soft mattress of a four-poster bed.

The newlyweds scrambled out of bed early, dressed, packed, ate toast, drank coffee and then took the seven o'clock northbound train to Sanford. Two hours later they arrived at the depot, walked to the dock, and boarded the *River Queen* for a trip up the St. Johns River to Palatka. Will and Rachel stood at the rail watching deck hands haul in lines as the old side-wheeler let out a hoot of steam and pulled away from the dock. As the boat crossed Lake Monroe, and headed for Palatka, seagulls followed, turning and diving for bread crumbs thrown by passengers. Facing the wind, Will held his bride's hand as she looked up at him. It was the same look he had seen before — unmistakable affection. He smiled. "You're probably wondering if we can afford this," he said.

"Can we?"

"It took every last cent, but nothing's too good for my bride."

"So, what do we eat when we get home?"

"Well, let's see. How about some of Billy's smoked possum? It's real cheap."

"Oh, Will."

He took her in his arms. "As long as I have you, I'm rich."

"Then, Mr. Taylor, you will remain quite wealthy, but let's not become a spectacle. Shall we go to our cabin?"

A week later, they returned to Orlando and moved into Rachel's room at the Adamsons' home. A letter marked "Personal and Confidential" waited for Will at the post office.

March 23, 1888

Mason, Thompson, & Thornberry
Attorneys at Law
249 North Peachtree Street
Atlanta, Georgia

Mr. William S. Taylor
C/O Postmaster
Orlando, Florida

Dear Mr. Taylor,

You are hereby advised of the death of Mr. Jonathan H. Fitch. Under the terms of his will, the deceased has bequeathed to Lucy Fitch Neal all citrus grove properties and equipment he owned in the State of Florida.

We are in the process of probating the estate. In that you currently manage the groves of the deceased, it will be necessary for you to travel to Atlanta to meet, in our offices, with Lucy Fitch Neal, the personal representative. Please advise, at your earliest convenience, the date of your arrival.

Awaiting your reply. I am, Your obedient servant,

George T. Mason

❦ 8 ❦

$\mathcal{A}$t the post office, Will folded the letter from George T. Mason walked to the street, and mounted Princess. Mr. Fitch, he thought, the one who gave him a job, brought him to Orlando, trusted him. Now, it was over. Lucy would sell the grove and he would end up a field hand, dragging Rachel down with him. Doctor Adamson was right: a married man should have a steady job. He tied up Princess and walked inside to tell Rachel the bad news.

Rachel read the letter, dropped it on her bed and moved closer to Will. "Lucy Neal. I remember you saying she accompanied her grandfather to Orlando. She was here with you. Tell me about her."

After a brief pause, he sat on the edge of the bed and began. "Lucy and I were classmates in Hogansville."

"Oh?"

"Yes. In fact, I think Mr. Fitch saw me as a candidate for a son-in-law, but it wasn't to be. Lucy was a good friend — that's all."

Rachel tilted her head. "Funny you never mentioned this before."

All the way to Atlanta, Will remembered his first train trip: the lonesome moan of the whistle; the clack of steel wheels that had driven him to bookkeeping school and a probable career in accounting, a future that had closed when he and Annabel made love. But, now, a new opportunity would also die, and with it the chance to make his way in a frontier town. And Rachel. What about Rachel? He wondered how she would react when the reality of his predicament settled over her.

As soon as the train pulled into Atlanta, Will checked into his hotel and hurried to Mr. Mason's office. Lucy was there, seated on a dark leather sofa in a mahogany-paneled reception room. Dressed in black wool with long tight sleeves, she wore a small cameo brooch at the neck. Sunlight funneled in from the window illuminating her auburn curls rolled up beneath a black bonnet.

63

"I feel terrible about your grandfather," Will said.

Lucy's voice was almost indistinct. "Thank you. It was his heart. He died in his sleep."

Will spoke softly. "All grove records are here for you and Mr. Mason. I'll do anything I can during the transition."

"Transition? You can't walk out, just like that. Where would I begin? I want you to continue managing the grove."

"I'm married, Lucy."

"That's not surprising. But that has little to do with the grove."

His mind churned. "All right, I will, but I'm left with nothing. Would you consider selling me five acres of the grove? I'll pay it off out of my salary."

She turned, walked slowly toward him, and nodded. "You and Mr. Mason settle on the price."

It was too easy. Did she really believe he was vital to the management of her grove? Why would she sell? He wondered. He reached out and took her hand. "Thank you, Lucy."

Just then, Mason opened the door to his office. "Please come in," he said, "we're ready to go over the records."

Will's train pulled into the Orlando depot at Church Street, screeched to a stop and released white steam. Rachel stood on the platform with head held high, waiting for her husband. He stepped from the car, dropped his bag and ran to her, his voice alive with excitement. "I still have a job managing the grove."

Rachel's jaw dropped. "What?"

"Lucy asked me to stay on and I agreed, with the understanding she would sell us five acres on the lake."

"Where will the money come from?"

"She's selling for two thousand dollars. She'll take it out of my pay — twenty a month."

Rachel sat in silence as Princess pulled the buggy down Church Street toward the Adamson place, halting at Orange Avenue for a yellow delivery wagon pulled by two large draft horses. Will popped the reins and they continued. "Rachel, I have no other job, and no money. I have to work for Lucy."

Rachel cleared her throat. "Well, here we are. Put Princess away and wash up. Lunch will be ready in a few minutes."

During the remainder of the day, icicles hung from Rachel. Ignoring her husband, she went about her daily tasks in silence. Will thought of pleading his case further, but he sensed that the more rational his argument, the more irrational she might become. He knew it wasn't a time for talking.

In bed, that night, Rachel turned her back and lay motionless on the edge of the mattress. Will moved close, kissed her shoulders and neck, and rubbed her back. When he had almost fallen asleep she asked: "Is Lucy very pretty?"

He turned her toward him and placed his face against her breast, kissed her, and whispered, "What am I going to do with you?"

With the thousand dollar loan Mr. Pendelton had approved, Billy helped Will build a three-room pine cabin on five acres at the northwest corner of the grove, thirty yards from the shore of the lake. The bedroom and kitchen were small, but the living room was spacious. Best of all, Billy built a brick fireplace. The place wasn't grandiose, but Rachel liked it and that's all that mattered to Will. The white paint on the interior walls had barely dried when new furniture arrived, a four-poster bed, tables, chairs, and a dresser with mirror. New dishes, pots, pans, kitchen utensils, and linens were put in place, all given by the Adamsons. Pink or white curtains hung from every window. Hooked rugs lay on living room and bedroom floors.

The cabin was finished and Billy Pastin was invited to sample Rachel's first attempt at fried chicken. Billy finished his fourth piece of chicken, wiped his hands on his shirt, put his feet on the seat of a chair, and lit a cigar. "You're really something, Rachel. Good looking, and you can cook, too. What a woman."

Rachel's voice was penetrating. "Listen, Billy, and you, too, my dear Will. This is a home. No one will bring dirty boots in here, or put their feet on furniture, or wear a hat inside. No bad language will be spoken here, and no alcohol will be served. That's the way it's going to be."

With that remark it became clear that Rachel Adamson Taylor was a force to be reckoned with. Will scratched his head. "Guess that settles that."

Billy's feet dropped to the floor. "Yeah."

In January, Will and Billy walked the grove examining limbs heavy with ripe fruit. "Looks like six boxes to the tree to me," said Billy.

Will nodded. "That means about seventy five hundred dollars for Lucy. She should be happy."

"Yeah, Guess she'll be coming to town to collect her money," said Billy with an impish grin.

"She'll be here next month with her new office manager, Bradford Hanson."

Pastin smiled. "And you'll be introducing her to Rachel."

Will frowned. "Yes, I will. You think that's funny?"

"Oh, no, no. Just commenting."

Will pointed his finger and shook his head. "Now, Billy, I've had enough trouble without your getting into it."

Billy shrugged and smiled like a Cheshire cat.

Will halved an orange and tasted the fruit. He wondered about Rachel and Lucy in the same town and wished he were anyplace else.

Bright sunshine greeted Lucy and Bradford Hanson as they stepped on the platform of the depot in Orlando. Gone were Lucy's black mourning clothes, replaced by a stylishly tailored traveling suit. Poised and confident, she looked directly into Will's eyes, held out her hand, and inquired about his wife. Will briefly held her hand, greeted Bradford, assisted with luggage, then drove them to the San Juan. There, Lucy changed to a light wool skirt, print blouse, and black riding boots. By three o'clock she, Bradford, and Will were in the grove, inspecting branches heavy with fruit. Lucy laughed as she picked an orange. "Granddaddy said, 'Money grows on orange trees.' I believe it; all that profit in just one year." Her green eyes sparkled as she looked at Will. "You're a miracle worker."

"Oh, no. Billy and I just do our job. Listen, Rachel and I are expecting you and Brad for dinner at seven at the San Juan."

"Thank you," she said, with a little smile. "I'm dying to meet Rachel."

At seven o'clock Lucy looked radiant in blue taffeta as she and Bradford Hanson entered the San Juan dining room. She made her way to Rachel and said, "I'm Lucy Neal. I've looked forward to meeting you."

Color flashed in Rachel's face. "Thank you."

"Well," said Will, "shall we have dinner?"

All evening the men talked business while Rachel sat motionless, a strained look stretched across her face. Finally, she turned to Lucy. "Your life must be very exciting, living in Atlanta."

"It is, but the city is so large. I envy you living in this beautiful place. And your husband — a genius. Whatever would I do without him?"

Rachel clenched her teeth as she listened, the words burning in her mind. Lucy — her auburn curls and green eyes. She would most certainly *do without* her husband. No longer would he be available to her.

Rachel's cheeks flamed as she sat facing her mother in the Adamson parlor. "I'm miserable, Mama, absolutely miserable. I cannot stand it that Will is working for a woman with whom he had a past relationship. I want to sell our place and buy a grove with the money grandpa placed in trust for me."

Mrs. Adamson sighed and carefully placed her cup in its saucer. "Darling. You must not overreact. You're Will's wife. He loves you."

Rachel stood. "No! Mother, I'm not overreacting. I'm simply asking for my inheritance."

Mrs. Adamson shook her head. "If you intervene, it will infuriate Will. He will know you do not trust him."

"What I know is that I cannot and will not live under that woman's yoke."

Mrs. Adamson closed her eyes as she spoke. "You are making a mistake, but I will not stand in your way."

Rachel took her mother's hands and squeezed them. "Thank you, Mama. I know what I'm doing." Rachel kissed her mother, left the house, sat very straight in her buggy, slapped the reins, and headed home.

That night, dinner dishes were washed and dried. Will lit the lamp on his pine desk, pulled up his chair, and turned pages in his ledger.

Rachel came from behind and placed her hands on his shoulders. "I want you to hear what I have to say before you say a word. Agreed?"

The tone of her voice was compelling. He turned and saw little lines of pain in her expression. "What is it, dear?"

"I want to sell our place and, with the money Grandpa Rand left me, buy a grove and build a home. Mama has agreed and," her voice trailed off to a whisper. "Oh, Will, I can't live in Lucy's grove. I can't!"

He stood and felt her heart pounding as he held her. His mind raced. If I say no, he thought, there will always be conflict. "We'll talk about it tomorrow," he whispered.

"No! Right now. Please!"

"All right."

She pressed closer. "When I'm twenty-five, the money is mine without Mama's permission. I would give it to you then to invest. But why not now?" She looked at him with tear-filled eyes. "Don't you see? I want you to invest all your energy, all your labor in our grove, not Lucy's."

It's not a matter of my pride, he thought. It's a matter of Rachel's pride. Encircled by Lucy's grove, she will always be tormented. He nodded. "All right. I'll write to her, offering our five acres, and my resignation."

Rachel's head fell on his shoulder.

August 20, 1889

Miss Lucy Fitch Neal
FITCH BROKERAGE COMPANY
100 East Harris Street
Atlanta, Georgia

Dear Lucy,

You were generous to give me the opportunity to manage your grove in Orlando. I appreciate that. However, for personal reasons, I hereby give notice of my intention to leave your service. Of course,

I shall be happy to continue until such time as you have employed new management.

I offer you first refusal on our five acres and home. Please let me know your wishes.

Your servant,

Will

Lucy dropped the letter on her desk and called Brad Hanson. He read it and slowly looked up. "Speaking as your friend, you should sell him the whole grove; it's for the best."

"For the best? What do you mean?"

"Lucy, we're in the fruit and vegetable brokerage business in Atlanta, a long way from Orlando. Besides, I knew he wouldn't stay with you. Rachel Taylor's expression told me that."

"Don't be silly. It's an excellent investment."

Hanson held her hands. "Yes, but not for you. Sell him the grove, Lucy."

She stared at him, then turned her back and walked to the window. People holding umbrellas dashed along Harris Street in morning rain. A white milk wagon pulled by an aging gray horse plodded along the street ... Will Taylor ... her first kiss ... under the big oak ... "All right. You handle it."

ᑤ *9* ᑤ

The aroma of Rachel's roast filled the air as Will and Billy washed their boots in the lake and then walked to the porch of the cabin. Pastin chuckled. "You happy?"

Will winked. "Huge crop and good prices, who wouldn't be?" But questions remained for Will as he considered making Billy a partner. Had Billy learned a lesson in Kissimmee? What about his drinking problem? Was he responsible? Well, he thought, there's risk in just getting out of bed in the morning, and there's no better grove man in Orange County than Billy Pastin.

As they stood on the porch drying their hands on towels, a light breeze blew across the lake brushing their faces. "Let's talk," said Will. "I want to expand, and I'm offering you a proposition. The more we make, the more you get. You manage the grove, and I'll be responsible for marketing the fruit and managing the money."

Billy looked dejected. "I ain't got no money."

"I know that. I'll invest the money, and you manage the grove for a salary of seventy-five a month plus ten percent of the profit we earn. What do you say?"

A broad smile came over Billy's wrinkled face. "Georgia Boy, you got yo'self a partner."

"Where do you think we should expand?"

Pastin rubbed his leathery hands together as he spoke. "Orlando's all right, but I want you to think about buying in Kissimmee. Down there they think cattle, not citrus. We can buy twice as much grove for the same money."

Will nodded. "Tomorrow let's go over and look around."

Billy headed for his horse. "Hey, Billy," said Will, "how about staying for some of Rachel's roast beef?"

Before he sat at Rachel's table, Billy removed his hat. When they were seated, he placed a napkin in his lap, passed dishes to the others, and waited for Rachel to pick up her fork before he began eating. When the meal was completed, he thanked Rachel, went out the door, and mounted his horse. Rachel stood in the doorway watching Billy ride away. She turned her head to Will. "Would you say I taught that roughneck some manners?"

In Kissimmee, the new partners rode several groves, examining trees and questioning growers. Jack Prosser, the scrawny, dark-bearded owner of the only packing house in town, told them to ride west two miles and look for a "For Sale" sign on a thirty-five acre budded grove. Prosser chuckled. "The owner, Ben Jacobson, is an ornery old duck. Can't get along with anybody. He'd rather let his fruit drop on the ground than pay a fair price to pickers."

Following Prosser's directions, Will and Billy plodded down a cow trail, winding through scrub oak and cabbage palms. Two miles down the trail they found a healthy, well-kept grove loaded with fruit. Billy remained mounted as he scanned the trees.

"Looks like at least six boxes to the tree. Let me do the talking."

"You're the grove man," said Will.

The owner, a fat little man of sixty or more, wearing faded over-alls, strolled out of his one-room shack. Billy dismounted, halved an orange, tasted the sweet fruit, and pointed to the For Sale sign. "You Mr. Jacobson?"

The old man frowned. "Yes. Why you want to know?"

"May want to buy your grove. What kind is it?"

"Sweet orange, budded on sour root stock, set fifteen years ago."

"How much you want, Mr. Jacobson?"

Jacobson stroked his gray beard and looked at his trees. "Five hundred an acre cash, and not a cent less."

Billy thought it was the best-cared-for grove he had seen anywhere. "Way out of line," he countered.

The muscles in Jacobson's crinkled face tightened. "Listen, my boy, there's at least twelve thousand dollars worth of fruit on these trees."

Billy smiled. "Why do you want to sell the grove? Could it be because local people won't pick your fruit? They say half your crop rots before you get it to market. Right?"

Jacobson's eyelids narrowed and his hands trembled. "The greedy scum in this town won't pick my fruit for a fair price, but that has nothing to do with the value of my grove."

Will and Billy rode every row, dismounting frequently to check for tree damage and fruit or leaf infection. It was nearly sundown when they returned to Mr. Jacobson's shack and found him sitting on a stump whittling an oak limb. "Nice clean grove you have," said Billy. "We'll be in touch,"

Will followed Billy back to town. They put their mounts away at Murray's Stable and checked into the Cattleman's Hotel. At one end of the dining room a hind quarter of beef roasted over oak coals in a stone fireplace. A cowboy drank beer as he sat alone at a pine bench table near the center of the room. Will and Billy took a corner table, ordered beef stew, cornbread, and coffee. Billy pushed his hat back on his head and said: "We can steal the grove for probably three-fifty an acre."

Seemingly preoccupied, Will said nothing as he waited for his supper.

Billy looked up. "You hear what I said?"

The owner approached the table and served stew on tin plates, poured steaming coffee in tin cups, and left. Will picked up his fork. "Is the grove worth four-fifty an acre?"

Billy dipped cornbread in his stew, put it in his mouth, and began chewing. "Course it is."

"Offer it. I'll work out the financing with the bank."

Pastin studied Will's face for a long time, then nodded. "All right, it's your money, but I don't understand."

"Simple. Never take advantage of a man who has no options."

The deal closed and within three weeks, Billy moved to Kissimmee to assume command of the southern flank of Taylor groves.

The population of Orange County had grown to nearly three thousand citizens. New groves appeared throughout the area, and increasing quantities of fruit were shipped from the new brick depot of the South Florida Railroad to cities all along the line, as far north as Boston. In January, school was dismissed for the day, permitting children from all over the county to join in the celebration of the laying of the cornerstone of the new red brick courthouse on Central Avenue in Orlando. New arc lights were installed in town and some streets were paved with clay.

From the first day he arrived, Will had felt "something special" about Orlando. It was more than just a beautiful town sprinkled with lakes and blessed with great live oaks. There was a spirit about the people, a sense of civic pride that set the place apart, an intuitive feeling that everyone was rowing in the same direction. "A land of opportunity," Mr. Fitch had said it. And yet, even though the place looked more and more like a city, it was still a country town.

Mrs. Adamson had warned Rachel a thousand times, "Don't hang out your wash for everyone to see," but in this community everyone knew everyone else's business. Everyone knew that Mr. Mitchell and Mr. Oakley had been brought before the Session of the Presbyterian Church for gambling; that Mr. Pendelton had been observed drinking whiskey at a bankers convention in Jacksonville; that Judge Cornelius White's daughter was seen dancing on a Sunday afternoon. But everyone also knew that Alfred Jackson's widow and her small children were in need. A bundle of food sat on her doorstep every morning.

By the summer of 1894, the Taylor family had expanded to four. Three-year-old John Adam and eleven-month-old Mary Ann had not only arrived but were, as Rachel said, "under foot."

It was June 10th and just about every little person in town was invited to the Adamsons' for Adam's birthday party. On the front lawn, fifteen screaming children played "Pin the Donkey" with Dr. Adamson. Mrs. Adamson watched with amusement as she held baby Mary Ann. Will and Rachel scooped vanilla ice cream on slices of white layer cake. "Look at daddy," said Rachel. "He's having more fun than any child at the party."

Will nodded. He thought of his grandpa, William Cummings. He, too, had been a large man, kind and gentle, who had loved children. But like everyone else in Will's early life, he died too soon. Family roots, that's what's important, Will believed.

The birthday party ended. Will and Rachel helped clean up, and then walked together to the shore of Lake Eola, her voice hinting of excitement as she spoke. "Things are going well. Can we build our family home? Can we do it? One more baby and you and I will be sleeping in the barn."

Will laughed as they continued their stroll. He knew a new home was needed and he could afford one. Fruit money had poured in. Dr. Adamson had said, "A man's home is his castle," but how large should it be? Where should it be located? What would it cost?

On Saturday morning, Will and Rachel pulled up at the Court Street office of Kenneth Martin Construction Company. Will helped his wife down and tied Princess to a rail. Mr. Martin, a tall man with long gray whiskers, greeted them at his door and ushered them to his office. Kegs filled with rolled blueprints literally surrounded Martin's stand up desk. Drawings of commercial buildings and residences hung on every wall.

Will began. "My father-in-law, Doctor Adamson, tells me you're the finest builder in Central Florida. That's why we're here. We want to build a home."

Martin held his hands together as he stood behind his desk. "Yes, yes," he fidgeted. "Nice of Dr. Adamson to say that. Now, tell me what you have in mind?"

Just as Will was about to answer, Rachel withdrew sketches from her handbag and placed them on Mr. Martin's desk. "Let me take you through my sketches," she said. "The front of the white brick home presents an entrance of eight-foot, double doors, and four columns rise from a veranda to support a gable. Inside, a pine-paneled foyer, featuring a crystal chandelier, opens on the right to a large dining room. The passageway from the dining area leads to a kitchen and pantry. The family breakfast room is adjacent to the kitchen. Here, to the left of the foyer is the music room, which opens to a spacious parlor featuring exposed beams in a high, vaulted ceiling. The centerpiece of the parlor is a stone fireplace, couched by leaded glass bookcases. Situated at the rear of the foyer, a spiral stairway leads to five bedrooms."

Martin grinned. "I see we have our architect. Where will we build this fine home?"

"On our grove, overlooking the lake," said Rachel. "Servants will occupy our present quarters." She folded her papers, glided back to her chair, and turned to her husband. "I'm sure you and Mr. Martin want to talk about financial matters. I know nothing of those things."

Will rubbed his chin with his fingers. "Our new home sounds like quite a place. We will, indeed, have to talk."

They said goodbye, climbed on their buggy, and started for home. Will shook his head as he spoke. "There's no way we can build a home like that — no way."

Rachel sighed. "Well, we can at least find out what it will cost."

"We can do that, but don't get your hopes up."

But as the weeks went by, Rachel left sketches of fine furniture, gilded mirrors, and crystal chandeliers around the cabin for Will to see. From Atlanta, she ordered a cherry wood clock for the wall of the cabin and a fine wool rug for the floor.

At the end of August, Rachel and Will sat across from Mr. Martin's desk as he unfolded drawings and specifications for their home. "All exterior wood will be heart cypress and I'll select only the finest pine for the frame and floors. Brick and roof tile must be brought in from Augusta." A half-hour passed and Mr. Martin paused. He ran his hand through his hair, his gray-blue eyes peering over the top of his spectacles as he focused on Rachel's face. "Nothing has been spared in the specifications of the finest home money can buy, and the price is a reflection of quality. I cannot build it for less than twenty-five thousand dollars."

Will blinked. "Has there ever been a home built in Orlando that cost that much?"

"Not to my knowledge. Your place will be one of a kind."

Will rose and extended his hand. "Thank you, Mr. Martin. We'll contact you in a few days."

The small hand of the clock pointed to ten, as Will sat nervously in an armless, straight back chair in Mr. Pendelton's office. Even though it was summer, the bank felt chilly and had a musty odor, like old treasure hidden in a cave.

"I have twenty-two thousand dollars on deposit," Will said. "Total debt is twelve thousand, payable five hundred each month, including interest. Total assets are forty-six thousand dollars. I'm sure I can repay a fifteen thousand dollar loan in thirty-six months. What do you think?"

The aging head of Orlando's largest bank wrinkled his nose and rocked back in his squeaking chair. "Will, I'm going to give you advice you may not want to hear. You're a good customer of the bank, and you, Rachel, and the Adamsons are friends of mine. I have an obligation to tell you precisely what I think, and I think you're going too far off shore into deep water. Experience tells me that farming is risky business. Think what would happen if a big freeze comes. Where would you be? Is building the finest and most expensive home in Orlando worth the risk of investing twenty-five thousand dollars? Why not cut back your plans to fifteen thousand. You'll sleep better at night." He rolled back his head. "Yes, your income is strong, and you have money in the bank, but why spend so much?"

Will sat motionless as he listened, then stood and extended his hand. "Thank you, sir. I'll sleep on your advice."

Will drove Princess to the barn and walked slowly to the cabin. During lunch, he told Rachel what Mr. Pendelton had said. He knew how much she wanted to build and, he, too, wanted a fine home, but twenty-five thousand dollars? He thought she would plead with him to go on with the plans, but no, she simply said that he was head of the family, and he should make the decision.

That night, he lay in bed and Rachel moved close to him, pressing her lips against his shoulder as she caressed him. *Too far off shore into deep water.* Mr. Pendelton's words, thought Will. She wants to live in the past, in her grandparents' home in Richmond. What would Paul and Martha think.

After breakfast, Will stood at the end of his dock watching wood ducks land in water near the shore. A light breeze cooled his face as he studied puffy clouds drifting overhead.

Hearing footsteps behind him, Will turned and saw a tall man with closely cropped hair, graying at the temples. He wore a tweed jacket over an open collar, freshly pressed cotton trousers, and brown walking boots.

"Mr. Taylor? I'm Colonel Aubrey Quinn. Your wife directed me to you, sorry for disturbing you."

Will offered his hand. "That's perfectly all right. I'm afraid I was in another world. How may I help you?"

"I'm recently retired from the British Army. Frankly, Mrs. Quinn and I came to Orlando seeking shelter from the dreary winters of England. Interestingly, we also found a booming citrus community. We're thinking of purchasing an orange grove and building a home. Mr. Pendelton, at the bank, said you might advise us."

Will nodded. "I'm a relatively new grower, but I'll tell you what I know. Please have a seat." Will leaned back on a post and began. "I suppose that growing oranges is somewhat like fighting a war — soldiers battling other soldiers. We growers fight freezes, infection, and root rot. Sometimes we lose, and when we lose, it can be devastating, but most of the time we win, and when we bring in big harvests, they can be very profitable. Frankly, I like the odds." For an hour Will continued, then he held out his hands and said, "That's about it, now tell me about yourself, Colonel."

Quinn described his years of service in Australia, South Africa, and Suez. "Civilian life will be a dramatic change for my wife and me, but we're ready for it."

"Look at that," interrupted Will. Near the dock, an eagle swooped out of the sky, snatched a fish from the water, and sailed over the grove with breakfast in his talons.

"Fascinating place, this Florida," said Quinn, as he extended his hand. "I should be on my way."

"Where are you staying?"

"The Arcade."

"I'll be in touch, Colonel."

During dinner, that night, Will told Rachel of his conversation with Colonel Quinn. Her eyes brightened as he finished his remarks. "Why don't you sell him part of our grove. If he wants it badly enough, we could use it to pay for part of our new home."

Will scowled. "Ridiculous! Why would we want to do such a thing?"

"Why not? He sounds like a gentleman. Think about it."

After the shock of Rachel's suggestion wore off, Will wondered how much the Colonel might offer for ten acres of his grove.

Investigation at the bank revealed that a letter of credit was issued to Quinn by Barclays Bank for fifty thousand dollars together with a letter of introduction from the president of the bank.

Within days, Rachel had arranged a small dinner party for the Quinns at the San Juan. During the evening she observed Aubrey Quinn: tall, handsome, polished, a perfect gentleman — and his wife, Margaret: modest, refined, and strikingly beautiful at middle age. Rachel was ecstatic. Here is the opportunity, she thought, to build her home, and also acquire exceptional neighbors.

On Monday, Will and Aubrey Quinn poured over records of the grove. It occurred to Will that the Colonel had far more than a passing interest. As he closed his ledger, Will said, "That's about all there is to it. We haven't done badly."

Quinn shook his head. "I'm astonished at the profitability, but do you think prices will hold up?"

"No one can answer that. Agriculture is risky business. I guess we've been lucky."

Colonel Quinn drew back in his chair. "Would you consider selling me ten acres? I'll pay ten thousand dollars."

Giving up ten acres of grove was like surrendering a leg, but Will smiled, and extended his hand. "Rachel and I are pleased to have you and Mrs. Quinn as neighbors."

In November, family and friends celebrated the ground-breaking of the Taylors' new home. "Imagine," said Mrs. Adamson, "a brick home, right here in Orlando."

Mr. Martin asked, "Who will turn the first shovel of dirt?"

"I'll handle that," said Will. He unwrapped a cypress name plate. "Our home will be named for the beautiful mother who lives here. It shall be called *Bellemere,* and that name will be placed on our gate."

A tear rolled down Rachel's cheek. "That was the name of my grandmother's home in Richmond."

Will grinned. "I know."

The foundation rose from the shore of Lake Ivanhoe. True to his word, Mr. Martin's promise that the Taylor home would be "the finest money could buy" was becoming a reality.

❦ *10* ❦

*I*nside the Taylors' cabin a freshly cut pine tree, decorated with candles and candy ornaments stood near the fireplace. It was Christmas day. Little Adam jumped from present to present like a frog hopping from one lily pad to another. When all the gifts were unwrapped, Will went to the barn and returned carrying a fluffy, honey-colored golden retriever puppy. Adam's eyelids widened as he let out a squeal and rolled on the floor with his new friend. "What's his name, Papa?"

"He's yours. You name him."

Adam closed his eyes and yelled in a loud voice. "I'll call him 'Pupsy.' Here, Pupsy. Come here, Pupsy!"

Rachel smiled as she held baby Mary Ann. "Come on boys, we don't want to be late for Grandma's Christmas dinner."

The sun shown brightly in a spring-like day, warm enough for cotton clothing. The Taylors piled into their buggy. Will slapped Princess's reins, and off they headed through the grove, and on to Orange Avenue. At the corner of Central and West Streets, the Taylors exchanged "Season's Greetings" with Chief Tyler McKenzie who rode past them on his huge white horse. When Will pulled up in the Adamsons' driveway Adam yelled, "Merry Christmas." He jumped from the buggy and ran to his grandfather's arms. Mrs. Adamson came out, took Mary Ann from Rachel, and hugged her granddaughter. Smiles and laughter continued as they made their way inside the house.

Will listened to the laughter as he led Princess to the barn. He remembered his first Christmas with Pastor Paul and Martha. They had taken him in, shared their home, made him their son. On Christmas Eve, he and Paul had cut a tree, and then killed and dressed a gobbler. Martha had prepared a Christmas dinner fit for a king. That night, Pastor Paul had told the Christmas story to his congregation. Will patted Princess, then walked inside to join his family.

Mrs. Adamson's dinner was prepared by her black cook, Melody, the granddaughter of Mrs. Adamson's mammy. Will knew that each time Rachel saw Melody, she thought of her Grandmother Rand's home and the receptions that had been held there before the war. Rachel had said that President Davis had been a guest, along with the establishment of Richmond. No place on earth defined heritage as well as Richmond. Will's thoughts were interrupted when Melody came into the parlor and whispered to Mrs. Adamson that Christmas dinner was ready. At the center of the dining room table, a roasted gobbler lay on an enormous white china platter. After Dr. Adamson had finished a long prayer, the family unfolded their napkins, and Melody passed a basket of hot rolls. The doctor rolled his sleeves, lifted a long knife, and surgically sliced the golden bird.

The meal was finished and, after coffee, the family moved to the porch. A gentle breeze swept off the lake in a cloudless afternoon of low humidity and temperature in the eighties. Robins had arrived earlier than usual; they flew about trees in the Adamsons' yard, chirping as they displayed their red breasts. Will looked at his wife, wondering what his life would have been without her.

"Penny for your thoughts," said Rachel.

Will grinned. "Good thoughts — very good thoughts."

It was nearly five o'clock when Rachel rose, kissed her mother's cheek, and said, "Thank you for a lovely day."

A golden sunset bathed Orlando as the Taylors waved goodbye and drove home with little Adam and Ann asleep in the buggy.

During the week after Christmas the harvesting of Will's fruit began. In the Orlando grove, black pickers stood on high cypress ladders in the trees, and filled canvas bags with ripe fruit. Others washed oranges, packed them in barrels, and hauled them on oxcarts to the depot for shipment north. By week's end, nine thousand boxes of fruit had been picked and sold to brokers at an average price of a dollar twenty-five cents per box.

Late Saturday night Will blew out the flame in his desk lamp, undressed, put on his night shirt, crawled in bed beside Rachel, and told her he had entered receipts of eleven thousand dollars in his ledger.

The Kissimmee harvest would bring at least sixteen thousand more. "No doubt about it," he said, "I'm carrying you across the threshold of Bellemere."

The humidity was overbearing on Sunday morning. Not a breath of air stirred inside the sanctuary of the Presbyterian Church. Except for Carey Hand Funeral Home hand fans, most of the congregation would have nodded off in the middle of Pastor Elwang's sermon. But finally, the service ended with a long prayer. The Taylors made their way to the street and started for their buggy. From dead calm, a brisk wind blew out of the northwest scattering leaves and clay dust along Main Street. Will looked up at thin gray clouds racing overhead, summoning black clouds from the horizon. He held Rachel's arm as she climbed on the buggy, and then handed up Mary Ann. Adam jumped to the seat beside his father and Will slapped Princess's reins and headed home. Within minutes of their arrival at their cabin, gale force winds accompanied blinding streaks of lightning, and booming thunder preceded a downpour of cold rain. During the hour, freezing wind from the northwest blew in, dropping the temperature to twenty-nine degrees by nightfall.

That night, Will moved the double bed and the children's beds close to the fireplace. He made many trips to the woodpile, keeping the fire blazing until dawn. At sunrise the temperature dropped to twenty-four degrees. Pumps froze and water pipes burst. Growers, fearing the worst, gathered at the San Juan Hotel, hastily trying to sell crops to buyers, who were attempting to get out of contracts to buy fruit. In the lobby of the hotel, a shouting match erupted between a fruit broker and Burton Mitchell. A fist fight followed as the reality of a devastating freeze set in.

Within days, it was apparent that no grove in Central Florida had escaped the frigid blast. All citrus trees were defoliating; and many trees, in the coldest areas, were killed. Buyers who had signed purchase contracts for fruit on trees vanished. People stopped buying everything except food and other essential items. Directors of the bank met, wondering how to stop a run on the bank.

A telegram arrived from Billy Pastin.

GROVES BADLY DAMAGED, BUT NOT DEAD ... BILLY

Will saddled up Princess and headed for Kissimmee. As he rode along the sand road, he told himself not to panic. Billy had said, "Freezes come and go, it's part of the business." Nevertheless, he felt a tight knot in the pit of his stomach.

When Will pulled up at the grove, he saw Billy sitting on an oak stump near the doorway to his pine cabin. Billy rose and spit tobacco on the ground. "Could be worse," he said. "We'll leave the dead stuff on the trees, then prune in April. After that, we'll just see what happens. Big question now is, what we gonna do for money?"

"Don't worry about the money. I have enough to see us through this."

Billy's black eyes opened wide. "You gotta be the smartest Georgia boy in the world. Nobody got any money now, except you. I know you don't drink, but come on in and watch me have a couple."

It wasn't a good sign when unseasonably warm days caused tiny green buds to sprout on limbs of damaged orange trees. Winter wasn't over. Another freeze, unthinkable as that was, could happen. "Don't worry," said Billy. "I ain't never seen two hard freezes in one winter. Besides, it's February. Nothing to worry about 'tll next winter." But on February seventh, an eerie silence preceded the appearance of black clouds in the northwest. Will stood on his porch watching the nightmare of December return. Wind blew slowly, at first, then rapidly gained momentum. A dazzling flash of lightning struck the top of a tall cypress tree at the far shore of Lake Ivanhoe. Intense rain obscured his vision as he hurriedly placed Princess in her stall and ran to the house. He stood dripping on the porch, looking at white waves lash the shore. In shallow water, cattails bent horizontally. Palm fronds ripped from trunks and blew about crazily as the storm raged into the night.

At dawn, the temperature dropped to seventeen degrees. The Taylors' ice-covered cabin looked like a Christmas scene in New England. In the grove, limbs stripped of leaves and coated with ice resembled ghostly figures, paralyzed in their reach for help. Will made seven trips to the woodshed gathering as much firewood as he could carry. Finally, he stopped. The full realization of what had happened hit him. He stood with Rachel on the porch, staring at the frozen grove. He turned his head to the ice-encased foundation of Bellemere, and thought of running out in the open and looking in every direction for help, as he had the night his mother died. But there was no relief. Nature had unleashed her fury, and had left a graveyard in her wake. He dropped to his knees, lifted his head to the led-gray sky, and cried: "Dear God. Why?"

In April, bleached orange tree trunks had split open to the ground, leaving long rows of ragged stumps. Before the freeze, the population of the area had been nearly thirty-five hundred. By June, fifteen hundred people had left the community for good. Many owners, including the Burton Mitchell family, abandoned their dead groves and returned to former homes in other states. The First National Bank declared bankruptcy. Jackson Foster closed his bakery, and Miss Marilinda Magee gave away the hats in her millinery shop before returning to Augusta. Work on Bellemere stopped; it stood there, by the lake, a solemn reminder of better days.

When summer rains began, Will discovered sprouts from living roots in the grove, green shoots, peering up from the sand — reminders of the past. "We still have the land, Billy. Now think, what's the best use of it?"

Pastin's expression turned sour. "Forget growing oranges. Let's plant corn and tomatoes. Winter crops bring good prices."

Will nodded. "Sounds reasonable. We need a cash crop as quickly as possible. If it freezes again we can replant, but I'm not getting out of the citrus business. Now, how do we get back in production?"

Billy scratched his ear. "Sprouts from roots can be budded at the ground and we could start a nursery from budded stock, but that's going to take a hell of a long time to get us back where we was."

"I know; but over the long haul, we'll never make it growing tomatoes and corn, will we?"

Billy spat chew on a black stump, then rubbed his nose with the back of his hand. "Yeah. All right, here's what we do. I'll start a nursery in Kissimmee. Once we get going, we'll set trees. In the meantime, we grow tomatoes and corn as a winter crop in Orlando. You understand that another freeze will wipe us out again."

They looked at each other for a long time. Will nodded. "I understand."

Under the leadership of Mayor Parramore, the city government of Orlando struggled to provide basic services to a dwindling community. But the strength and endurance of a few dedicated families became the fabric of the economic, political, and religious life of the town. Working together, they slowly rebuilt.

The Baptists dedicated a new sanctuary at the corner of Main and Pine. New roads cut through Orange County, providing work for starving citizens. A refurbished Opera House opened. Cattlemen came to Central Florida, grazing herds where orange trees had grown. Growers bought new citrus stock in south Florida for replanting in Orange County. Charles Shiller opened a grocery store on Central Avenue. At the Blue Drug Store on Orange Avenue, folks buried their problems in dishes of Doc McElroy's homemade ice cream.

Long days in the grove darkened Will's skin and hardened his hands as he and Billy uprooted stumps, cleared and burned rotting trees, and set tomato plants, corn seed, and new orange root stock.

Rachel fed the men and cared for the children. She also washed clothes, sewed, cleaned the cabin, and tended her garden, tasks which had previously been performed by Mrs. Adamson's servants. No Rand woman had ever been reduced to such a state, but then, every family in Orlando was similarly distressed. She lifted her chin and went on, knowing she had it to do.

Sunday afternoons were special times, times for Will and Adam to fish on Lake Ivanhoe. They rarely got a bite; it was mostly a time for a father and a son to be together, to tell stories about Jake Summerlin, "King of Florida Crackers," the pioneer cattleman who supplied half the Confederate Army with his Florida beef, and about Fort Gatlin, which became the village of Jernigan and later, the town of Orlando. Before the pioneers came, Spaniards had come to Florida in great sailing ships bringing orange seeds, which became wild orange trees. And before the Spaniards, there were only Indians, who had hunted deer, bear, and panthers. Eagles flew overhead in warm blue skies, and fish filled a thousand lakes. But mostly, Will told stories about family. "After all," he said, "family is everything." He told about Pastor and Mrs. Bentley, Mr. Fitch, Troupe County, and of his father's bullet wound at the battle of Peachtree Creek.

Adam frowned, his sun-bleached hair blowing about in the wind. "Why didn't Grandpa Taylor die when the Yankee soldier shot him?"

Will mopped his head with a bandanna, then pulled his line out of the water and threw it on the other side of the row boat. "He almost did. Your grandma saved his life. If she hadn't, you and I wouldn't be sitting out here in the hot sun catching nothing."

Adam laughed as he checked his bait. "Did you know Uncle Billy killed three bears with his bare hands?"

Will looked up out of the corners of his eyes and said, "He told you that?"

"Yes sir, and the bears were ten feet tall."

Will scratched his chin. "Well, one thing is sure, Uncle Billy tells tall tales."

∞ *11* ∞

1905

*W*ithin two weeks after Rachel gave birth to Charlotte Patricia Taylor, big, round Elizabeth Johnson and her skin and bones husband, Baker, arrived at the Taylor's door. Baker stood with hat in hand asking for work. Obviously annoyed by the interruption, Rachel clutched her screaming baby and shouted: "I can't hear a word you're saying."

Elizabeth stepped forward, held out her hands, took the infant in her huge arms, and began humming *Jesus Loves The Little Children.* Perhaps it was Elizabeth's broad smile or the richness of her voice; whatever it was, Rachel stood in stunned silence, unable to account for her willingness to give her baby to a strange black woman who instantly put little Charlotte to sleep.

Baker interrupted. "Ma'am, we looking for work. We picks fruit."

Ignoring the black man, Rachel stared at Elizabeth "You've been a mammy to white children, haven't you?"

"Yes, ma'am, many little children." She looked tenderly at the baby. "Prettiest little thing I ever seen."

Rachel reclaimed Charlotte, then glanced at Baker. "Come back in the morning. My husband may have work for both of you."

The sun had been up just thirty minutes when Baker and Elizabeth stood in the presence of Will and Rachel. As they related their childhood, it was obvious they had not overcome the spirit of slavery. As the children of slaves on the Williford plantation, they had watched most blacks run away when Yankee soldiers killed Colonel Williford and sacked his mansion. But their mother had stayed on with the white family and nursed the Williford children to adulthood. When the last child left the old home, Elizabeth and Baker had followed crops and picked vegetables in Georgia and oranges in Florida.

Rachel called Will aside. "I want the mammy for Charlotte, and you can always use another man in the groves."

Rachel had lost weight. Will knew the children and years of hard work had drained his wife's strength. He remembered what Mrs. Adamson had said: "You can't possibly handle three children by yourself." Elizabeth was needed. She and Baker could live in the barn.

In the grove, on Lake Ivanhoe, Billy Pastin peeled an orange. "We gonna pick a little crop, Will."

Will took a deep breath. "Yeah. We've been lucky."

Pastin spat tobacco juice, then tasted the orange. "Way I figure it, the harder we work the luckier we get."

Will nodded as he glanced at the foundation of Bellemere. He knew he should complete the house before further erosion occurred. The ten thousand dollars Colonel Quinn had paid for ten acres was secure in his strong box and the Kissimmee grove had also come back into production, but the ten thousand dollars was his only reserve.

"Finish up the house," said Billy. "You owe it to Rachel. If we ever get another freeze like '95, I'll just ignite all the moonshine in Orange County and burn the freeze away." With a wry smile, he added, "Besides, now that I taught you how to work, they ain't no way you gonna go broke."

Will grinned. He knew he owed Rachel nothing short of sound financial planning, and yet, the money was there. He could do it, and it would please her.

That night Will checked his cash position — nine thousand, with six thousand coming from the fruit on the trees and ten thousand more resting in his strong box. After all, he thought, bills were paid. Including Billy's share, he calculated he would have twenty thousand left.

When the bank opened the next morning, Will stood at the door. He walked straight past teller windows to Mr. Pendelton's desk and stood there waiting for acknowledgment.

Old Mr. Pendelton shifted about uncomfortably in his chair, drummed his gnarled fingers on his desk, and said, "I suppose you're looking for a loan?"

"Yes, sir. Fifteen thousand dollars."

"Bound and determined to build it, are you?"

Will squared his shoulders. "Yes, sir."

The old man cleared his throat, picked up his pen, wrote on a loan application form, and pushed it across his desk for Will to sign.

Mr. Martin and a crew of ten workmen began building Bellemere. After the subflooring was completed, wooden frames rose on all sides. Massive stone chimneys with fireplaces on each floor were built at the center of the north and south sides of the house. With the house dried in, townspeople gathered to watch the laying of white tile on the roof and white bricks coursing up exterior walls. Outdoors, broad wooden stairs led to a thirty-foot-wide veranda facing the lake. Four cypress wood columns supported a broad gable. Double hung windows were installed. Oak floors were laid, and doors were hung. After the house was painted and the floors varnished, the Taylors moved in on September 15, 1906.

Rachel and Will finished their coffee in the breakfast room of their new home. "Thank goodness for Elizabeth," said Rachel. "Adam and Ann are running wild, and there's so much to do with furnishing, decorating, and landscaping. And you, my love," she winked at her husband, "require a great deal of attention."

Will chuckled, put on his straw hat, picked up his keys, and left for Kissimmee.

With Elizabeth and Ada, the new cook, in place, Rachel concentrated on furnishing and decorating Bellemere. The conversation piece of the home was the newly refitted and wired crystal chandelier, hanging in the foyer. Given to Rachel by her mother, the heirloom had been buried by slaves in the cellar of the Rand mansion in Richmond. Everything else had burned when the Yankees leveled the city.

Soon after the last painting was hung in the parlor, Rachel invited her mother to Bellemere to see the re-creation of the Rand mansion. As she moved from room to room, Mrs. Adamson realized the degree of influence the Rand name exerted on her daughter. In the parlor, she seated herself on a damask-covered wing chair, a replica of chairs that had graced her mother's home. Beneath her feet lay a beautifully patterned Oriental rug. She observed a pair of delicately designed, blue Wedgewood vases, much like the ones given to her mother as a wedding present by the governor of Virginia. She wandered into the spacious dining room, wondering how many times the immense mahogany table would seat fourteen guests.

Rachel guided her mother back to the parlor, seated her at a small maple desk, withdrew an invitation list and said, "We're planning a reception. Please look over the list, and see if we have omitted anyone."

Mrs. Adamson read more than three hundred names on the list. "Rachel," she scolded, "You are undertaking entirely too much. Why must you plan such a large party? Everyone in town is on your list."

"For heaven's sake, Mother, this is our first party. Of course we are including everyone. We simply cannot reduce the list."

"If you ask me, I'd say it's going to be a carnival. I think you're making a mistake!"

"Please relax. You and Daddy will be the last to leave the party. Wait and see."

Mrs. Adamson put on her hat and prepared to leave. "No one we knew in Richmond would have invited _everyone_ to a party," she declared. She closed the door behind her and walked stiffly down the steps to her buggy.

At five o'clock , Mr. Etheridge, the tailor, arrived at Bellemere, and Will was livid. "Rachel, this is ridiculous! I am not buying a tailor-made suit. That is final!"

In a quiet voice she began. "I've dreamed of a home like Bellemere. A home that my family and the entire community could be proud of, an uncommon place that would be the forerunner of other fine homes in Orlando. I want my family to dress accordingly for this special occasion." She paused, moved to his side and whispered, "Please, do it for me."

Will glanced at Mr. Etheridge, standing nearby with a tape measure around his neck and said, "Let's get on with it."

On the night of the party, everything was in readiness for entertaining guests. Dressed in a black and white uniform, Elizabeth hurried to the foyer, her face glowing with excitement. "You and Mr. Taylor looks mighty pretty. This is gonna be some party."

"Thank you, Elizabeth," said Rachel, rather stiffly. "Now, please go and help Ada in the kitchen." Rachel placed a carnation in the lapel of Will's new jacket. "You're a darling for being patient with me," she said.

Will watched his wife standing beneath the glittering chandelier, adorned in white silk, with small white orchids woven into her lustrous hair. Soon, he thought, she would graciously greet arriving guests, knowing precisely what to say, how to hold her head, and what to do with her hands. He recalled his first impression on the night they met — a vision of southern charm.

In a low, calm voice, Rachel said, "Our guests are arriving. Stand beside me."

On Monday, Will and Billy sat in front of the fireplace at Bellemere, eating leftover party sandwiches. "Where do we go from here, Billy?"

Pastin breathed deeply. "Chance of another freeze like '95 is small, but it's your money. If it was my money, I'd forget about farming and buy a case of good bourbon whiskey, a box of Havana cigars, and sail to Europe with a fine woman."

Will chuckled. "You probably would. Seriously, what do you think?"

Billy stared at the burning logs. His long hair and beard were nearly white. Lines in his face had grown deeper, but his mind was finely honed like the blade of the fruit knife he always carried. "Well," he said, "I wish I could have a drink at your house. I think a lot better with whiskey in my belly." He looked at Will. "Buy all the land you can afford and let's plant orange trees. If we get lucky, you'll be a millionaire in a few years, and I'll be in pretty good shape too. You once said, 'You'll never make it growing tomatoes and corn.' You're right. If a freeze comes, those crops can only hold you over."

A warm expression came over Will's face. "For fifteen years we've been partners. It's worked out pretty well. Buy two hundred acres in Kissimmee and a hundred in Orlando."

On his way out, Billy sat in Will's new Model T Ford. "I'm sixty-five years old. Never thought I'd ride on anything but a horse. Lord, here I am perched up on a gas buggy. How about taking me for a ride?"

∞ 12 ∞

The Orlando Evening Star reported the arrest in New York of a woman smoking a cigarette in public. And it was rumored that Jake Martin had driven a buggy into a head-marker at Greenwood Cemetery.

By the end of March, the last of Taylor Groves fruit was harvested, and Billy had located a hundred-acre tract on Lake Apopka between Winter Garden and Oakland. To Will, twenty dollars an acre seemed high; but the land lay on the south side of the lake, the drainage was good, and besides, the tract was just a mile from the railway line. Fruit could be processed in the field and shipped to market with little effort. The deal was made.

At the bank, Will signed a cashier's check made out to the seller for two thousand dollars, handed it to Billy, put on his hat, and started out. "What's your big hurry?" questioned Billy. "Ain't you got time for coffee?"

"Nope. Ann's birthday party. Gotta go."

All the way to Bellemere, Will thought of Ann — already fourteen years old. At the party, she would wear the new white dress purchased at Dickson-Ives. She would run, jump, and laugh with the other children until the dress was practically ruined. Rachel would scold, but it would have little effect. Little Annie had a mind of her own.

Ann was the first to greet Will as he parked near the barn. "Papa, Papa. What did you bring me?"

"Bring you? Now, why would I bring something to you?"

Her dark eyes sparkled like stars. "Papa, tell me!"

Will glanced at Baker who stood by the barn.

"Anything in there for Ann?"

Baker opened the door and led out a saddled palomino gelding. Ann screamed, "Thank you, Papa," as she ran to the horse and hugged

95

its neck. Baker helped her mount, and then she held the reins and walked the animal down the path to the road and back.

From the porch, Rachel shook her head; then she moved to Will's side. "Big mistake, giving her a horse. You never gave one to Adam."

"I've not shown favoritism. Adam didn't want a horse."

That afternoon the children arrived and played games until everyone was out of breath. After the cake and ice cream had been eaten, Will pumped water for the children standing in line to wash their hands and faces. Ann was last. She stood before the pump and tilted her head back, "Papa, wipe my face."

Before he could answer, Rachel intervened. "He'll do no such thing. You're old enough to care for yourself. Hurry on now, with the other children."

Ann stared blankly at her mother and then turned and ran away.

Will frowned. "Even on her birthday, you give her no slack."

"That's right. You're spoiling her to death."

"If spoiling her means showing a little warmth, then I'm guilty."

Rachel's expression softened. "You're a push over, Will Taylor."

Will shook his head as he dried his hands.

The party ended, and Will drove to the post office for his mail. Among his letters was one from Pastor Bentley in Hogansville. Inside, a note was wrapped around a small envelope addressed to:

> Mr. William Taylor
> General Delivery
> Hogansville, Georgia

> This letter was given to me by the new postmaster. Apparently, it had been lying around his office for some time.

> Paul Bentley

Will carefully unfolded the letter and began reading the artistically penned words.

December 9, 1907

Dear Will,

Remembering that you lived in Hogansville, I send a letter that should have been written long ago. I pray it reaches you. When you came looking for Annabel McCoy, so long ago, she had returned to her parents' home in Athens. Soon thereafter, she discovered her pregnancy. After her parents shut her out of their home, she returned to me in Atlanta and gave birth to the child, and they remained with me until Annabel's death last November. Her baby, Gail, the little girl you fathered, has no one except me, and I am destitute, unable to carry on as her surrogate mother. Gail will not come to you. Like her mother, she is proud and unwilling to face her situation. Whatever you can do, please do it soon.

Sincerely,

Mary Beth Livingston

Will closed his eyes. Deep in his mind he felt Annabel's presence. So long ago, she had listened as he read before her. And when she had touched his hand, he felt a shock. They had crossed paths again in Atlanta. He remembered the warmth of her body as she clung to him. Nothing had mattered except the moment, no thought of consequences. She had remained hidden in Atlanta, left alone to bear the baby and raise the child. Why had he not confronted Mary Beth, again and again, demanding information on her whereabouts? Now Annabel was dead. How many times had she wanted him, only to be turned back by her unyielding pride? Will folded the letter, and mumbled, *"Christian Gentleman."*

"You just see a ghost?" hollered Billy Pastin as he walked up the steps of the post office.

Will's face turned scarlet as he waved Billy off. He walked to the telegraph office to advise Mary Beth of his arrival in Atlanta on Friday.

That night, at the dinner table, Rachel listened as Will made his announcement: "It's business — sort of an emergency. I must be in Atlanta on Friday, but don't worry, I'll return on Thursday, in time for your dinner party."

Rachel patted his hand. "Be certain of it. I do not wish to be deserted at my own party."

Will placed his napkin on the table, rose, and walked to the porch. Cypress trees at the far shore of the lake were silhouetted by the last glimmer of light in the sky. Now he carried Annabel's cross, tasted the gall, felt the pain she had endured. What would he say to Gail? Hello. I'm your father, missing through all the years - the father who never held you in his arms, dried your tears, or read stories. He walked slowly down the stairs and moved along the path to the shore. He stopped, looked up, and saw the sliver of a new moon positioned low in the darkening sky. "Tell me what to do, Lord. Tell me," he whispered.

A steady rain poured from gray skies over Atlanta. Will hurried from Union Station, hailed a carriage, and directed the driver north, past the newly completed Piedmont Hotel, and on to Mary Beth Livingston's address on Ponce De Leon Avenue. Upon arrival, he tipped the driver generously, buttoned the collar to his rain coat, and ran with suitcase in hand to the porch of the old brownstone home located in a once fashionable neighborhood. He rang the bell and waited for what seemed an eternity. At last, the door opened. A plain looking woman, whose youth was nearly washed away by the years, stood momentarily silent in the doorway. Will removed his hat and raincoat. "Mary Beth. Your letter remained in the post office for months. I just received it and I came as quickly as I could."

A little smile crossed Mary Beth's lips. She extended her hand. "Come in, Will. Come in. Let me take your things."

The room was large and cold, almost void of furniture, except for a tattered sofa, a straight back chair, and a small round tea table sitting on bare wood floors near the fireplace.

Mary Beth lit a lamp on the mantel. "Sorry we have no electricity. Really can't afford it."

"I understand."

"Will you have coffee?"

"No, thank you. Tell me what happened to Annabel."

The lines in Mary Beth's face deepened. "Sit here beside me," she said. "From the moment I learned of her pregnancy, I begged her to go to you, pleaded to let me contact you, but she refused. After her parents tuned their backs on her, I took her in and helped raise the child. We lived on my meager nurse's salary, along with the money she earned by taking in sewing. My parents passed away seven years ago and left this house to me. We three lived here until Annabel died of typhoid fever, last November."

Will breathed in deeply, exhaled, and slowly shook his head. "And where is Gail?"

Mary Beth glanced at the brass clock on the mantel. "She should be coming in from school any moment."

"Does she know about me?"

"Oh, yes. She knows everything."

"I'd like that coffee now. Black for me, please."

Mary Beth rose and started toward the kitchen just as the front door flew open and Gail raced in out of the rain. "Aunt Beth," she shouted. "Aunt Beth." Then she saw Will, who stood when she came in. She stopped abruptly and took a step back, like a fawn sensing danger.

The dreadful silence was broken by Mary Beth. "Darling. This is Mr. Taylor, a good friend of your mother. He's here for a visit."

Will looked at his daughter's bright eyes and proud chin, the embodiment of Annabel. Her brown curls were parted at the center and held by white ribbon at the back of her head. So lovely, in the bloom of her youth. He shook his head and took a step forward. "Sorry, Mary Beth, evasions won't do. Gail, I'm your father."

With an air of serene discipline she nodded. "I know."

"Now then," interrupted Mary Beth. "Coffee will be ready in a moment. Sit here with Mr. Taylor. He wants to hear about everything you've been doing."

Gail made her way to the chair and sat uneasily on the front edge of the seat, her eyes shifting anxiously about the room.

Will grinned. "I'm just as speechless as I was the first day I met your mother. She told me I must read before the class, and I almost collapsed from fright."

Gail's eyes opened wide. "Mother was your teacher?"

"Yes," Will laughed, "I was a problem for her, but I did learn to read. She was a wonderful teacher, patient and resourceful. In Atlanta, after my school days, we became the best of friends — drawn to each other in so many ways."

Gail settled back in her chair. "But you never married her."

Will closed his eyes. "No, I did not. I wanted to marry your mother, but she was ashamed of what we did out of wedlock. She hid herself from me, and never let me know her whereabouts."

"Did you love her?"

"Yes. I'll never forget your mother."

Mary Beth entered the room carrying a silver tray. She placed the tray on the tea table, offered napkins, poured the coffee, and beamed at Will. "Thank you for coming. I knew you would want to see your daughter."

"You were so right to contact me." He looked at Gail. "Tell me about yourself. Tell me about school."

Speaking in a low, self-assured voice, she sat erect, looking directly into Will's eyes. "I am first in my class. No one is even close to my grades."

"I'm not surprised," said Will, "Your mother was also very bright."

"Yes, but she had little opportunity to use her intellect. I intend to rise above what men expect women to become."

"I'm sure you will," nodded Will.

Gail smiled. "Do you have a family?"

"A wife, two little girls, and a sixteen-year-old son. We live on a lake, and I grow oranges for a living."

"You must be very happy," said Gail.

"Yes. Come live with us," he said softly. "I want you with us."

She stood, and moved to Mary Beth's side. "It's very nice to know you, Mr. Taylor, but Aunt Beth is my family. I am quite happy here. May I go to my room, Aunt Beth?"

After receiving a nod, Gail quickly ran up the stairs. Mary Beth set her cup and saucer on the tea table. "You understand, don't you?"

"Of course. I knew this would be difficult. She's so much like Annabel."

"I know. A proud little darling."

"Tell me what you need."

Mary Beth walked to the window, pulled aside the heavy drapery, and watched the rain as it continued to pour from the sky. "More than anything, she wants to attend the University of Georgia."

"I'll make inquiries, and take care of everything. I'll also send a monthly check to you for your support. What else can I do?"

"Tell me you really loved Annabel."

He walked to the window and stood beside her. "I did love her with all my heart."

Mary Beth patted his hand. "Thank you. You must stay the night with us. I'm serving country ham and grits."

He nodded. "I cannot resist."

Will's train pulled into the depot at Church Street. Billy Pastin stood waiting for him on the platform. "Good trip?" said Billy as they walked to Pastin's wagon.

"Yes." But there was a detached sound to his voice.

"Some big deal?"

Will said nothing as he kept walking.

"Guess you don't want to talk about it."

"That's right, Billy."

They reached the wagon, and Billy took the reins. "I thought we were partners."

"It's a personal matter, nothing to do with you and me."

Billy looked squarely at Will. "Everything that happens to you affects me."

Will nodded.

"You and Rachel O.K.?"

"Fine, Billy."

At Bellemere, Will grabbed his bag; then he turned and touched Pastin's arm. "Thanks, Billy, you're my best friend, but I must work this out alone."

Will looked up and saw beautiful Rachel standing in the doorway. Was she protecting her sanctuary, shielding her status from intrusion? All he could think of was the maelstrom that would open when he told her about Gail.

Rachel's Friday evening supper party was a topic of conversation for many who attended services at the Presbyterian church on Sunday.

"As far as I can see, she's taking over Orlando," said Mrs. Pendelton, as she walked with friends to her pew in the sanctuary. "Yes," echoed Mrs. Ramsey, "and it's about time someone took the lead. She has taken Orlando out of the swamp. I love her parties and everything else about her. If it were not for Rachel Taylor, Orlando would be a very boring place."

Will had overheard the conversation. Young as she was, he knew that Rachel was socially well established, admired throughout the community. Knowledge of his past transgression would deliver a terrible wound from which she might not recover. But no secret would remain between him and his wife. No mask would hide the truth, whatever the cost.

At Bellemere, luncheon dishes were removed, Charlotte was put down for a nap, and Adam and Ann were sent out to play. After a long silence, Rachel spoke, "When will you tell me what's troubling you, darling?"

"Obvious, isn't it?"

"Quite."

Will rose from his chair, and walked to the window. His temples throbbed, and he swallowed several times attempting to restore moisture in his mouth. "Long before I knew you, I had an affair with a girl in Atlanta named Annabel McCoy. Ten days ago I received a letter from Mary Beth Livingston, Annabel's closest friend, telling me that Annabel had died. She also informed me that I was the father of a nineteen-year-old girl — the result of one night with Annabel. I was not in Atlanta on business last week. I met with Mary Beth and my daughter, Gail, a beautiful and highly intelligent girl. I became convinced that the right thing to do is underwrite the expense of her college education and to financially assist Miss Livingston, Gail's surrogate mother." Will breathed deeply, then turned to face Rachel. "I did not know there was a child until I received the letter."

Rachel remained remarkably calm, but a cynical expression formed on her face as bitterness seeped through her eyes. She folded her hands in her lap, then nodded several times. In an even voice she said, "Tell me how many more 'yard children' are out there? Perhaps you and Lucy Neal have produced a few. And are there other women in your life?"

"I have told you everything."

"Come now. You're quite the ladies' man. Tell me."

He knew she would press the matter, push until all the poison was spent. But it was out, there was nothing more to say. He remained at the window, looking out, watching the sun try to break through the rain clouds hanging over the lake.

Rachel sat erect in her chair as she spoke. "Don't you ever bring that girl to my home." She rose from her chair and walked softly to the staircase. The only sound was the ticking of the clock hanging in the foyer.

⌘ *13* ⌘

Adam Taylor began his freshman year at The University of Florida in September 1911. At eighteen he was, as Rachel had said, "a catch." His six-foot frame, dark brown eyes, and irresistible smile had had half the girls at Orlando High falling over themselves to be near him. In his senior year he led the baseball team in hitting and served as president of the senior class. But beyond that, it was his warm personality and humility that everyone in Orlando admired.

Neither Adam nor his roommate, Tommy Lane, had lived away from home before. Elizabeth wasn't there to "pick up" after him, and the cooking certainly didn't compare to the food Ada prepared at Bellemere. He had known every student at Orlando High; but in Gainesville he hardly knew anyone except Kappa Alphas, who treated "Rat Taylor" just like a rat. They shaved his head and paddled his rear end. He washed the "Brothers'" clothes and shined their shoes.

Tommy Lane entered the dormitory room and flopped down on his bed. He looked at Adam and said, "The homework's killing me. I'm ready to go back home and forget this college education stuff."

Adam nodded. "Yeah, I know, it's crazy. Never thought college would be like this, but listen, buddy, don't even think about pulling out. Now, shut up. I've got to read *Evangeline.*"

"*Evangeline,*" said Tommy. "Who in the world cares about *Evangeline?*"

"Well, son, let me tell you about her. She's the heroine in a poem about two lovers who become separated in exile. During the remainder of her life, she looks all over the country for her man; at last she finds him, an old man, on his death-bed. And that, my boy, is precisely what I predict will happen to you if you don't get busy and read this poem — kicked out of the university, and someday, I may find you bent and broke in a flop house."

Tommy sat up in his bed. "If I read the poem, will you go with me to get a soda?"

Adam shook his head. "Read it, Lane."

Gainesville was a time of preparation for becoming one of a new breed of scientifically trained citrus growers. Adam learned new grafting and budding techniques. He acquired valuable information concerning soil nutrients and insecticides. But more than that, he was on his own, out of Rachel's cocoon and into the world of responsibility. No one at Gainesville cared whether or not he did homework, or how late he stayed up. What he wore was his business, not Rachel's. He could eat green peas with a knife if he wished. But when he thought of Papa, remarkable Papa, he felt his presence all around him. Do it right ... tell the truth ... never overreact, all part of Papa's bible. Many nights Adam walked the campus, looking up through pines at skies filled with white stars, wondering about the choices he had made and what Papa would think.

"Hey, Taylor," yelled Tommy Lane as he ran down the steps of Peabody Hall. "I made a B on the English final. Made my grades. You made an A, didn't you?"

Adam chuckled. "Just got lucky."

"What you gonna do with all those high grades after you graduate?"

"I'll be the best educated field hand at Taylor Groves."

"Oh, sure," laughed Tommy. "And in rags, I'll bet. Come on, I'll buy us that soda."

As they walked to the malt shop Adam considered his remark: *field hand.* It wasn't a joke. With Papa, you start at the bottom and work your way up — no other way.

The school year passed quickly for Adam. He had asked to live and work in Kissimmee with "Uncle" Billy Pastin, who lived deep in the grove in a weathered, two-room cabin looking more rustic than any Adam had seen. Rough cut pine flooring was bare and dirty. A rickety old wicker chair stood before a soot-covered fireplace. Above the mantel hung a mangy bear's head. A cypress table doubled for food preparation and gun cleaning. The black wood-burning stove looked as though it hadn't been cleaned since the Civil War.

During breakfast, on the day after his arrival, Adam flashed his report card. Three A's and two B's brought a broad grin to Billy's face. "Gettin real smart, ain't you?"

Adam's eggs got cold as he explained everything he had learned at the university about growing citrus: when to plant, how to plant, how to fertilize, and when to pick. In his earlier years, Billy would have pinned Adam's ears back for being so authoritative. Now, more tolerant, he listened to a continuous lecture on the latest techniques in citrus culture. But finally, Billy had enough. He wiped his mouth with his sleeve and said: "Well, what do you know. You college boys are learning lots of good stuff up in Gainesville. I guess about all we need to do is push buttons, and zoom, out comes oranges." Billy grinned and put his arm around Adam as they walked outside where black Ben waited in the wagon. "Son, I want to introduce you to the most important agricultural tool I know, a shovel. Ben and I use it to throw manure on the grove. Now, you fellas get going, and I'll see you back at the cabin around sundown."

"Yes sir, Uncle Billy."

Sheepishly, Adam climbed up on the smelly fertilizer wagon and sat next to Ben, whose bottom almost filled the wide wooden seat. As they moved down the sandy road, Adam said: "You think I've been talking too much?"

All of his white teeth showed, as a grin covered Ben's black face. "Yassah."

At 4:00 a.m., Saturday, Billy shook Adam. "Wake up boy. Time to go fishing."

Adam dressed quickly, ate bacon and grits, and asked, "How big is the lake, Uncle Billy?"

"A lot bigger than them little ponds in Orlando, and the fish we gonna catch make Orlando fish look like minnows." As they paddled in a small inlet, Billy whispered, "Throw your line near the shore, over by them lily pads, and wiggle your pole every now and then." When a large fish took Adam's bait, the water churned and his cane pole nearly bent double as he maneuvered the black bass into Billy's hands.

"Look at him. He must be six pounds. Put another shiner on your hook, and let's get some more."

By noon, the summer sun baked the lake and the fishermen wrapped their lines around cane poles and made their way to shore. The fish string was so heavy, Adam strained to lift it into the wagon. They cleaned all the fish they could eat and gave the rest to field hands in Kissimmee. Late that afternoon, Adam watched as Billy built a wood fire in his stove, rolled fillets of bass in corn meal, heavily sprinkled with salt and pepper, then dropped pieces of fish into a huge black skillet half-filled with hot grease. Crackling sounds and the aroma of frying fish filled the cabin as Billy rolled hush-puppy dough in preparation for the frying pan.

"Son, you ain't never gonna eat as good as you will today. Wait 'til you taste my fried bass and hush puppies, and you know what? You gonna get a bottle of my home brew, but don't tell your Mama, she'd have a conniption fit."

As the days of summer passed, Adam's tan deepened, his hands hardened, his back ached. He realized that only a small part of his education took place in the classroom. Beneath the creases in Uncle Billy's leathery forehead rested a mountain of knowledge. He understood nature and had developed a "feel" for plant life. He knew precisely when to fertilize, irrigate, and prune. He sensed changes in the weather and spotted infestations from a distance. He knew things about growing citrus that had never been printed in textbooks. To Adam, Uncle Billy's life was the real thing; the way fruit men should live.

Just before bedtime on a Friday evening in August, Adam watched Uncle Billy clean his double barrel shotgun by the light of a kerosene lantern. "How long have you known my Papa?" Adam asked.

Billy put his gun on the table and looked thoughtfully at Adam. "Your Papa came to town in 1887. He was just a snip of a boy. A little bit at a time, I taught him how to grow oranges, but I'll tell you something, he taught me a lot more than I taught him."

Adam leaned forward. "What?"

Billy picked up his gun and began rubbing the stock with linseed oil. "I watched him. He does things right, never overreacts, does a lot of listening and bends over to help the other fellow. Best way I can describe him is to say he's a straight shooter. You grow up like him, you'll make a man." Billy grinned. "Want to go fishing in the morning?"

"Yes, sir."

"Better go to sleep. I'll be waking you up at four o'clock."

A summer of hard work mixed with fishing, listening, and learning from Uncle Billy ended in September. The fall term at the university had rolled around and Adam was packed and ready to leave Kissimmee.

"Uncle Billy, if you'll have me, I want to come back next summer."

The old man's eyes glistened. He took Adam's hand and squeezed hard. "I'd be proud and pleased to have you, son. I feel like you're part mine."

↶ 14 ↷

At eighteen, Adam Taylor's sister Mary Ann became a young image of her mother. She not only had inherited her mother's beauty, she had also developed her temperament.

Through the years, Will had read stories to Mary Ann, kissed her bruises, played her games, and hung on her every word. "Annie," he would say, "Annie, my little sweetheart."

On a shirt-soaking early September evening, Will and Rachel finished their coffee. Ada removed dishes from the table and then began serving bread pudding.

"None for Ann," said Rachel. "She's getting chubby."

Ann's voice was frigid. "Mother, the gentle, reassuring one. She knows what's best for everyone. May I be excused, Father?"

Rachel raised her voice. "No, young lady, you may not!"

Ann carefully folded her napkin, rose from her chair, and without a word, left the dining room.

Rachel stiffened as she looked at her husband. "Notice how she speaks to her mother." She stretched out her arms to little Charlotte, "Come to Mommy, honey. At least I have one lovable daughter."

Will pushed back in his chair. Rachel and Ann, so much alike, he thought. Two actresses, intoxicated with pride, hurling lines at each other, competing for the upper hand.

Later that night, Will stood at the foot of Rachel's bed. "Why can't you and Ann enjoy a normal mother and daughter relationship?"

Seated before her mirror, Rachel stopped brushing her long, black hair and softly placed the silver-backed brush on her dressing table. "I have asked myself that question many times. Whatever it is, I do not enjoy her."

"Don't say that. She's our daughter and I love her."

Rachel looked at her husband's reflection in the mirror. "That's a large part of the problem. You say you love her, and yet you spoil her.

She's rotten, and you, my dear, had better straighten her out before she ruins our lives."

"You antagonize her. She rebels against you because you treat her as if she were an opponent instead of a daughter. Why do you do that?"

A chilling expression crossed Rachel's face. "So you side with our unmanageable child. You believe I'm responsible for her behavior."

"Rachel. Listen to me. I love you." He placed his hands on her shoulders.

"Please, don't."

The afternoon sun had dropped below the horizon, painting the western sky pale gold, Will and Ann walked near the lake's edge, neither knowing how to begin a conversation. Finally, Will said, "How's school going, Annie?"

"Oh, Papa. School's fine, it's Mama. Mama's my problem. She hates me, and I hate her."

Will took her hand. "Don't say that. I don't know why you and Mama feel the way you do about each other. It hurts me so much."

"Papa!" she exclaimed, her face filling with anger, "she's mean and cunning, and she twists you like a ribbon around her finger. Don't you see that?"

Will placed his hand on her shoulder. "Long ago, when I was a small boy, I watched my mama die. She didn't always show it, but she cared for me and loved me. At the funeral, my foster father read from the Bible. He ended by quoting *'Charity beareth all things, believeth all things, hopeth all things, endureth all things.'* We're going to work it out, Annie. Help me."

Ann nodded and then rested her head on her father's broad shoulder.

The sweltering heat of September had passed on the day Colonel Quinn's wife, Margaret, called to tell Rachel their son Jeffery had arrived on the train from New York. He had recently graduated from The Royal Military Academy at Sandhurst and was on extended leave before joining his regiment in the British Army.

"Please come for dinner on Friday evening," said Mrs. Quinn, "and by all means, bring Ann."

Bored with the thought of a dull evening, Ann reluctantly agreed to join her family in greeting Lieutenant Quinn, but on Friday, from the moment of their introduction, the lieutenant's rugged blond looks made it clear to her that the plain blue dress she wore was too casual.

After dinner, Mrs. Quinn led everyone to her parlor. Jeffery sat beside Ann on a sofa facing the fireplace. It wasn't just the uniform or Lieutenant Quinn's handsomely chiseled profile that so completely hypnotized Ann; it was also his voice. All evening she rode a magic carpet as he spoke in the grandest of English.

"Cirencester," he said, "the place of my birth, is England's greatest wool market. As a boy, I played in the park in summertime, and in autumn, I walked among the oaks, beeches, and chestnuts draped in brightly colored leaves." He looked at Ann. "You should see the beige limestone houses of the Cotswolds, hear the peal of ancient bells, breathe the aroma of rich earth, see the fog as it rolls across the meadows."

"I'd love to be there," Ann whispered.

Jeffery smiled. "So would I, but soon I'll be off to join my regiment in India."

Rachel glanced at the clock on the mantel and rose. "Well, we simply must be going. Thank you for a lovely evening." She turned to Jeffery. "How nice it is to know you. Your parents are among our closest friends. Please come see us while you're here."

"Thank you, Mrs. Taylor. I certainly will." He turned to Ann. "May I see you tomorrow?"

"Oh yes. I'll be at home all day."

As the Taylors drove the short distance to their home, Rachel sighed. "That was the most forward behavior I have ever witnessed. You practically threw yourself at the young man. What in the world must the Quinns be thinking?"

Ann said nothing. She retired to her room immersed in thoughts of Jeffery Quinn. Through her open window she gazed into the night at moonlight reflecting on the lake, wishing he were near, wondering what India was like.

In the morning, Jeffery dismounted his father's black stallion, tied his horse at the Taylors' post, and knocked at the door of Bellemere. The cherrywood clock in the foyer struck ten.

Ann jumped at the sound. "Go to the door, Elizabeth, and see who it is."

"You knows well as I does who it is. All you been talkin' 'bout all mawnin' is Lieutenant Quinn."

Elizabeth opened the door and gawked at the young officer's dark eyes. Clad in khaki riding breeches, brown leather cavalry boots, and brass-buttoned jacket, he looked like the prince in Miss Charlotte's story book.

"How do you do. I'm Lieutenant Jeffery Quinn. May I come in?"

"Yes sir. Come right in and sit in the parlor."

Elizabeth waddled to the foot of the staircase.

"Miss Ann, Lieutenant Quinn here to visit you."

Upstairs, Ann bit her lip as she heard Elizabeth yell to her. She looked at Rachel and whispered: "Listen to Elizabeth. Jeffery's going to think we're the most unrefined people in America."

"If that's what he thinks, he may be right. After your performance last night, there's no telling what he may be thinking. Now, stop primping, and for heaven's sake, exercise restraint when you're with him."

Rachel shook her head in dismay as Ann bounced down the broad stairway and rushed into the parlor to meet Jeffery. Displaying no reserve, she moved to his side, her expression conveying an obvious message. He took her hand, but the magic moment vanished as Elizabeth shuffled into the room with a tray of tea.

"Mrs. Taylor says English folks always drinks tea, even in the mawnin."

Jeffery replied. "Thank you, Elizabeth, very thoughtful. We English are indeed an odd lot." He winked as Elizabeth left the room. "Ann, ride with me this morning."

"I'd love it. Let me speak to mother."

In her bedroom, wearing a soft pink dressing gown, Rachel listened carefully as Ann asked for permission to ride with Jeffery.

"Very well," said Rachel, "but you will confine your ride to a radius of one mile of Bellemere. There will be no dismounting, and you must return no later than one o'clock."

Jeffery sat straight in his saddle as he and Ann rode past huge cypress trees standing at the water's edge on the far side of Lake Ivanhoe. He looked strong, fearless, and confident. She smiled and followed his lead.

At the end of the week, Jeffery and Ann began their morning ride. "Let's go to my parent's place," he said. "I want to show you something."

They rode at the edge of the lake to the Quinns' porch; there, Jeffery helped her dismount. His hands around her waist created a warm, but helpless feeling. Color appeared in her face and her heart pounded. She wanted to remain in his arms, to be taken to India, or any other place. Hand in hand they entered the vacant house.

"Come with me. I want you to see my room," he said in a soft but compelling voice.

She stopped. "What about your parents?"

"They won't be here until late afternoon."

They entered an oak-paneled foyer that led to a great room. Over the mantel of the fireplace hung a silver shield crossed with cavalry sabers. Jeffery led the way up a carved oak stairway that led to a hallway at the upper level. Paintings and photographs of battle scenes, along with portraits of British Army officers, lined the corridor leading to his room. Ann's mind screamed as he opened the heavy door, entered, and guided her to his bedside. He placed his hands around her waist and said, "There's not much time. I'll be leaving soon."

"When?"

"Day after tomorrow."

"Jeffery, I ..."

"I wish I could take you with me."

Overwhelmed by his possessive voice, she looked away knowing the message in her eyes would betray her. Then he kissed her lips and almost without realizing it, she sat on the edge of his bed. In his arms, her mother's lectures were now forgotten. He stretched out his hand and loosened a white bow at the back of her head, releasing dark ringlets which fell loosely about her shoulders. In a clash of virtue and passion, convention washed away. All that mattered was the moment, his presence, his touch ....

The clock struck one. As she lay beside him she whispered: "It's late, I must go. Please take me with you. Please."

"The minute I learn of my assignment, I'll send for you and we'll be married. I promise."

The tone of his voice and his words sounded so believable. Ann smiled as she visualized herself dressed for traveling, leaving for New York where she would board a steamer for Bombay. She would become Mrs. Jeffery Quinn, and half a world would separate her from Rachel.

Weeks went by and no letter from Jeffery. Morning sickness told of new life forming within Ann's body. Her mind raced from one alternative to another: Adam could hide her in Gainesville; Papa would know what to do; anything, anyone except Mama. Mama must never know. But no alternative was acceptable, all of them led to the same conclusion — *trapped.*

Rachel was so preoccupied with preparations for her Thanksgiving party that she failed to notice her daughter's symptoms, but Elizabeth knew. In an attempt at an explanation, Ann said. "I must have a touch of fever, it's not serious."

"Miss Ann, you ain't foolin' me. I knows mawnin' sickness when I sees it."

"Hush up, Elizabeth. You don't know anything."

"Yes'm I do, but I ain't saying nothin' to yo Mama. Lawd know, she gonna throw a fit when she find out."

"Now you listen to me, Elizabeth. Mind your own business. You ... you ..." Her voice broke as tears ran down her cheeks. "Oh, Elizabeth. What am I going to do?"

Elizabeth took the child-woman to her massive breast and whispered. "Hush now, baby. Hush. It gonna be all right."

Christmas passed, and the New Year came, but still no letter from Jeffery. The very thought of sharing the secret with her mother was unthinkable, and yet.

The evening meal was completed. Rachel finished her tea and was about to rise, when Ann began. "Mother, I want you and Papa to remain for a few minutes. I have something to say."

Unable to face her mother, Ann's gaze fell upon the portrait of her maternal grandfather, John Ashton Rand of Richmond. The treasured painting reminded Rachel constantly of the pride and social prominence of the Rand side of her lineage, so deeply entrenched in the culture of Virginia.

Ann sat on the edge of her chair and with no hint of remorse, revealed her pregnancy. "I have no regrets," she said, as she looked directly into her mother's eyes. "I love Jeffery, and he loves me. Soon, he will send for me and we will be married."

A dreadful silence fell over the room as Rachel sat erect and motionless. Her normal glowing color became chalk white. The agony of what she had heard imprinted on her face. "You say he intends to marry you. Has he written?"

"No, not yet."

"Does anyone else know of this?"

"Only Elizabeth."

"You little fool. Jeffery will not be sending for you. You were merely a soldier's plaything while he was on leave. Now, for the first time in the history of the Rand family, a child will be born out of wedlock. Our shame will be the topic of whispered conversation in every home in Orlando. You will bear that shame, but all of us are ruined."

Will stood. "All of us need time to think. Good night, Ann. We'll talk tomorrow."

Rachel's mind raced as she lay beside her husband. How could Ann do this to her family? Could her secret possibly be kept? To what degree would the family be socially isolated if the truth were known? Where could Ann go? She thought of the Rands — Anna Rand— Cousin Anna. Of course! She would arrange for Ann to stay with Anna, in Richmond.

It was nearly dawn when she fell asleep.

∽ *15* ∽

*L*ittle conversation took place between Rachel and Ann dur
ing the train trip to Richmond. In the dining car, Ann sat
across from her mother and remained calm, seemingly resigned to her mother's decision to place her in Anna's home during
her pregnancy. Inwardly, a gnawing pain held her, as the thought of
her abandonment and the resulting humiliation of bringing a fatherless
child into the world became a reality. After barely touching her food,
she returned to their compartment, buried her face in a pillow, and
tried to sleep; but it was no use. She should be with Jeffery in India, an
officer's wife, on his arm, and dressed in white. Where was Jeffery?
she wondered .... The train rolled on in the night.

At dawn, Anna's chauffeur helped with baggage as Rachel and
Ann stepped from a Pullman car at Richmond Station. He loaded the
bags in a Cadillac sedan and drove the ladies to a grand old three story,
brownstone home on Franklin Street, a centerpiece in the mosaic of
Richmond.

Anna Rand, a wealthy, forty-six-year-old spinster, lived alone. Like
Rachel, she had deep violet eyes and dark hair parting at the center and
rolled out at the temples. But Ann soon discovered that that was where
the similarity ended. She immediately felt the warmth of a caring person.

Anna held out her arms. "Ann, let me look at you. You're so lovely.
I'm pleased that you wanted to visit me." She kissed her niece's cheek
and then turned to Rachel. "I'm sure you're worn out, so please go up
and rest. Maude will serve lunch at one."

Rachel's smile was affectionate. "Thank you, Anna. You have no
idea what your acceptance means."

Ann and her mother climbed a broad circular stairway leading to a
suite of two bedrooms connected by a white tile bathroom. The walls
of Ann's room were painted light pink, complementing window drap-

eries of a floral design. A cream-colored quilted bedspread covered the huge four-poster bed that stood high off polished oak floors. It was a sumptuous bed, Ann thought. A Rand bed.

After lunch, the ladies sipped tea in the parlor before a warm fireplace. Rachel pulled at the hem of her handkerchief as she began the conversation. "Ann is four months along. The father is a young officer in the British Army, on leave, visiting his parents in Orlando. There has been no communication from him since his return to duty, so we assume he has deserted her. Of course, we will place the child for adoption."

Anna looked at Ann and spoke in a gentle voice. "How very difficult this must be for you. Dreadful as it seems, things like this happen, and we must carry on. This will be your home, and I will care for you as if you were my daughter."

Her daughter. Ann knew there was no daughter or son in Aunt Anna's life. The love of her life had died of cholera, and her father had fallen at Fredericksburg; she had no brothers or sisters, no one to share her home. Except for Rachel, the Rand bloodline would have become extinct. But now, Anna's home would be her home, and Rachel would not be there.

In the months that followed, Ann absorbed Anna's love; this was the mother she needed, the understanding she craved. She told of her love and admiration of her father and shared her times of frustration and humiliation as the target of her mother's outbursts. "Aunt Anna," she said, "Mama will never know how I feel. She'll never try to understand me."

Anna listened, then began speaking softly. "Your mother is a Rand and very proud of our heritage. The family first came to Virginia in 1731. Over the years, some of our men rose to high government office; others served distinguished careers in the military. Before the war, my father built a fine business in Richmond and accumulated considerable wealth. But notwithstanding what you may have heard, all Rands were not pristine. There were mulattos on Rand plantations, and more than one Rand girl studied abroad for a year. What you did was wrong, but you are not branded. You must keep your head high, and remember that God loves you."

It wasn't until the last week in May that Rachel and Will returned to Richmond, just two weeks before the baby was due. The scene was far better than Rachel expected, and in accordance with her request, arrangements for adoption were settled by Anna's attorney.

While Ann rested, Rachel, Will, and Anna had lunch at a quiet table in the dining room of the Jefferson Hotel. The white brick structure built on Franklin Street in 1895 featured a Carrara marble statue of Thomas Jefferson standing in the splendidly appointed Palm Court. And the grand stairway leading from the court down to the Rotunda provided an impressive descent for Richmond's most prominent families. Rachel believed no place more appropriately defined the gentility of Richmond than did the Jefferson.

At the table, Rachel placed her hand on Anna's arm. "Thank you for working a miracle with Ann. I have never seen her in a better mood. Soon, this will be behind us and we will be on our way."

Anna smiled graciously. "You are fortunate to have such a lovely daughter. I wish she were mine."

A half-smile crossed Rachel's face.

When Ann's pains of birth began, Anna's chauffeur drove the family to Memorial Hospital. Ann's water broke as a nurse wearing a long white uniform wheeled her into a brightly-lighted delivery room. The nurse helped her onto a table, and swabbed her with solution of iodine.

At exactly 11:24 a.m., Dr. Stallings emerged from delivery nodding his head. "It's a seven pound boy."

A boy, thought Will. A boy. But he won't be ours. He won't be a Taylor. He'll be given away. Now the image of Gail streaked through his mind. Another Taylor child would bear some unknown name — become a stranger to its kin. He cleared his throat and walked swiftly to Ann's bedside.

Rachel had given strict instructions: "Under no circumstances is the baby to be taken to Ann."

But Ann begged: "I want to see my baby."

Rachel stood beside the bed. "It would be unfair to the baby's adoptive parents. Let's put this behind us and thank God everything has gone so well."

"I want my baby! Aunt Anna — don't let her do this."

Anna cringed. "Please, Rachel, let her hold the baby, just for a little while. There are no right answers in situations like this."

Rachel shook her head. "It's wrong, but if that's what you want, go ahead." She turned and left the room.

Anna watched as the infant was placed in his mother's arms. She knew that the life of a beautiful son was justification enough for the anguish of bearing an illegitimate child. Rachel didn't want them. Ann and her baby could remain in Richmond, live in her home. A daughter and a grandchild would fill her life with happiness. Her position in the community, her name would overcome the stigma of the baby's illegitimacy. The child would have every advantage, take his place in Richmond, become a part of the heritage of his blood line. Anna wiped tears that had streamed down her face, and she smiled as she touched the baby's tiny hand.

On Thursday, Ann wanted no food. Beads of perspiration popped out on her forehead as her temperature reached 104 degrees. Twitching and turning, she moaned in agony and bled profusely. The Taylors had planned to return to Orlando the minute Dr. Stallings released Ann, but by noon Ann had developed chills along with fever, profuse sweating, and listlessness. Her pulse was rapid, and she continued bleeding from the uterus. Sharp abdominal pains persisted and her temperature edged higher and higher. Dr. Stallings realized that a bacterial infection was present in her body, gaining momentum, as the fever raged out of control. Nurses applied ice bags to her forehead in an attempt to comfort her. She was given injections of morphia and infusions of digitalis, but to no avail.

Monday. Ann became delirious. Will, Rachel, and Anna sat by her bedside, and for a few moments, Ann's eyes opened. She whispered, "Oh, Aunt Anna, I'm so tired." Slowly, her head turned toward Will. "Papa, don't give my baby away."

Will placed his palm on her burning cheek. "Please, Annie, save your strength and try to sleep."

A faint smile crossed her lips, and then she closed her eyes and slept. But she did not awaken the next morning.

Rachel and Will sat quietly in Anna's parlor. Soon they would return to Orlando, bearing Ann's body for burial at Greenwood Cemetery. "Should we tell the Quinns?" Will asked.

Rachel's face was expressionless. "No. It would serve no purpose. Ann died of pneumonia. It is over."

Tears filled Will's eyes as he departed the room. He put on his gray morning coat, adjusted his hat, and left the house. Aimlessly, he walked along the sidewalk of Franklin Street, passing many fine homes, some featuring black wrought iron fences; owned, he guessed, by Richmond's most celebrated families, fine people, no doubt, who had also experienced tragedy. There's no promise that lives can be led without suffering. God has a plan for everyone. Who are we — who am I to question Him? Suddenly, he stopped. An inner voice was clear.

Don't give my baby away ... Ann's final words.

He had convinced himself that adoption was in the baby's best interest. He had also considered bringing the baby to Orlando and raising him as a son, but he wanted no confrontation with Rachel.

Ann was gone, but her son lived. The child was his blood, his link to the future. Hurriedly, he returned to the house and found Anna in her parlor. In a firm voice he asked, "Where is the baby?"

"Why do you want to know?"

"I'm adopting the child. He will return with us to Orlando and live in our home."

Anna's glance was mischievous. "What does Rachel say about that?"

"I haven't told her, but it doesn't matter. The decision is made. The boy is ours, and I'll not give him up."

Anna's eyes sparkled. "Well, the fur's going to fly when you tell her, but I'll tell you something, it so happens that an adoption has not been arranged. The baby is still in the hospital."

"You guessed what I would do?"

"No. I wanted him, and Ann, too, but I'm so proud of you for taking a stand and giving the child your name. Now go, and face Rachel."

"I love you, Anna."

Will found Rachel in the bedroom, packing for the return to Orlando. His abrupt entrance caused her to flinch. "What is it?"

He closed the heavy oak door behind him and stood in the center of the room. His voice was clear and direct. "I've come to my senses. Our grandson is not going to be placed for adoption. He's ours. We'll name him Andrew, after his great grandfather, and we'll raise him as a son."

Rachel breathed deeply and then sat on the edge of the bed. "I know how you feel. I, too, share the pain of giving up Ann's baby, but consider the alternatives. Here, in Richmond, he will be adopted by a young couple who will give him their name. He will be legitimate and live a normal life. If you desire, you can provide funds for his education, as you did for Gail. But in Orlando, he'll be branded and ridiculed all of his life. Is that what you want?"

Will squared his shoulders. "Your fear is not for the boy's reputation. Your concern is what you think people will say about us. Frankly, I'm not concerned with what people say. Those who say ugly things behind our backs are not friends. I'm going to honor Ann's final wish and take the child to Orlando to live with us."

Rachel's chin quivered, as her voice reached a high pitch. "Don't you understand what you're doing? You're planning to *ruin* us! For the sake of a little bastard, we will be ostracized!"

Will stood motionless. "I love you Rachel, but the decision is final."

Rachel wiped tears from her eyes. "Another Taylor *bastard*, this one living right under my roof, a reminder of the stain on our family. My only comfort is that his name is not Rand. You know I am unalterably opposed to what you're doing. The responsibility for the infant is solely yours."

When Rachel stepped off the train at the depot in Orlando, Mrs. Adamson held out her arms and embraced her daughter. Rachel brushed away a tear. "Oh, Mama, it happened so quickly. She — we — I."

With the baby in his arms, Will interrupted. "Say hello to your family, Andrew. They're here to greet you."

When the shock wore off, Dr. Adamson stepped forward. "Why, he has the hands of a surgeon. Let me have my great-grandson." The doctor took the infant in his arms and everyone crowded in for a look at the newest Taylor.

Will stepped back and watched as Mr. Carey Hand and two of his assistants removed the coffin from the train, placed it in a hearse, and slowly drove away toward the funeral parlor. Annie had come home. The news washed in a wave over Orlando. At two o'clock on Wednesday, hundreds of neighbors and friends stood as the Taylor family entered the sanctuary of The First Presbyterian Church for Ann's service. Arrangements of summer flowers covered the chancel, and a spray of red roses adorned the casket. Dr. Stagg stood in the pulpit, speaking of family and of life everlasting, but mostly he spoke of God's love for all his children. When the benediction had been pronounced, friends surrounded the Taylors, showering them with expressions of sympathy and kindness. Rachel responded in her usual gracious manner; but, for the first time, Will saw lines and shadows in her face.

∽ 16 ∽

*W*ill Taylor's new office wasn't exactly imposing. When he first saw the two story building on Pine Street near the corner of Main, the room smelled of stale tobacco, which Mr. Ramsey said was left over from the cigar store that had previously occupied the space. But the building was structurally sound and adequate for an office. Will's roll-top desk sat on the first floor, near the back wall on an uncovered pine floor. Behind the desk were two, wooden file cabinets that held letters, invoices, and ledgers, records of every transaction Will had made since his arrival in Orlando. A six-foot unpainted table stood at the center of the room surrounded by four captain's chairs Rachel had found at Bumby's Hardware Store. Plastered walls were painted cream, and bare except for an Orlando Bank & Trust Company calendar which hung near the roll-top desk.

Will and Billy sat at the table, reviewing monthly bills. Will initialed the last invoice and pushed back in his chair. "We own 520 acres in three counties. The business is getting too big for us to be separated by twenty miles. I want you to move to Orlando. You can live upstairs, over the office."

Billy scowled. "I don't like a whole bunch of folks crowding me and besides the fishing's good down there. I ain't moving to the city."

Will cleared his throat. "Listen, my friend, you could die out there in the middle of nowhere and no one would know it. I need you and Adam here, with me."

Billy flared. "You're trying to be a mother hen."

Will looked over the top of his new steel-rimmed glasses. "I'm firing you if you don't move to Orlando."

Billy's scowl turned to a little smile. "Since you put it that way, I ain't got no choice."

"Now listen, I want you to go with Rachel and me to the Growers and Shippers meeting in Tampa. They tell me the people at the experiment station found outbreaks of canker in Miami; it sounds serious."

Pastin frowned. "Hadn't heard that. All right, I want to hear what they have to say." Pastin got up and started to leave.

"How's Adam doing?" said Will.

The old man smiled. "The boy knows exactly what he's doing. He's irrigating the groves like crazy, and that's increasing fruit production; but that's just the tip of it. He's all over the place morning and night. Never saw a man learn so fast. He could run the whole field operation right now."

Will shook his head. "He's just getting his feet wet, he hasn't faced the problems you have. He needs an old warrior to keep him in line."

Pastin pulled at his beard. "Well, maybe I can help him a little, but you're overpaying me."

Will scoffed. "You're worth ten times what you get. There wouldn't be a Taylor Groves without you."

Billy stood, picked up his hat, and grinned. "Aw, shut up, Will."

Will nodded. "The Tampa meeting begins two weeks from Friday. Write yourself a note."

"You think I'm getting old and nutty? I can still lick a bear."

"Yeah, I know. Ten foot tall bears. That's what Adam says. Right?"

Growers from every citrus-growing county in Florida filled the grandiose ballroom of the Tampa Bay Hotel. Built by Henry B. Plant in 1891 on the west bank of the Hillsborough River, the sprawling showplace reflected a near-eastern theme as its Moorish spires stood impressively in the sky above Tampa. Mr. Plant had imported treasured antiques and pieces of art from practically every continent to furnish his masterpiece of construction.

Lloyd Tenny called the meeting to order. "Gentlemen, we are here to review a report on Canker written by Dr. H. E. Stevens of the Agricultural Experiment Station at the University of Florida — Dr. Stevens."

"Thank you Mr. Tenny. Let there be no mistake, canker is a serious threat to the entire citrus industry in Florida. The cause of the disease has not been determined, but we know the malady is infectious and probably more injurious to citrus than any fungus known. Do not confuse canker with scab. Canker appears as small, circular spots. They are light brown and composed of a spongy mass of dead cells covered by a thin membrane that finally ruptures and turns outward. The spots appear on leaves, fruit, or twigs. The disease has been found only in Miami, but I caution you, canker is very infectious; once introduced, it may be expected to spread rapidly. Any grower finding canker symptoms should notify us immediately. Diseased trees must be removed and burned."

The meeting broke and Will turned to Billy. "Have you seen anything that looks like canker?"

"No. Our groves are clean, but you better believe Adam and I will look at every leaf on every tree."

"Good. I'm going up to get Rachel. Meet you in ten minutes for lunch."

Will walked to the lobby and started up the oak staircase.

"Will Taylor!"

The voice came out of the past. He spun around. It was Lucy Neal.

"Lucy!" He stared at her pretty face. "Why — where did you come from? You haven't changed a bit."

Color rose in her cheeks. "Still in Atlanta, running Fitch Brokerage Company. We have much at stake with the canker scare, that's why I'm here. I wondered if you would be here."

It wasn't a casual compliment. Lucy really hadn't changed. He saw no lines in her face, no strands of gray in her long auburn curls, no blemishes in her complexion. He started to speak, then he looked up and saw Rachel walking slowly down the staircase.

"Rachel," said Will, as he cleared his throat, "look who's here."

Rachel attempted a smile. "Why, Lucy Neal. What a surprise."

"Thank you," said Lucy. "You look so pretty. Perhaps we could have dinner one evening,"

Rachel nodded. "By all means."

The awkward moment ended when Lucy excused herself and glided down the corridor to join a friend.

At lunch, Rachel picked at her salad. "How long since you've seen Lucy Neal?"

Will paused. "I really can't remember. I lost track of her years ago."

"I doubt she lost track of you."

Will chuckled. "Did I ever tell you how beautiful you are when your eyes turn green?"

Rachel's stare could have frozen Tampa Bay.

During the afternoon meeting, Lloyd Tenny harped on fruit loss due to spoilage. "Nearly one third of the oranges arriving at market are bruised or rotten. There must be a way to improve picking, packing, and shipping practices; it's costing all of us."

The meeting broke for dinner and Tenny approached Will. "I want you to chair a committee to find solutions to the damaged fruit problem. Put together a group of growers and let's get started on this thing. Get Lucy Neal to work with you, representing the brokers."

All day Wednesday, the committee worked around a large table in a meeting room near the main ballroom of the hotel. The consensus was that more emphasis should be placed on training pickers and more care given to cleaning and sorting. Fruit should be stored in shady, open air areas, and the interval between picking and shipping should be reduced.

Across the table, Lucy studied Will. He'd always been strong and handsome, she thought, but now he's mature and confident. She forced herself to look away and think about damaged fruit, but it was no use.

At five o'clock the meeting broke and Lucy was drawn to Will's side. "You look the same," she said. He touched her shoulder. "And you look wonderful, Lucy."

She glanced over his shoulder and took a step back. Will turned and saw rage in Rachel's eyes as she stood motionless in the doorway.

"Thank you for your invitation, Miss Neal, but my husband and I will not be joining you for dinner." Rachel turned and moved swiftly down the carpeted hallway.

To Will, the train trip back to Orlando seemed endless as Rachel stared out the window of their car. Finally, Will remarked, "What you thought you saw, wasn't there."

Rachel continued to stare. "You know what I've been through. It never occurred to me you would be attracted to another woman."

"I am not attracted to Lucy Neal."

Her eyelids narrowed. "You're so naive. I heard it in your voice. Do you find her more appealing?" Her lips trembled.

"Rachel." He reached for her hand.

"Don't *touch* me."

Women, thought Will ... totally unpredictable ... never want to talk it over when they're upset. Billy and I always settle things when we're mad. Women.

In bright morning sunlight, Will looked uncomfortable as he sat with Billy on his dock and stared across the lake. "What's wrong with you, Will? Moping around like a calf with colic. What is it?"

"Oh, I don't know. Rachel and I ..."

"Rachel and you, what?"

"She thinks I'm attracted to Lucy Neal."

"What? Squeaky clean Will Taylor." Billy roared with laughter.

"It's not funny."

"I know it's not."

Billy stormed into the house, found Rachel in her kitchen, and said, "I want to say something."

As she folded her hands together she seemed annoyed. "What?" "You and Will are having trouble over Miss Lucy Neal. Right?"

Rachel lashed out. "That's none of your business, Billy."

"Yes it is! You, Will, and your kids are the only close friends I have in this world, and I'm not going to let anything come between you. Lord, woman, if there was ever an honest, straightforward man, it's Will Taylor. In all the years I've known him, he ain't never messed around with another woman, ain't never told a lie. The man is loyal as an eagle. You ought to go apologize to him."

"I certainly will not." She turned on her heel and left the room. At bedtime, Rachel lay silently, beside her husband. Finally, she spoke. "Remember Cadet Stanley Edwards?"

"How could I ever forget him?"

"You were terribly jealous."

"Yes."

"Then you know how I feel."

"Rachel." He turned and held his cheek against her shoulder. She whispered. "Do you love me?"

"Of course I love you."

Much later, Rachel heard the clock in the foyer strike three.

Billy Pastin's seventieth birthday fell on the second Saturday in February and Ada baked a huge coconut cake for his party. The Taylors gathered around the dining room table to watch Rachel light the candles. Will glanced at Billy. "All right, old friend, you must make a speech."

Billy sat up as straight as he could, but he looked withered. His eyes watered, and his voice scraped like sandpaper as he looked at Adam and Charlotte. "I've been hanging around this family since 1887. Never had a dime before your daddy came to town. Never knew a man like him: smart, upstanding, and honest. Oh, we fussed and fumed at first, before I realized how much he cared about me." He turned to Rachel. "And you, Rachel — prettiest girl in town when you married, still are. All I got to say to all of you is, thanks for putting up with me all these years."

Will lifted his glass. "I propose a toast to the best citrus man in Florida, Uncle Billy Pastin."

Billy frowned. "Oh, for crying out loud. Nothing but iced tea to drink. Rachel, ain't you ever gonna loosen up?"

You could almost cut the humidity with a knife on Tuesday afternoon. Adam entered the Pine Street office, breathed heavily, and looked around to be sure no one else was present. "Uncle Billy, we have a problem."

Billy put his coffee cup aside. "What is it?"

"I just drove in from Kissimmee. There's canker in the northwest corner of the grove. I thoroughly checked it and compared it to drawings in my files. Listen, Uncle Billy, state law says we have to call in a Canker Inspection Team, but there's no telling what they might do. We could lose the whole grove. Why don't we cut out the infected trees, burn them, and pick the grove? They'll never know about it."

Billy's wintry eyes glared as he rubbed his white-bearded chin. "So you think that's the best solution. Cut out a few trees and save the crop?"

"Uncle Billy, there's twenty thousand dollars worth of fruit on those trees."

"Twenty thousand — twenty thousand dollars." A dark look crossed his face. "You discover canker in the grove, and for twenty thousand lousy dollars you would expose the entire citrus industry in Central Florida to infection. After all the education and all the upbringing you've had, you ain't learned nothing!" Billy sat back in his chair, then pointed his finger at Adam. "The day we bought that grove I told your Papa we could steal it for a whole lot less than it was worth. Good business I thought. The owner was ornery and nobody liked him. You couldn't do business with him. We could have really taken advantage of the old man, and I was shocked when Will told me to offer him a fair price. But as time went by, I learned from your Daddy the most important lesson in the world. Do what's right. You hear me? Now, go tell Will to call in the inspectors."

"Yes, sir."

State canker inspectors came quickly; they condemned eighteen acres of Taylor groves. After trees were removed, sprayed with oil, and burned, Will received a letter from the Florida Citrus Canker Committee.

Dear Mr. Taylor,

Although you lost acreage, your sacrifice may have saved the citrus industry in Central Florida. For that, the growers will always be grateful ....

D.C. Gillett, Chairman

Will smiled as he handed the letter to Adam. "I'm so glad you came straight to me. We paid a small price."

Adam nodded, then walked to Billy's desk. "How about lunch?"

"Sounds good," said Billy.

In silence, they ate soup and sandwiches at the San Juan. Adam wanted to say something, but what? he wondered. He had not only been wrong, he had been dishonest. What would Papa think if he had known? Adam took the last swallow of coffee and picked up the check. "It's mine. Small price to pay for a terrible mistake in judgment."

The old man's voice rattled as he looked up. "We all make mistakes, son. You know how I feel about you."

"Thank you Uncle Billy."

Late that night, Billy Pastin died in his sleep.

∞ 17 ∞

September 1917. Second Lieutenant John Adamson Taylor's train would leave at noon for Camp Wheeler at Macon, Georgia. He dressed in his uniform and glanced around his room. A framed picture of the 1909 Orlando Tigers Baseball Team hung on the wall; his Kappa Alpha Fraternity beer mug sat on his dresser; Ann's photo taken near the rose garden was pinned to the closet door. He fastened the leather straps to his valise and walked downstairs where Rachel, Will, Charlotte, and Andrew sat at the breakfast table, waiting for him.

Ada's hair was nearly white. She shuffled to the table and served Adam's favorite breakfast: juice, grits, eggs-over-light, and biscuits. She poured his coffee and then placed a brown bag on the table. "These biscuits is for you and Mr. Tommy to eat on the train."

"Ada," said Adam, "when Tommy Lane and I get promoted to general officers, we're making you head cook of the whole army. Nobody makes biscuits like you."

"Oh, Mister Adam," she said tearfully, "I gonna miss you."

Rachel cleared her throat. She had read reports of thousands of casualties in France, young men bleeding to death on the battlefield. She waved a finger. "Promise me you'll take the heavy wool socks and the scarf to France. You have no idea how cold it gets over there. Promise me!" She dabbed a tear running down the cheek of her lined, but still beautiful face.

Adam reached for Rachel's hand. "Of course I will. We'll win the war in no time, and I'll be right back home — you'll see."

"No, I don't see why our boys have to fight in a foreign war. Woodrow Wilson should be ashamed of himself."

Adam frowned. "They're sinking our ships; it's our war now."

Will pulled a gold watch from his vest pocket saying, "Time to go." The family packed into the Dodge sedan and as Will drove through the grove, Adam took a last look at the trees and said, "Big crop."

135

"Big crop is right," answered Will. "Thanks to you and Billy, this may be our best harvest, maybe seven boxes to the tree."

Adam smiled. "Save me a job. I may be home by Christmas."

Rachel said nothing. Her face drawn as she pulled at the hem of her handkerchief.

At the depot, hundreds of family members and sweethearts of Orlando's National Guard gathered to see their men off to Camp Wheeler. Helen Pendelton was there. Rachel had tried her best to promote a romance between her son and Helen, the granddaughter of Harold J. Pendelton, Orlando's wealthiest citizen. But with each not so subtle attempt, Adam had brushed aside his mother's overtures. "Mama, we're at war, this is no time to get involved."

Mayor Giles wore a white linen suit and a black ribbon bow tie. He stood on a wooden box facing the station house and praised the "brave young men making the world safe for democracy." The Orlando Brass Band struck up *The Stars and Stripes Forever*. Men cheered and mothers wept as Captain Bradford Allison led "C" Company on the train. Little Andrew Taylor sat on Will's shoulders waving a small American flag, and Rachel held a handkerchief to her lips as the engine pulled out of the station with whistle blowing.

Will lifted Andrew from his shoulders, placed him on the ground, then held the little fellow's hand firmly in his grip. Most able bodied young men in Orlando were on the train. But as Will stared at the last car moving down the tracks, the reality struck. *His* boy was on the train. He told himself that only women shed tears at times like this. He sniffed, then cleared his throat. "Come along, come along," he said, "let's get back to the car."

The sun was nearly down when noisy buses carrying "C" Company troops pulled in at headquarters of the 31st Infantry Division at Camp Wheeler. White canvas army tents stood in long rows beyond the clay parade ground. Soldiers clad in olive drab uniforms darted about. Wooden barracks, classrooms, mess halls, and armories were under construction everywhere.

A bronze-tanned sergeant major with a chiseled face and intense dark eyes saluted Captain Allison. "Welcome, Captain. You and other officers will please enter division headquarters building for orientation. Enlisted men will follow me."

Adam grinned as he looked at his former college roommate, Tommy Lane. "Remember the time you wanted to quit school in Gainesville? Well, Lt. Lane, you ain't getting out of this one either. We're in for the duration."

"Thank you very much for that information. I thought we were here just for the weekend."

At 0700, Colonel Armitage, the diminutive, gray-haired Assistant Division Commander addressed all newly arrived officers. His voice was deep and clear. "Gentlemen, you of the National Guard represent some of the most experienced officers in the army. All of us want to get into the fight: but for now our mission is training soldiers for action. The Germans are combat veterans of three years of war. We have been in it only a few months; therefore our training must be thorough and rigorous. How well we do our job will determine how many men return alive from Europe."

From Florida, Georgia, Alabama, and South Carolina they came, recruits from schools, farms, factories, and offices. Their hair was cut short. They received olive drab uniforms, army shoes, rifles, bayonets, steel helmets, and canteens; they ran or marched everywhere they went; they ate tasteless army food, drank bitter army coffee, saluted commissioned officers, learned to use the weapons of war, and how to take cover from enemy fire. They had come to Wheeler as green recruits. They left for ports of embarkation ready to fight.

In France, Operation Michael began in March 1918. Six thousand German artillery pieces rained gas and high-explosive shells on British and French troops along a broad front from the Somme River to the Marne. Undercover of an enveloping fog stretching across the battlefield, fifty German divisions sliced through Allied defenses, threatening Paris. During four years of fighting two million British and French soldiers had died on battlefields from Flanders to St.Mihiel. Now, the Allies faced a new offensive. Newspapers all across America questioned whether the Allies could hold out until fresh troops from the United States arrived.

"Tell you what's going to happen," said Tommy as he lay on his cot at Bachelor Officer Quarters. "We're never going to France. Our grandchildren will read about how we choked breathing clay dust in Georgia. We're stuck here, training all the future heroes. And Lord knows, the girls in Macon run the other way when they see me. You'd think I was contaminated. But they go to you, Taylor, like bees after sugar water. Boy, you must wear some kind of male perfume. I can't figure it out. Tell me your secret, boy."

Adam squirmed, as he lay on his cot. The last thing he wanted to be reminded of was his long tenure at Wheeler. The next to last was Tommy's preoccupation with women. "Lieutenant Lane, I will personally award you the Medal of Honor if you will just shut up and go to sleep. By the way, you and I are invited to Atlanta for a weekend at the home of friends of my parents. They have two daughters, that should make you happy. You better apply for weekend leave on the double."

Tommy threw up his arms. "You, sir, are a savior. Forget what I said. Just get us out of here."

"Turn out the light, Lane."

Will's Atlanta banker, Sheldon Nelson, and his wife, Kathleen, waited at their home in Buckhead for the arrival of the young officers. The taxi turned and made its way up a private drive lined with pink dogwood. Ancient live oaks towered over beds of lavender azaleas, framing the veranda of the Nelsons' colonial home. A warm feeling came over Adam as the image of Bellemere flowed through his mind.

Mrs. Nelson, wearing an ankle-length ivory lace dress, received them in her parlor. A hint of gray in her bouffant hairstyle was becoming, and her smile was infectious.

"Adam. Come in, come in," she said.

"Thank you. This is my friend, Tommy Lane."

Mrs. Nelson extended her hand. "Hello, Tommy. We're delighted to have you men as our guests. We want to hear everything about Orlando. But now Thomas will show you to the guest house. Hurry back, the girls will be down in a few minutes."

Thomas's black face was framed by white hair and white sideburns. He wore a white cotton coat, white shirt, and black bow tie. Silently, he took the men's bags, then ushered them through rooms richly furnished with dark antiques, to a covered walkway and past formal gardens surrounding a cottage suite of two bedrooms, bath, and sitting room. Thomas placed the bags at the foot of each bed, and then slowly backed out of the room.

Tommy flopped on a pink sofa in the tastefully furnished bedroom. "This doesn't remind me much of Camp Wheeler, ole' buddy."

Adam looked around and grinned. "Yeah. I think we can fit into this. Listen, Tommy, I know they have one attractive daughter about our age and another who is college age. You, old pal, get the student."

Tommy sneered. "Lieutenant Taylor, we shall see if the looker can resist my charming personality. I make no promises."

Before dinner, the Nelson sisters made their appearance. Tall, slender Carolyn Nelson led the way into the parlor wearing an off-the-shoulder, black sheath that accentuated her figure. Her stylishly bobbed hair and warm brown eyes combined to produce a striking image, one that did not escape the notice of the young officers. Alice, the younger sister, dressed in a blue, puffed-sleeve cotton print, followed in Carolyn's wake, glowing with the color and brightness of her twenty years. The luster of her blonde, bobbed hair framed clear blue eyes reflecting the look of innocence.

In a voice that was unmistakably Atlanta, Mrs. Nelson made introductions, announced dinner, and led everyone to her dining room. The centerpiece of the room was a multi-tier crystal chandelier hanging majestically over a long mahogany table. Sterling flatware and Limoges china lay on a white lace tablecloth of intricate design. A bouquet of pink azaleas arranged in a crystal bowl graced the center of the table. At each end of the sideboard, glowing white tapers stood tall in sterling candelabra.

After soup bowls were removed, Thomas served slices of Chateaubriand with red wine sauce, spears of asparagus, and lyonnaise potatoes.

During the meal, Mr. Nelson paused. "We're so proud of you men in uniform." He looked at Adam and said, "Tell us about the training at Camp Wheeler."

Adam told of long marches, blistering heat in the field at the rifle range, simulated battlefield exercises, close order drill at the post. "Actually," he concluded, "it's pretty boring."

Tall, gray-haired Sheldon Nelson, handsomely suited in charcoal black, white collar and blue silk tie, carefully placed his dessert spoon on his plate. "Boring now, but chances are you will soon be in France, fighting the Huns. By Gad, I wish I could go with you. Do you know when you will sail?"

Adam shook his head. "No sir. No orders yet."

"Well," said Mr. Nelson, "we'll see to it this weekend is special for you. Atlanta's a big city and I want you men to see it. I've planned a grand tour for tomorrow."

"Darling," interrupted Mrs. Nelson, "let's retire and let the young people visit with each other." She glanced at Adam. "If you like, after you see the city, Sheldon can arrange dinner at the Club for you and the girls."

Adam smiled. "Thank you. We would like that very much."

In the parlor, Carolyn slid beside Adam on the sofa. An impish smile appeared on her face as she spoke. "Tell me about those Florida alligators, Lieutenant Taylor. Do they really devour little girls?"

She's definitely the looker, he thought, but also a flirt. "No, not if a gentleman is present."

A tinge of color rose in his face as her fingers touched his hand. "In that case, I'd be safe with you, wouldn't I?"

Carolyn talked about her debut at the club, her summer in Canada, Christmas with snow at the Greenbrier. He wanted to ask questions, but she never stopped talking. Finally, Adam rose and said goodnight, but Carolyn glanced at Alice. "It's much too early to retire, sister. Let's show them the garden."

A pained expression appeared on Alice's face as Tommy moved to her side.

Carolyn placed her hand on Adam's arm and led him out into a moonlit night. As they walked, through the Nelsons' grounds, Carolyn continued her chatter. Was the Atlanta visit a big mistake? he wondered. Finally, Adam said, "Tommy, Mr. Nelson will have us up for court martial if we keep his daughters out any later."

"Don't be silly," said Carolyn."

When they returned to the foyer, Alice said goodnight and quickly ran upstairs, but Carolyn remained. Her eyes fixed on Adam. For heaven's sake, he thought. Surely she expects no more of me. He patted her arm and hurried off.

In their room, Tommy began, "Well, great alligator-slayer, she practically threw you on the floor. Some guys have all the luck."

"Yeah. Now, tell me old friend, how did you do?"

As he turned out the light, Tommy said, "Shut up."

Mr. Nelson's tour of Atlanta began early. On and on they traveled, from the Peachtree Creek Battlefield to Stone Mountain, from Decatur, then south to the Macon Road. Finally, the odyssey ended when Nelson drove his Pierce-Arrow into his driveway and parked under the broad canopy. Adam and Tommy expressed their appreciation, went to their room, and fell into chairs. Tommy laughed. "It was a lot more than I ever wanted to know about Atlanta. What I'd rather have is Carolyn Nelson giving me a massage." Adam threw a pillow in his face.

At seven, the young officers escorted the Nelson girls to dinner at the Piedmont Driving Club. Its membership drawn from the highest levels of Atlanta society, the club provided the ambience, delicious steaks, and strains of soft music that made Camp Wheeler seem far away. Caroline looked stunning in peach silk as she and Adam gracefully danced across the floor. Fascinating, he thought, but too game, too eager. The music stopped and they walked to the table. "Here she is, Tommy. It's your turn."

Adam turned to Alice and smiled. "Would you like to dance?"

She looked up, and answered in a barely audible voice, "Yes."

Silently, they glided across the floor to the rhythm of the music. She seemed different from her sister, so unassuming and modest, a delicate flower. When the orchestra broke, Adam and Alice walked onto the veranda.

"Carolyn says you're a student at Agnes Scott," he said.

"Yes. A senior, majoring in history."

"History. If we would only learn from the past, there would be no war."

She looked up beyond tree tops. "Tragic, isn't it?"

"Were you born in Atlanta?"

"Oh, yes. Our family has lived here for three generations. Daddy was literally born into banking."

Adam stopped walking. "My grandfather was almost killed during the battle for Atlanta. Do you suppose we're distantly related?"

She laughed, and then looked at him with clear bright eyes and smiled.

For a moment he was speechless; then he returned her smile. "You can't imagine how great it is to be here with your family."

She quickly looked away and said, "When will you be going overseas?"

"I hope not too soon. I want to see you again."

Her face flushed. Summoning the last ounce of courage, she replied, "Will you be coming to Atlanta again?"

"I will," he nodded. The music began and they walked inside to dance. Later, at the table he described how Billy Pastin had taught him how to care for citrus, how to catch bass, and how to drink beer. Alice smiled, laughed, and seemed totally relaxed. When the orchestra leader announced the last selection, he held her as they danced to the strains of *Goodnight Sweetheart*. Adam didn't want the evening to end. He wanted to hold her even closer, but she seemed so innocent, so chaste. Instead, he touched her cheek and said, "You're very pretty." He drew her close, but without a word she turned away.

Four days after Adam and Tommy had returned to duty, the telephone rang at Alice's dormitory at Agnes Scott. Lillian Anderson poked her head in Alice's room . "There's a long distance call for you downstairs, from Adam Taylor."

Alice dropped her book and ran to the telephone.

"Alice, this is Adam."

She swallowed, "Where are you?"

"At Camp Wheeler. I have orders. We're off for Fort Dix, New Jersey. We arrive at the Atlanta train station Monday morning at eleven; we'll be there about an hour. Can you meet me?"

"Yes. Of course I'll be there."

"I can't tell you how much I want to see you."

"I've been thinking about you." Her voice quivered as she spoke.

"That's good. Goodbye."

Before noon, on Monday, thirty crowded buses pulled in at Atlanta station and fifteen hundred khaki-clad officers and enlisted men unloaded their gear and rushed inside.

Adam looked everywhere for her; then, finally, he saw her standing on the other side of the huge station room. She wore a demure brown dress with plain white collar, a dark beret, and short white gloves. She stood alone, waiting for him. He wanted to race across the floor and take her in his arms, but he restrained himself. He walked to her side and held her hands. Her smile was so natural, so sincere.

"Alice. I'm so glad you're here. It looks like we're on our way to France. I had to see you before I left."

She looked up into his eyes. "I had no idea it would be so soon."

They walked to a small cafe' filled with noisy soldiers wolfing down sandwiches and beer. He understood that loneliness travels with men in uniform. Falling in love was common among soldiers going off to war, but it wasn't loneliness that drew him to her. Beneath the veneer of a shy, unaffected girl, he recognized the qualities of a lady. He glanced at his watch; it was time to leave.

Holding hands, they walked to the platform. The conductor's shrill whistle blew. "Alice, I'll write as often as I can."

"Please do that."

When the whistle blew again, he took her in his arms and kissed her lips.

Slowly, the train made its way out of the station, into the Georgia countryside, and northeast through North Carolina and Virginia. Late that night as they passed through Richmond, Adam thought of Aunt Anna, living in a rarefied world. He had been with her only a short time during the week of the funeral, but he felt her warmth and strength. He imagined the pain Papa and Mama felt as they stood by Ann at the end. And Andrew, Ann's little son, had brought new life to the family. His family would like Alice. He knew they would. How could they not like a perfect girl?

Troops unloaded at Trenton Station and packed into buses for the seventeen mile ride to Fort Dix. As the convoy crept along the highway in early sunlight, buds appeared on trees and some flowers bloomed. Spring had just arrived and the morning air felt cool and damp. Adam recalled his mother's remark, "Woodrow Wilson should be ashamed of himself." He laughed. The German offensive had driven all the way to Chateau-Thierry. Now, it was up to the Americans to save France.

Buses turned in at gate 3 of the sprawling replacement depot. Thousands of soldiers waited there for ships; they slept, smoked, played nickel poker on canvas cots, read magazines, and wrote letters, but mostly they thought of home and the girls they left behind.

The day before the *Leviathan* sailed, Adam wrote:

Dear Alice,

Can't say when we sail, that's classified information. I can say that you're always in my mind. I'm not certain how you feel about me, perhaps not much, but when this thing's over, I want to be where ever you are.

I love you,

Adam

∞ 18 ∞

*F*n convoy, the *Leviathan* sailed under cover of darkness from Hoboken, transporting eight thousand officers and men to France. At sea they stood in food lines, shower lines, and latrine lines. Men rotated from below deck to open deck for periods of exercise and training. It was a time of reflection and self-examination. A time of prayer. A quiet time before the rage of battle began.

Adam and Tommy shared a small cabin. It was 2:00 a.m., but Tommy knew Adam was awake. "You're really stuck on Alice, aren't you?"

Adam chuckled. "Yeah. But there's a war to fight. You scared?"

"You bet. They say that's a good sign. If you aren't scared, you're not alert."

"Glad to hear that. Let's stay good and scared and soldier our way through this thing so we don't get planted in France."

Tommy nodded. "That's right. We go home together."

At dawn on the eighth day at sea, the convoy sighted the French coast. Adam stood on deck gazing at Belle Isle, silhouetted by the rising sun against the dark Atlantic.

"War's getting a little closer," shouted Tommy above a brisk breeze.

Adam nodded. "Yeah. Captain says we should pull into the Loire River sometime today. Listen, Tommy, if by some crazy chance I don't make it home, I want you to stay close to Andrew, be his big brother." Adam paused, lit a cigarette, and continued. "Go to Alice. Tell her — well, tell her how I feel about her."

Tommy snickered. "You big old softie. What was all the crap about not getting planted in France? I'm the one that walks in your shadow. You're supposed to be the confident one. If anybody gets it in the rear end I'm sure it'll be me."

Adam doubled his fist and pounded his chest as he choked with laughter. "That's what I like about you. You don't take life too seriously."

In late afternoon, troops disembarked at St. Nazaire. Bronzed fishermen wearing blue denim coveralls and black berets unloaded their catch on wharves streaked with sea water. Long columns of American soldiers streamed down gangways from the hull of the ship and loaded onto trucks. The convoy moved out of the city on cobblestone streets, past houses built of stone with slate roofs. In the countryside old men tended fields; women wearing coifs, long white aprons, and wooden shoes, herded fat milk cows; and children waved as the convoy rumbled down the road.

All through the night, soldiers unloaded at a camp near Nantes. Now, at first light, Adam saw a sea of canvas tents housing at least twenty-five thousand replacements, all positioned to refill ranks of American combat units. Soldiers washed, shaved, cleaned weapons, smoked, and talked in an atmosphere of restlessness. No one said it, but Adam saw it in their faces. The enemy waited, somewhere out there. Somewhere.

Two days after arrival, Adam and Tommy received orders to report to the 42nd Infantry Division Training Camp at Rimaucourt. Only a skeleton force of cadre was present when they arrived. The remainder of the division was engaged at Chalon-sur-Marne. At Rimaucourt, training became an exercise in seeing who could avoid falling in slime, spring rains having turned the area into a quagmire. Even coffee and beans tasted gritty.

"This isn't battle, it's a mud fight," said Tommy as he stood in ankle deep mud outside his tent. "We're just one war too late. If we'd been in 'Jeb' Stuart's cavalry, we could have ridden stallions and kept our feet dry."

"Yeah, lieutenant," replied Adam, "But you'll recall that we lost the Civil War. A little mud won't hurt us."

Using his bayonet, Tommy scraped mud from his shoes. "Hey, that's pretty funny. You're loosening up. You just might make it out of here."

Orders arrived on July 22. Two thousand replacements boarded trucks for transport to the front. Adam joined First Platoon, "C" Company, 168th Infantry. Tommy replaced a severely wounded platoon leader in "D" Company.

The 168th unloaded in a batter of mud near the village of Chateau Thierry. First and second battalions formed skirmish lines and moved to the German-held village where enemy machine gunners hid behind stone walls, fallen trees, and partially destroyed houses. At 1420, red flares lifted into the sky signaling the attack. Entrenched enemy machine guns opened fire, killing hundreds of American soldiers. Near a broken wall, an exploding mortar round decapitated Adam's platoon sergeant, but through the torrent of enemy fire the 42nd kept moving toward the village.

It was nearly dark when Adam's platoon halted and found shelter in shell craters and behind broken walls. As he opened a flat tin of potted beef, Adam remembered Tommy's remark during their last days at Camp Wheeler. "Tell you what's going to happen, we're never going to France. Our grandchildren will read about how we choked on clay dust in Georgia."

The morning air was cold and damp as Adam led his men through a stand of leafless, skeleton-like trees. At the bottom of a deep crater a German soldier lay face down, half submerged in mud. The regiment moved on, reached the banks of the Ourcq River and stormed the enemy's main line of resistance. As they poured through a breech, American casualties mounted, but reserves from the 4th Division arrived. A final assault forced a full scale German retreat. The enemy fell back, abandoning heavy weapons, ammunition, and supplies, but the price of victory was terrible. One-fourth of the 168th fell at Chateau Thierry.

The smoke of battle had not completely cleared as Adam made his way to Lane's platoon. He looked everywhere, but no Tommy. He stopped a soldier and held him by his arms. "Where's Lieutenant Lane?"

"Looking for me, Lieutenant?" Adam turned and saw his mud-spattered friend. Their eyes locked as they slapped each other on the shoulder. "If you want to, you can feed me some hot chicken soup and rock me to sleep," said Tommy.

The 168th pulled back, ate hot meals, and slept. They stripped for fumigation, bathed, received clean uniforms, and read mail from home. Adam received a letter from Alice; included was a photograph of her standing in the Nelsons' garden behind a row of white lilies. She didn't really say much except that she missed him, but the letter was signed, "Love," a large concession, he thought, for a shy girl. If only he could hold her, touch her. He looked up. In the distance, heavy clouds hung low, signaling more rain and more mud. He stared at her picture. She looked so natural, so fine. He placed it in the pocket of his jacket, next to his heart. After the war, he would invite her to Bellemere; they would ride by the lake shore, lunch at the San Juan. He would introduce her to everyone in town.

September 26. The 42nd Division boarded trucks for Meuse-Aragone, a salient sixty miles away. The dense Aragone Forest anchored the left flank of an eighty-mile front, the winding Meuse River providing the boundary on the right. The division assembled at Montfaucon Woods, a ghostly place where low-lying fog concealed a wasteland of splintered trees and mud filled craters.

General Pershing had sent a message to his corps commanders: "Break the Hindenberg Line protecting enemy rail lines near Sedan and end the war."

Adam drank black coffee as he cleaned his automatic pistol. He had read stories of Gettysburg and believed Meuse-Aragone would be like that, a barbaric struggle in which thousands would die within an all-pervading code wherein patriotism overcomes fear. No matter what came, he would make Papa proud.

He thought of Alice. She had worn a simple brown dress with plain white collar. He had walked to her side and held her hands. He recalled Rachel's words. "Take the heavy wool socks and the scarf to France." He smiled. The socks were worn out and the scarf in his kit bag was filthy.

The objective of the 168th was Cote-de-Chatillon, a heavily fortified position at the center of the front that General MacArthur had committed to fight to the death to win.

When dawn came, rain poured from dark skies, soaking every soldier. Whistles blew, signaling the attack, the front exploding in blinding white bursts of artillery shells and machine gun fire. The men of First Platoon moved forward in an upright position; but when bodies dropped, the others stooped and moved forward foot by foot, taking cover wherever they found it.

Adam's head throbbed as he led his platoon forward. Flanking the enemy, he crept within ten yards of a German machine gun placement and lobbed two grenades into the bunker, killing three soldiers. He entered the pit and turned the gun on the enemy, pouring shells into their flank. Smoke covered the battlefield, partially blocking his vision, but as the rattle of gunfire continued, he heard screams. He emptied the gun and listened, but there was no sound. The remainder of his platoon followed as he waved his arm forward, signaling a continuation of the attack. When the Americans neared the crest of the knoll, the enemy fired point-blank from fortified positions.

Now, it was hand-to-hand combat — a savage melee of explosions, screams, and pouring rain. A gray-coated German came out of a trench, threw Adam to the ground, raised his rifle and fired, shattering Adam's right elbow. Feeling no pain, he rose and fought his way forward to the crest, firing his pistol at retreating Germans. But soon a wave of numbness, followed by failing vision, overcame him. Drenched in blood and soaked with rain, he collapsed near a splintered tree.

By late afternoon the battlefield fell silent. The Americans had won Cote-de-Chatillon; all along the front the enemy was in full retreat.

Tommy searched for Adam, but no one knew what happened to him. Frantically, he uncovered long rows of corpses lying on the field. It was nearly dark when he found Adam on a cot at Regimental Field Hospital, his right arm amputated at the elbow. Adam opened his eyes and offered a thin smile. "Surgeon told me somebody made a tourniquet from my scarf — kept me from bleeding to death."

March 12, 1919. Troops of 1st Battalion stood at attention at 168th Infantry Headquarters, Remagen, Germany. Brigadier General Douglas MacArthur stood before Adam, turned to retrieve a small box from his aide. He opened it and pinned a Distinguished Service Cross on Adam's chest. The general saluted, and then placed his hand on the decorated hero's shoulder. "I am proud to have served with you, Lieutenant Taylor. I wish you well." After speaking briefly with his aide, the general entered his staff car and departed.

The Battalion Commander dismissed the troops, and Adam was mobbed. "You're a hero, Taylor," said Tommy Lane, "and I'm buying."

"Well, what do you know, guys? I have to lose an arm to get Lane to buy beer." Everyone cheered as they walked down a narrow, cobblestone street to the Steiger Inn, which reeked of highly seasoned sausage, entered, and drank until a bugler played Retreat.

The party ended, but Tommy stayed. He placed his arm around Adam's neck. "We sail for home tomorrow. Sounds like a miracle, doesn't it?"

"Yeah. Another miracle is that I didn't lose both arms."

"That's right. Concentrate on that thought."

Adam's eye lids narrowed. "I can handle it."

Tommy ordered more beer. A fat woman with straw-colored hair played a polka on an out-of-tune accordion. Adam stared at the flame of the table lamp, wondering what Alice would think of a one-armed man.

"Well, Adam said, "at least we didn't get planted in France, and after tomorrow we won't have to listen to polkas anymore."

A soft rain fell from gray skies as tugs slowly pulled the *Leviathan* up the Hudson River to a berth at the Port of New York. Few civilians were there to greet the victorious 42nd Division. Adam wondered if anyone even knew they'd been to war. He had written to Alice, and to the family, telling them of the loss of his arm; but now, he thought, they'll see the empty sleeve. The muscles of his jaw tightened.

The giant gray ship came to rest and lines tethered her to the pier. With gangways secure, soldiers poured from the ship's hull and into the arms of their loved ones.

Adam was near the last of the 168th to leave the ship. He glanced back and forth across the crowd as he walked down the gangway. There they were: Mama, Papa, Charlotte, Andrew, and Alice, all frantically waving as they stood under umbrellas. He dropped his bag and raced to his mother's arms. The family crowded in, holding him. Rachel and Alice were crying.

Adam turned to Alice, believing no angel in heaven could be more beautiful. Her pink felt hat fell to the pier as he held her. He hadn't planned to ask, the question just blurted out. "Will you marry me?" When she lifted her head, raindrops fell on her face and trickled down her chin. "Yes. Oh, yes," she said. Then she pressed her face against his shoulder and wept.

The family watched in silence, then Charlotte piped up. "This is really getting mushy. Let's get out of here before we all drown."

❦ *19* ❦

September 1920. Charlotte Taylor began her sophomore year at Rollins College in Winter Park. More than anyone, she resembled Grandmother Taylor, not pretty, but she did attract classmate Jack Melvin. He liked the way she walked and talked and teased. Her stylish, blonde bobbed hair and breezy personality went well with her shapely figure. She was part of a "new age" of college women who had no intention of conforming to codes set forth by previous generations. Some coeds smoked cigarettes, drank, wore "revealing" bathing suits, and danced "ridiculous" dances. "After all," Charlotte had said to her mother, "this is the twenties."

Since its founding in 1885, Rollins had embraced a classical liberal arts program of study, which appealed to the parents of northern students who were generally a part of the upper echelon of wealth and social prominence in their communities. Moreover, the excellence of the faculty and the ambiance of a small private college, located on the shore of beautiful Lake Virginia, where fall weather remained throughout the winter, made the high tuition quite acceptable.

Charlotte spent most weekends on campus with student friends, but at Rachel's insistence, she had stayed overnight at Bellemere. It was Saturday morning. Will and Rachel sat on their porch watching a gator float near their dock. A stiff breeze from the west raised white caps on the lake and blew through the grove, jostling green fruit on the trees. Instinctively, Will looked north, scanning the horizon. No worry, he thought, it's only September. He settled in his rocker and began reading the Saturday Evening Post.

Tanned, slender Jack Melvin drove his yellow Buick roadster into the driveway, came to a stop near the porch, and waved. He wore a tweed cap, white cotton trousers, and a blue turtle-neck shirt. His friends at Rollins called him "Money Bags," a title conveyed when a fraternity brother had visited the grand Melvin estate in Wilmington, Delaware.

153

Charlotte flew out of the house, threw an overnight bag on the seat, and jumped in the car. Without a word they sped off.

"Where are they going?" asked Will.

Rachel didn't look up from her book. "They're off for a weekend at Daytona."

"Where will they stay?"

"At Betty and Tom Murdoch's house. Betty is Celia Warren's aunt. They'll be well chaperoned."

"Are you sure the Murdochs are at the beach?"

Rachel looked up and answered crisply. "No, I'm not, but I trust Charlotte. She's completely responsible."

Will nodded. "I hope you're right. I'm not as confident as you are."

Twenty miles from Daytona, near Deland, Jack pulled his roadster off the highway and followed tire tracks one mile to a weathered shack set among palmettos, oaks, and cabbage palms. He entered the rear door and came out carrying two quart Mason jars filled with gin. Charlotte puckered her lips. "Gimme a little sip, honey."

Jack placed the jars on the back seat, then slid his hands around her waist. "You'll get plenty of everything before the weekend's over." She giggled as he started the car and raced off to the highway.

Jack had rented a three-room white cottage facing the ocean, isolated, far north of Daytona. As they entered the place, Charlotte chuckled. "Perfect." They talked and laughed as she lightly sipped gin, but all afternoon he drank heavily until the sun disappeared. Smiling seductively, she lifted her short filmy skirt and rotated her shapely hips. "Anybody want to dance?"

He breathed heavily as he stared. "Not now," he grunted, as he groped his way through the room — "Need air." Puffy flesh surrounded his watery eyes as he threw open the door, staggered down wooden stairs to the beach, and wandered in darkness toward the water.

Like a whining puppy, she followed. "Jack! Wait! Please come back. Listen to me. Sit down!" The cold wind prickled her face, but her body felt like flame. Like a mechanical man, he entered the surf and continued walking deeper into the ocean until he disappeared under breaking waves.

"Jack! Oh, my God, Jack!" She thrashed about in rising and falling swells, reaching, and groping. She swam to shore and ran in darkness looking for help, but the beach was deserted. Wind whipped her hair as she fell on wet sand, exhausted. It was a bad dream, she thought, a terrible little play that did not happen. Soon I'll awaken, and it will be over. But slowly, the wind cleared her mind, and she knew it was not a dream. She scrambled to her feet and returned to the cottage, washed her face, brushed her hair, drove to a small diner, and called her mother.

Rachel listened, then she answered in an erratic voice. "Stay at the diner, I'll leave at once."

Will must not be told, she thought, not yet. She had never driven the Cadillac beyond the city limits of Orlando, but now she must manage. She dressed quickly, left a note, and drove into the night. As she crossed into Volusia County, she blinked, but there it was, in the darkness, an image of Bellemere in flames, an inferno roaring out of control. In the mirage, a circle of friends watched as walls collapsed, and great timbers crashed through the floors destroying the foundation. A shiver ran through her heart.

At the beach, Rachel parked near the oceanside diner, now closed and dark. The car lights illuminated Charlotte sitting alone at an outside wooden table. Charlotte rose and walked slowly to the car, opened the door and sat next to her mother. In a quiet voice, she told everything. When she had finished, she became very still. The only sound was that of waves breaking on the shoreline.

Rachel drove to the cottage, placed her daughter's things in a leather bag, closed the door, and began the long drive back to Orlando. Rain pelted the windshield as they crossed the St. Johns River bridge.

Where will it end? Rachel wondered. What will Anna Rand think? Once again, seven generations of prestige tainted by a daughter's poor judgment.

Charlotte's voice was barely audible. "What will happen when they find out?"

"Does anyone know you were with Jack — anyone at all?"

"No."

Rachel nodded. "Actually, you have been at home, with us, all weekend."

Charlotte fell into a deep sleep as her mother drove on in the rain.

Rachel pulled into the driveway of Bellemere. In the distance, her headlights beamed on her home. Thank God, we're here, she thought. He'll ask a thousand questions — must be calm — stay in control. She dabbed her face with a handkerchief.

Will opened the car door and asked, "Where in the world have you been? I've been out of my mind."

Rachel knew a terrible thing was written on her face as Will helped her out and followed her inside. She hurried her daughter to her room and closed the door. After twenty minutes, Rachel tiptoed out and stood in the hallway, pulling at the hem of her handkerchief, her eyes filling with tears. The wounded feeling had been there before, but now, for the first time, she felt old and drawn. Will held her in his arms and whispered, "What is it?"

Her head lay on his shoulder. "Jack Melvin is dead. They were not at the Murdochs' cottage; they were alone at a place he rented on the beach. Jack drank heavily, went berserk, and drowned himself. Charlotte tried to save him, but couldn't."

"When did he drown?"

"Early last night."

"Where?"

"The cottage is about two miles north of the pier."

"Did she find the body?"

"No."

"Did you call the police?"

"No."

"I'll notify them."

She pulled away. "No one knows they were together. No one saw them at the beach." Her color was gone. "Will, please, leave it alone." She sobbed hysterically as he lifted her and placed her in bed. He pulled a spread over her shoulders, kissed her cheek, left the room, and placed a call to the Daytona Beach Police.

At the Volusia County Courthouse in Deland, Charlotte testified before the Grand Jury. Her plain, navy blue dress with a high, square neckline contrasted greatly to the stylish clothing in the remainder of her wardrobe.

State Attorney Brian Pope's eyes fixed on Charlotte. "You have said that you and the deceased were alone at the beach cottage on October fourth. Was there a lover's quarrel between you?"

"No, we never quarreled."

"Are you aware of any other woman in his life?"

"No."

"You say he drank gin all afternoon, until he lost his senses. Why were you not similarly affected?"

"It tasted terrible, like swallowing acid, or something. I couldn't drink much of it."

"So, you were sober, and he was drunk. You could have stopped him from entering the water. Why didn't you?"

She trembled as she tightened her fists. "I tried to stop him, but he was out of his head. He just kept on, and on. I couldn't stop him." She placed her hands over her face and slumped in her chair.

Pope paused and placed the fingertips of his right hand on his temple. Then he turned and gripped the wooden railing separating him from the Grand Jury. "Ladies and gentlemen, the state finds no cause to indict Charlotte Taylor."

As the weeks of winter went by, Rachel observed changes in Charlotte. Her selection of dress was more conservative than before; her speech was less compelling. And even though her daughter's classmates at Rollins avoided her, she seemed resigned to her isolated state. Only Charlotte's roommate, Jo Ann Warren, came to Bellemere on weekends. Jo Ann, thought Rachel, poor little creature, the personification of homeliness, but thank God for her.

At Rollins, first semester grades had been posted on Dr. Walter Eubanks's classroom door. Charlotte beamed when she saw the "A" in Drama written by her name. She rushed to her dormitory room to share the news with Jo Ann. "Look at this," she said. "No one brings meaning to the play like Dr. Eubanks. When I read lines in his class, the rest of the world is far away. I am the character. I feel the setting and want to laugh or cry as the plot unfolds. Don't you see? I now know where I belong."

Jo Ann blinked. "Charlotte, that was beautiful. But what are you talking about? Where do you belong?"

Charlotte placed her hands on Jo Ann's bony arms. "The theater! New York. Go with me and be my roommate. We'll share everything."

Jo Ann looked at her roommate in wonder. "You're serious, aren't you?"

"Yes. There's nothing here for us."

A little smile crossed Jo Ann's face. "There really isn't, is there?"

In her bedroom, Rachel sat in a soft yellow chair by the window, knitting a vest sweater for Andrew. Charlotte rested on her mother's bed, fingering the fringe of a white wool blanket folded neatly at the foot of the bed.

"You're not happy, darling," said Rachel, as she continued her knitting.

"No. Not at all. Except for Dr. Eubanks's class, Rollins is a nightmare. He says I'm good, Mama, good enough to make it in the theater. Do you remember the school plays? When I had the leading role, nothing made me happier than hearing the applause."

Rachel dropped her knitting and looked up. "The theater?"

"Yes. The theater in New York. Dr. Eubanks says I could study drama at New York University while I pursue a career."

"Alone, in New York? Papa would not stand for it."

"Jo Ann wants to go with me."

Rachel shook her head. "Jo Ann in the theater?"

"No. No. She would continue her English major."

Rachel felt the excitement in her daughter's voice.

"I'll talk to Papa."

"Tell him there is no place for me in this town."

That night, long after dark, Rachel lay beside her husband recalling Charlotte's words: *No place for me.* Friends of the family had been considerate, much more considerate than Charlotte's friends who turned their backs, but she knew that gossip across bridge tables continued. Charlotte was guilty of no crime, but her persecution would never end.

In the morning, at breakfast, Rachel carefully selected her muffin as she spoke. "Charlotte is miserable at Rollins. She wants to leave Orlando and study drama in New York."

Will lay his paper aside and looked up over his glasses. "Of course she's miserable. It's the price of poor judgment."

"Her friends have deserted her. She must get away."

"Charlotte is irresponsible. I'll have no part of her living in New York."

A grim look settled on Rachel's face as she placed her fork on her plate. "Years ago you made a final judgment about Andrew's future. It turns out you were right. Now, I say Charlotte continues her education in New York, and that is final."

Will wiped his mouth with a breakfast napkin, pushed his coffee cup aside, and stared at his wife's deep blue eyes. "You're making a terrible mistake."

"You simply do not understand. She cannot remain in Orlando."

❧ *20* ❧

*F*t was a good year — 1924. Boom times had arrived in Orlando. The eleven-story Angebilt Hotel had opened, and two "sky-scraper" banks, ten stories each, rose along Orange Avenue. No longer the quiet little village nestled among oak and orange trees, Orlando was now a flourishing city, and the roots reached out in every direction.

Eleven years earlier, after Colonel and Mrs. Quinn returned to England, Will had purchased their home on Lake Ivanhoe and subsequently closed it up. Rachel said the place would have looked even lonelier had Baker not mowed the grass, tended the shrubs, and painted the house. But the lonely look disappeared in 1919 when Adam and his bride, Alice, moved in.

It was obvious that Alice had a green thumb. Her red poinsettia, blooming at Christmas time, lined the driveway to the front entrance of the house. Azaleas and camellias surrounded the home, bursting in pink and white blossoms in February, and amaryllis raised their heads in April. Alice had selected light yellow paint for the house, like the morning sun. Wallpaper of a pastel print decorated the foyer, and patterned draperies hung from every window in the parlor. An oil portrait of Alice's parents found its place in her bedroom, and on her bedside table lay Grandmother Norton's Bible. It was indeed Alice's home, every aspect reflecting her personality.

On Sunday afternoon, Rachel and Will sat on their porch watching Adam and Alice's three-year-old daughter, Kathleen, laugh and run with twelve-year-old Andrew. Her glossy black hair, deep violet eyes, and beautiful face were pure Rand, but her quiet and gentle disposition was her mother's. "You must not call her 'Annie,'" Rachel scolded. But the clock had turned back for Will. It was "Little Annie" he watched, so full of life, like the little girl he had played games with, fed, and rocked to sleep so long ago. Must not spoil her, he told himself. Must not give her too much, too soon. No matter how much he wanted to.

Kathleen ran across the lawn and jumped in Will's arms. "Papa, Papa," she said. "Play with us."

As he held her closely, he turned away from Rachel's stare and whispered, "I love you, Annie."

At the Pine Street office, Nathan Finley, Jr. unrolled a plat plan before Will and Adam. "Gentlemen," he said, "I've been selling real estate for fifteen years and I have never seen anything like it. Orlando is the most exciting market in the country. People from all over are pouring in here, buying everything they can get their hands on." He licked his lips. "I put together three parcels in South Orlando totaling two hundred acres, three thousand feet on Lake Conway; it's a steal at a hundred and fifty thousand dollars. Lakefront lots alone will recoup the investment. The remaining acreage could be sold for another hundred and fifty thousand."

Will peered over his glasses and said, "Wonder when the bubble will break."

Adam broke in. "Papa, everybody's making a mint of money on land. Why shouldn't we?"

Will glanced at his son. "Because we're citrus growers; that's our business. When the bottom falls out, and it will, that's when we'll buy land."

Finley scratched his head, then rolled up his plat. "Hate to see you miss a great opportunity, Mr. Taylor."

Adam saw Nathan to the door and said: "I'll call you." He walked slowly to his father's desk. "Can't pass it up, Papa. I'm buying the Lake Conway property. Ten thousand cash, one hundred forty thousand in a fifteen year mortgage."

Will shook his head. "Hate to see you follow the mob into land speculation, but if that's what you want, I won't stop you."

"Times have changed, Papa. You're missing a sure thing."

Will ran his fingers through his thinning hair as he grunted. "Well, we'll see. Just don't neglect the groves, son. Don't do that."

"Have I ever, Papa?"

Will put his hand on his son's arm. "No. No you haven't."

Six weeks after the Lake Conway deal closed, Finley called Adam. "I have a buyer for the acreage I sold you. They're offering two hundred thousand. What do you say?"

"Sell it. Listen, Nathan. You once asked if I wanted to join you in selling real estate. Is the offer still open?"

"Absolutely. Whenever you're ready."

"I'll meet you at your office at noon."

Within three months after Adam joined Nathan Finley, Jr., land prices skyrocketed. Developers platted subdivisions, built sidewalks and streets throughout Orange County. Like children in a candy store, buyers snapped up acreage. Low-lying cypress tree land, under water during most of the rainy season, sold at premium prices. Sellers accepted "no money down" binders, and some properties changed hands three times in a single week.

By the summer of 1925, Finley & Taylor Company sales reached six million dollars. Like a fire out of control it continued. Buses from all over the country arrived daily, unloading excited buyers. Men wearing straw hats and white duck trousers jammed real estate offices all along Orange Avenue and Pine Street, eager to make quick profits. There was no end to it. Money flowed into Florida like water from a silver fountain. Adam bought a new Packard and insisted that Alice redecorate their home. The Taylors and the Finleys vacationed together at Palm Beach, and regularly dined together at the Country Club of Orlando.

1926. It happened without warning. The land boom carousel ground to a halt. No one seemed to know why, but like falling dominos buyers reneged on contracts. Banks called loans. Signers and co-signers disappeared. Subdivision deals fell. The straw hats and white duck trousers left town and so did Nathan Finley. He departed Orlando, bankrupt.

Adam had personally endorsed promissory notes totaling four hundred thousand dollars. He sat with Will on the porch of Bellemere, overlooking the lake. Perspiration soaked their cotton shirts as they watched heat waves shimmer above the water.

Adam shook his head. "I tried Papa, I really tried. I wanted to make it on my own, like you and Uncle Billy."

Will stopped fanning himself and poured more cold lemonade into his glass. "You went too far off shore. That's what Mr. Pennington said when I wanted to build Bellemere before I had enough money in the bank. You thought you saw a shortcut to a pot full of gold, and you went for it. Like so many others, you got swept up. Now, you're deeply in debt. So, what do you plan to do?"

"Bankruptcy."

Will rubbed his hands together. "You think that washes away your responsibility?"

"No, sir, but I have no alternative."

"Yes, you have. You can borrow from the bank and pay it back, month by month, as long as it takes. If you give your word to meet your payments, I'll endorse the note."

"Can't ask you to do that. I got myself into this."

Will frowned. "I'm fully aware of that. You're gonna sweat blood to pay back every penny of it." Then he smiled. "More lemonade?"

April 1929. Milk was first delivered in wax paper cartons. The New York Yankees began wearing numbers on their uniforms. All over the country, movie theatres were installing sound equipment, and prohibition was in effect.

In a speech to the Rotary Club, Dr. Calvin H. Hardee said: "Eleven years ago we celebrated the end of a World War. It was a war to end all wars, to restore peace, justice, and brotherhood to the world. Now, we might ask ourselves two questions: What have we learned? And how will the decade of the 20s be remembered? Prohibition has made bootleggers millionaires. Gangsters gun down people in the streets of our large cities. Gambling is commonplace. Intelligent men mortgage everything they own to invest in the stock market. Young women smoke cigarettes and dress themselves revealingly. Are we a land of sensible, God-fearing men and women, or the personification of moral seepage? Is this the American dream?"

Will thanked Dr. Hardee and walked back to his office. He knew it was coming, like a dark funnel on the horizon, an economic storm of epic proportion, sweeping forward, engulfing everyone. But an economic storm wasn't all of it; medflies had been found in John Morrison's grove. The state had stopped shipments of all fruit out of Florida and the citrus industry was in panic.

On Monday, Will sat in John Lockner's office. He leaned forward as he spoke. "You've been president of Orlando Trust Company for fifteen years, and my close friend for more than that. What do you see ahead?"

Lockner stood up, walked to the window, and looked across Pine Street. Like ants, people scurried about, seemingly unconcerned that a crisis lurked that had the potential to ruin lives. He thrust his hands in his pockets and turned. "First comes the land boom bust, now the stock market is at an all-time peak. People are going crazy, risking every-thing. It can't last. Even beyond the medflies, something terrible is about to happen. It's not spotty, it's the whole economy. But, if people like you pull out of the bank, there won't be a bank. The top people in town are watching each other, waiting to see who blinks first."

"So you think we're in for a crash?"

"Perhaps, but the bank is rock solid. Stay with me, Will."

Will stroked his chin, then adjusted his glasses. "All right, count on me."

During dinner that night, Rachel said, "Mary Lockner called this afternoon and insisted we come for dinner on Saturday."

Will nodded. "I called on John today. My better judgment tells me I should pull out of the bank and invest the money in Postal Savings, but I won't. I don't want to start a run on the bank. And besides, John is my good friend."

"Why in the world would you consider withdrawing our money?"

Will finished the last of Ada's tomato soup and touched a napkin to his lips. "Years ago, Billy Pastin said something I've always re-membered. 'Watch a deer,' he said. 'He knows when danger's near. Does he see it? Hear it? Smell it? He just knows it.'"

"You sound like a person who thinks the country's coming apart."

"It's greed, Rachel, greed. Land and stock speculators created an immense bubble that's about to break."

Rachel glared. "Do we own stocks?"

Will shook his head. "We're growers. We invest in land."

Rachel touched Will's hand. "You're a fine business man, Will Taylor. I feel very secure."

October 20, 1929. Everyone cheered as President Herbert Hoover and eighty-two-year old Thomas Edison arrived on the Baltimore & Ohio train at Dearborn, Michigan to join the Lights Golden Jubilee celebration honoring Edison's invention of the electric light bulb, fifty years earlier.

Henry Ford had arranged a lavish banquet and invited five hundred guests to honor the great inventor. The list included, John D. Rockefeller, Jr.; Charles Schwab, Chairman of Bethlehem Steel; and Julius Rosenwald, Chairman of Sears, Roebuck, all giants of American industry, all sharing a belief that America would lead the world into the future. The dinner program read: *"Here at last is a democracy that rates greatness of achievment principally in terms of social service."*

Those attending the dinner believed that America's commercial and industrial future was strong and vibrant, positioned to achieve even greater affluence for all Americans. Walter Chrysler, Chairman of Chrysler Corporation had said, "I can see nothing but good signs along the road of business for the present year."

But author Sinclair Lewis saw things differently. He wrote: "The hair-raising plunge is just ahead. I can see it, feel it, smell it in the air." Roger Babson had said, "Sooner or later a crash is coming and it may be terrific. Wise are the investors who now get out of debt and reef their sails."

The end came on October 29. Everyone at the University Club in Orlando talked about the stock market collapse. Billions lost. Fifty percent of the value of stocks in the index lost. *The Orlando Sentinel* reported that an investor in New York had shot himself, others jumped out of hotel windows to their death.

It didn't happen in a day; earlier in October the market dropped, but rallied on the following day. Another deep plunge came on October 23, followed by a near crash on the 24th. J.P. Morgan moved to support prices and restore confidence. President Hoover declared: "The fundamental business of the country is on a sound and prosperous basis." But on the following Monday, the market fell apart. No one could stem the tide. Then came Black Tuesday — October 29. After the crash, growing pessimism ruled the marketplace. Businessmen slashed capital investment, inventories, and payrolls. Those who retained jobs took substantial pay cuts.

At the bank in Orlando, John Lockner began calling loans, blaming Herbert Hoover for the collapse. Everyone wondered what had caused the disaster. Was the burden of World War debt to blame? Excess consumer debt? Inequitable distribution of the wealth? The income of twenty-four thousand American families, one-tenth of one percent of the population, equaled the income of the bottom forty-two percent of the nation. All people knew was that like a tidal wave the depression rolled in, washing away jobs, and depriving families of necessities. Millions of people were jobless; thousands of families were evicted from their homes, unable to meet mortgage payments. Men wandered about the country in search of work.

The Orlando city budget was slashed, and property taxes were cut. The police force was reduced; the city recreational department was eliminated; and many city library employees were laid off. Retail food prices decreased: Campbell's soup sold for five cents a can, pork & beans sold for seven.

Swamped with non-performing loans, The Orlando Trust Company closed in July 1930, and with the bank went Taylor Groves deposits of three hundred thousand dollars. John Lockner quietly left Orlando to accept a position with a bank in Baltimore. The circle was complete: busted real estate boom, stock market crash, closed banks. The economic impact of the '95 freeze would recur.

On his signature, Will secured a small loan at Reedy National Bank, enough to meet payroll, but as fruit prices declined, cash also dwindled, forcing slow payments to creditors and layoffs of Taylor Groves field hands.

Adam and Andrew worked in the groves, disking, fertilizing, pruning, irrigating, and overseeing harvesting. When Andrew complained about ten-hour days and multiple aches, Will laughed. "These are short days, son. For years, Uncle Billy and I worked from sun up to dark. Work's good for a man."

Benton Foster, President of Reedy National Bank, ushered Will and Adam into his office. His round face glistened, and his deep-set eyes sparkled, but his voice was forced. "Gentlemen, have a seat. Thank you for coming. Cigar?"

Will held up his hand. "No, thank you."

Foster plopped down in his chair. "These are terrible times, absolutely terrible. It seems that all we bankers do these days is bring bad news to business people." The pudgy banker opened a file, laid it on his desk, and began reading. "Taylor Groves has a twenty thousand dollar note, and Adam Taylor's note balance is two hundred thousand. Your Groves' statement shows accounts payable of one hundred thousand. Receivables are thirty thousand. Of course you own six hundred acres of bearing groves, but demand for citrus is weak and prices are quite depressed." Foster sat back in his chair and held up his hands. "Frankly, our board is concerned. We must know how you plan to meet your obligations." Will breathed deeply. He knew this was no time to swell up in indignation. It was a time for composure. The bank could call their loans and he would be forced to sacrifice the groves. "Of course I understand," he said. "I'm grateful for the bank's patience; but like everyone else, we're strapped, unable to make principal payments. The question is, will the bank work with us by accepting interest payments only, until the economy strengthens?"

Foster smiled, then nervously drummed his fingers on the arms of his chair. "I wish we could. But there's a way out. An investment group out of Boston wants to buy your groves. They're offering seven hundred an acre, a fair price that will pay off your obligations and leave you sixty thousand dollars. That's a good sum these days."

Now it was clear that Benton Foster had no intention of arranging any kind of payout. Will had always heard that it was "business is business" at Reedy National Bank. Now he had a taste of it. He rose from his chair and said, "Thank you Mr. Foster. We'll contact you right away."

Foster rushed to his feet. "We think the world of you, Mr. Taylor. I hope you understand our position."

Will adjusted his hat and nodded. "Oh, yes. Perfectly."

In silence, Will and Adam left the bank and walked to Adam's car. "It's all my fault," said Adam, as he turned the ignition key and pushed the starter. "I have ruined the family."

After a pause, Will looked straight into his son's eyes. "When you returned alive from France, I told myself that nothing in this world would ever get me down. I meant it. All I want now is time to think." He patted his son's knee, and then looked to the north horizon. Dark clouds had formed, and gusts of wind blew papers about Orange Avenue.

At Bellemere, Will closed the door to Adam's Ford, said goodbye, then walked to his dock. He glanced at orange trees growing near the lake, now towering in full maturity. He remembered what he had said to Billy Pastin, on that day so long ago, when dead orange trees covered his land: "I'm not getting out of the citrus business." He and Billy had dug out dead stumps, reset budded stock, and nursed the trees until they produced fruit. Now, after more than forty years of blood and sweat, the groves had expanded to six hundred acres. He had overcome the vicious freeze of '95, but now, the threat was different, it was self-created.

It rained all night at Bellemere. Will heard every drop of it.

The rain had stopped on the following morning. Chilling wind from the north pushed gray clouds out of sight. Rachel dressed and then reached for a shawl before going down to breakfast. Will stopped her at the door, and said, "Sit here with me. I have something to tell you." Methodically, he disclosed every detail of his meeting with Benton Foster, then he paused. "I'm not sure we can save Bellemere."

An angry look appeared on Rachel's face. "Well, you and Adam have created quite a mess, haven't you? You tried to save John Lockner's neck and you cut off your own. Why didn't you follow your instinct and withdraw our money from his bank? Now, you tell me I might lose my home. Let me tell you something. I will not move out. Sell the groves, if you must, but remember, I will not leave Bellemere."

Will nodded. "I must go. I'll try to arrange refinancing."

At the Pine Street office Will and Adam assembled a plan specifying a one hundred thousand dollar loan, providing twelve months moratorium on principal payments. Under the plan, Taylor Groves creditors would freeze past due accounts for six months. Adam and Will would receive salaries of two hundred a month each until the business was capable of making note payments along with regular payments on past due trade accounts.

Will made his first presentation at First National Bank of Orlando. He finished by saying, "There is every indication that demand for fruit will strengthen. We know the citrus business, and we know how to make money."

President Harold J. Pendelton, III listened attentively. "My father, and my grandfather, always spoke highly of you. I'm sorry you are not now a customer of the bank. Of course I will submit your loan application to the board, but frankly, I cannot imagine their approving your request. We barely have enough deposits to accommodate our regular customers. Considering the urgency of your needs, I suggest you contact other financial institutions."

Bankers in Tampa, Jacksonville, and Atlanta shook their heads to Will, saying, "Sorry, we have no money, there's nothing we can do."

On Friday, back in Orlando, Adam met Will's train at the depot. Will sighed and shook his head as he stepped off the car, saying, "Nothing doing in Atlanta."

"Papa." said Adam, "We're not finished. Sell out. You can buy another grove. You, Andrew, and I can start all over. We'll do all the work ourselves. I'll sell my house, and we can all live at Bellemere until things turn around. We can do it, Papa."

At that moment, Will saw the fire that had always burned in himself reflected in Adam. And even though the war had cost his son an arm, his mettle was in full view.

"All right. We bend and twist, but we don't quit. We stay in the citrus business. I'll call Mr. Foster."

When the bank opened on Monday morning, Foster's greeting was almost fawning. "Please be seated, Mr. Taylor. Delighted to see you, and how is Mrs. Taylor?"

Will thought the banker looked like a priest about to offer last rites to a man before a hanging. "Fine," said Will. "Let me get right to the point. I'm here to accept the offer to purchase my groves."

Foster's chair creaked as he pushed back, then he folded his hands together, his left eye twitching as he began. "I regret to tell you there has been a change in the buyer's offer. Now it's five hundred an acre."

It flashed through Will's mind that the bank was out to make a profit, but what difference did it make? If he accepted the lower offer he was insolvent; if he refused, the bank would foreclose. Either way he was ruined. After promising to tell Foster on Wednesday what he would do, he walked slowly to his office. His mind wandered back to Atlanta and the night he was fired from the Southern Tavern for accidentally dumping gravy and mashed potatoes on Sergeant Slattery's face. Out in the street, he had had just enough money to return to the safety of his home in Hogansville, but that was long ago. Now, he faced the reality of the present — no credit, no place to turn. He knew he must sell to the bank and somehow pay off his creditors. Bankruptcy was out of the question, even if it meant sacrificing Bellemere.

That night, after supper, the Taylors gathered in the parlor. Deliberately, with no emotion, Will told of his predicament. Finishing his remarks, he looked at Rachel and said, "At the price the bank offers, there is no way to avoid insolvency. But I will sell with the understanding that we keep our homes. Adam, Andrew, and I must find jobs as quickly as possible."

"Papa," said Adam, "they're stealing your groves."

"I know," replied Will, "but there's no market. I have no choice."

After a long silence, Rachel asked if anyone cared for coffee. Everyone declined. Then one by one they excused themselves, leaving Will seated alone in his chair by the fireplace.

Will placed a "For Sale" sign in his office window, put on his coat, and started for Reedy National Bank. On his way out he stopped to answer a ringing telephone.

"Mr. Taylor, this is Harold Pendelton. I have good news. Please come to the bank at your earliest convenience."

Within thirty minutes Will entered Pendelton's office. Seated beside the president, John Lockner rose to his feet, and extended his hand. "Will. Good to see you."

As he took Lockner's hand, Will shook his head. "John. I thought you were in Baltimore."

"I am. I'm with Atlantic National Bank. Shall we sit down?" Lockner rubbed his chin with his fingertips before he spoke. "Nothing hurt me more than your loss at Orlando Trust Company. It wouldn't have happened if I had not used our friendship to keep you from with-drawing your money. When Harold called to tell me about your situation, I caught the next train."

Harold Pendelton broke in. "Mr. Lockner wants to guarantee half of your one hundred thousand dollar loan. The bank will accept your signature as collateral for the remainder."

Lockner's jaw tightened. "It's all I can do, Will, but it's also the least I should do."

∞ 21 ∞

Charles Lindbergh's child was kidnaped and later found dead; President Herbert Hoover was "booed" at a baseball game. In Florida, the medfly had been eradicated. And even though the depression lingered, Taylor fruit was once again moving out of the state to markets.

It was July. Tommy Lane sat in Adam's office and lit a cigarette. "They laid me off at Dickson-Ives. I need a job, and I'm willing to do anything."

Adam laughed. "From men's clothing to field hand."

"It's not funny, Adam. I'm forty years old and pretty desperate."

"Yeah, I know. I was kidding. Seriously, if you want to be in the citrus business, you start at the bottom, there's no other way. Ten hour days in the sun is normal."

Tommy chuckled. "I wouldn't know the top if it landed in my lap. Everything I've started has been at flat bottom. Here I am, boss, ready to go to work."

"O.K. You start at fifteen a week and you work right along with a field crew until you learn what it's all about. Sure you want to do this?"

"Positive."

"I'll put you with Andrew. He's working in the Kissimmee grove this summer."

Tommy picked up his hat. "I really appreciate you and your friendship. I'll get the job done."

Adam smiled. "Hey, you're gonna be my strong right arm."

Tommy pulled up to the barn in the Kissimmee grove. There stood eighteen-year-old Andrew, six feet of muscle, bone, and extraordinarily good looks.

"Tommy," yelled Andrew. "Good to see you. Welcome to the vacation spot of America — Taylor Groves."

Tommy laughed. "Adam said you could teach me everything I need to know."

"Oh, sure. What he means is, I know what slave labor is." Andrew glanced at Tommy's feet. "Those nice shoes and clothes don't fit out here in the hot sun. Better wear boots and a big straw hat."

Tommy smiled. "In other words, this ain't downtown Orlando."

"Right," said Andrew with a grin.

They sat on a bench in the shade of the tractor barn. Andrew began. "You've grown up around citrus and probably know more than I do, so if I tell you stuff you already know, just nod. Papa's groves are made up of Hamlin, Valencia, Parson Brown, and seedling. This is a thirty-five acre Valencia grove. Moses and I fertilize, prune dead stuff, and dust for rust mite with sulphur. The crotalaria you see growing between trees isn't disked until October. Picking usually starts in March. To tell the truth, there's not too much work in summer months. And just in case you're interested, Moses and I wet a line in the lake once in a while, but don't tell Adam."

Tommy chuckled. "Now that's the last thing we want to do." The Taylor men, thought Tommy, always playing it straight; each generation building on the last; all caring for friends, neighbors, and family — salt of the earth.

The heat hadn't slacked a bit, but summer vacation had ended for Andrew. He packed and got ready to leave for Gainesville. The family, including Tommy Lane, had gathered at Bellemere for lunch. They sat around the dining room table surveying the spread Ada had prepared. Fried chicken and hot biscuits never looked so good to Andrew.

When the family was seated, Will's eyes traced the full length of Rachel's gold brocade window draperies; then he gazed at an Italian tapestry covering the south wall of the dining room. Sterling flatware flanked Haviland china and Waterford crystal. Unimportant, he thought, as he glanced at Rachel. Willingly, he had permitted her to surround the family with opulence. While wealth alone didn't bring on moral seepage, he believed overemphasis upon material things detracted from

matters of real value. He bowed his head, vowing to be more charitable. "Dear Lord, we thank Thee for all our many blessings."

When the meal was finished, Alice helped Elizabeth clear the table.
The men moved to the parlor to smoke. Will glanced at Adam. "You
think these boys are going to make citrus men?"

Adam suppressed a smile. "Well, they're pretty soft, but another
five years in the grove will harden 'em up."

Will chuckled. "We better all harden up. Things are looking up,
but we're a long way from recovery."

Through the dining room window, Rachel watched a taxi pull into
her driveway. A young woman, dressed in a wrinkled cream-colored
suit, stepped out, came to the porch and rang the bell. Rachel opened
the door and looked at a thin and strained face. "Charlotte!" She fell
into her daughter's arms.

Charlotte spoke softly. "Oh, Mama. I don't want anyone to see me
looking like this. May I go upstairs?" She brushed past the family and
hurried off.

Rachel followed and hesitated at her daughter's door before entering. One look had said it all. Cast into a highly competitive culture
dominated by talented people, Charlotte was overwhelmed, unable to
cope. But now, Charlotte had come home.

Rachel opened the door, sat on her daughter's bed, and listened as
Charlotte began. "I couldn't make it in the theater, Mama. After years
of whoring for the spotlight in bit parts, I became miserable and drank
myself to sleep every night; that really finished whatever career I might
have had. I stopped answering your letters because I was too proud to
tell you I had failed. There were men, Mama, terrible men. I can't tell
you how awful it was. I swore I'd never come home, but here I am,
back on your doorstep, broke and looking terrible." She closed her
eyes and lowered her head.

Rachel held her daughter. "Oh, baby, it's all right. What's important is that you're home." She kissed her daughter's cheek and said,
"I love you. Freshen up and come down."

Charlotte buried her face in her hands. "Not now, Mama. Not now."

Rachel stood and took her daughter's hand. "When you're ready,
darling." She closed the door to Charlotte's room behind her, drew a

deep breath, and reflected on the moment. Everything had changed. Tongues would waggle, people would stare, friends would ask carefully selected questions. One thing was certain, she would not let Charlotte out of her sight.

At nine o'clock on Monday morning, Elizabeth shuffled into Charlotte's bedroom carrying a breakfast tray of orange juice, scrambled eggs, bacon, grits, and toast. "Honey, you thin as a rail. I want you to eat every last bite."

Charlotte took a deep breath as she looked at the massive breakfast. "I'll try."

"After breakfast, yo' mama taking you to town to buy new clothes. I so glad you home, honey."

"Oh, Elizabeth. You don't know how good it feels."

Baker brought the Lincoln around and drove to Dickson-Ives Department Store. He parked in front, let the ladies out, and walked across the street to talk with the doorman at the San Juan.

Inside the store, Rachel became the center of attention as she led Charlotte through an entourage of clerks from millinery to lingerie, from street apparel to dressy attire. Charlotte stood before a full length mirror wearing a stylishly pastel silk dress. The clerk held up her hands and remarked, "You look lovely. Why, I'll bet you're not thirty years old."

Rachel's stare was pitiless. "You're right, she's not." She turned to her daughter. "Take off that ugly rag, it's much too matronly."

Color immediately rose in the clerk's cheeks.

Hours later, Rachel came out of the store with Charlotte trailing her. A policeman's foot rested on the running board of her Lincoln. She glared as she spoke. "Young man, what do you think you're doing?"

"You're getting a ticket, ma'am. You're overparked."

Rachel gazed cooly at him. "Please take your foot off my automobile and listen to me. I have lived in this town for fifty years. No policeman has ever given me a traffic ticket. Now you take your ticket down to Chief Billings and tell him Mrs. Will Taylor will not accept it." She whirled around and motioned to Baker. "Please go inside and get our packages. We're going home." Rachel wrinkled her nose as she adjusted her broad straw hat. "Disgusting, isn't it? A servant of the people imposing himself on us."

Baker opened the trunk and placed the packages inside. After seating the ladies, he started the engine and sped off. In his mirror he saw the policeman standing motionless on the curb.

"Well, now," smiled Rachel. "There's a party at the club on Friday. I want to see you wearing the pretty things we bought."

Before the sun came up, Will finished his breakfast, put on his coat, and headed for his car. Charlotte followed him. "Take me to the office with you, Papa. I want to see what you do."

Will hesitated, believing his daughter could not be serious. The Pine Street office offered little resemblance to the towers of Manhattan. He hunched his shoulders."It's not very exciting, but jump in."

As they rumbled down Orange Avenue, Will spoke softly. "Mother never gave up, but after all the years, I thought we'd lost you. There's been so much heartache in our family, and family is all there really is."

Charlotte looked straight ahead. "I knew I'd never take Ann's place. I'm your black sheep. I'm sorry."

"Don't say that. I love you." He reached out and took her hand.

"I know you do, Papa. I'm so adrift. Give me a little time."

At the office, he explained his bookkeeping and filing system in great detail. "I do it all and don't mind the work, but I hate to write letters."

"I know how to type. Let me write them. I need something to do."

"You want to go to work?"

"Yes, I really do. I had to eat, so I worked part time at an insurance company."

"You've got yourself a job. You're office secretary. Ten dollars a week with room and board. And Charlotte," he nodded, "we work every day, except Sunday."

She kissed his cheek. "Thanks, Papa."

He chuckled. "Stop the office romance, and let's write a few letters."

As the weeks went by, Charlotte did far more than type letters at the Pine Street office. She reorganized Will's bookkeeping and filing system and purchased a new Remington typewriter. She rearranged furniture, brought a hooked rug from her bedroom, and hung a photograph of Bellemere behind Will's desk.

Will gazed at the picture. "Wonder what Uncle Billy would say if he could see this office?"

"I can hear him now," said Charlotte, as she wrinkled her brow. "Lord knows Will, you done let your little girl turn it into a tea parlor."

Will smiled. His hand shook as he began signing payroll checks.

Tommy Lane's family had once owned a fifty-cow dairy in south Orlando, not rich, but they lived well. Mrs. Lane had said, "Tommy could milk before he walked." But everything had changed in 1925 when Mr. Lane sold the dairy, and followed the crowd into real estate. He had accepted a hundred thousand dollar note from a Chicago speculator who later defaulted after selling off the cows and all the dairy equipment. All that remained was two hundred acres of land that nobody wanted. The Lanes became renters, and all they had was help from Tommy, the money Mrs. Lane earned from taking in wash, and the vegetables that Mr. Lane grew on his repossessed land.

As a teenager, Tommy had become another son at the Taylor house, always present at meal time. He and Adam, always together, had ignored little pig-tailed Charlotte, who was constantly in the boys' way, always wanting so badly to be included in everything they did, always to be endured. But now, Adam and Tommy were in business together, and Charlotte was one of them — not to be excluded.

No one had been more surprised than Rachel when Charlotte announced her engagement to Tommy. She wondered if her daughter really fell in love. Perhaps, over time, she simply drifted toward him as they played tennis, fished, walked, or dined together. He was a little too heavy, a little too short, and his hair was thinning on top, but he was always available. More than that, he was dependable. Charlotte would be safe with him. Rachel was sure of that.

The wedding was outdoors at Bellemere, near the rose garden, in view of the lake. At Charlotte's insistence, only the closest friends of the family were invited. The rest could "go to hell," Charlotte said.

During the wedding ceremony, Alice and Adam stood beside the bride and groom. The Taylors and the Lanes sat on wicker chairs behind the wedding party.

Dr. McNair asked, "If any man knows why Thomas and Charlotte should not be joined in holy matrimony, let him speak now or forever hold his peace."

Rachel felt a little shock of fear that someone might actually speak. The ceremony ended and everyone moved to a large white canopy placed in the center of the lawn; there, on a table covered by a white linen cloth, stood glasses filled with ginger ale punch. Adam tapped on his glass with a spoon. "Here's to the bride," he said. "She reeled her man in like a big bass on light tackle — very skillfully." Everyone roared.

When the wedding party moved to the parlor, Rachel pulled at the hem of her handkerchief as she watched her daughter dance with Tommy to the music of a string quartet. It may not be love, she thought; it may be a twenty-nine-year-old girl looking for companionship. That's all right, as long as she's happy. I want her near me. Will can build them a home, here on the lake. He'll do that for me. She cleared her throat and announced dinner.

∞22∞

November 1936. Winter weather came early, browning the grass at Bellemere and sweetening fruit in Will Taylor's groves. At the breakfast table, Will took the last bite of his biscuit, opened his paper and said, "Look at this, Andrew."

PRESIDENT ROOSEVELT REELECTED IN LANDSLIDE

"Pretty obvious," continued Will. "With his socialistic schemes, he bought votes from labor, grain framers, minorities, and just about everybody else. Of course, the rest of us are paying for it with high taxes. But we sure don't want a Republican in the White House. At least Roosevelt is putting people back to work."

Rachel chuckled. "Yes. Back to work," she whispered. "Ada wants eight dollars a week. What's wrong with Republicans?"

Will placed his fork on his plate. "Since the Civil War they have sucked millions of tax dollars out of the south and sent back little or nothing in return. They think federal taxes are the sole possession of Yankees."

Andrew frowned. "Papa. Where do you think the money comes from to pay C.C.C. and W.P.A. workers in Orange County?"

Will glared. "That's not what I'm talking about. The government never gave me a cent for not planting orange trees and I never wanted it, but they pay farmers out west for plowing up wheat and corn. They call it the 'New Deal.' Finish your breakfast. Adam wants me to see a grove in Clermont, and I'd appreciate your driving me out there."

Andrew cranked up his '33 Ford pickup and headed west on the Winter Garden Road. Half way to Clermont, Will remarked, "You don't look like your mama, but every now and then I hear a little red pepper in your voice that reminds me of her."

Andrew grinned. "She had a mind of her own, didn't she?"

"Oh, yes. She and Rachel were at each other all the time."

Andrew chuckled, then turned his head toward Will. "We've been over it many times. I know my mother died in childbirth, but what about Jeffery Quinn? Have you ever heard from him?"

A distant look crossed Will's face as he rolled down the window to let in fresh air. Every time he thought of Quinn a vial of poison emptied in his heart. "It was a classic example of seduction. A soldier took an innocent girl's virginity, then sailed away with a smile on his lips. There has never been a word from him."

Andrew squeezed his father's arm. "It makes no difference. You're my Papa."

Andrew drove west, past Winter Garden, on the road to Clermont. Flat land became rolling hills and sandy soil turned into orange clay. Citrus trees covered with ripening fruit stood in long rows on hillsides, their green leaves shining in bright sunlight.

"Beautiful out here, isn't it?" said Will.

Andrew nodded. "Wait till you see the Valencia grove Adam and I have been looking at."

They bumped along in Andrew's pickup truck on a clay road to the south shore of Lake Minnehaha. "There it is, Papa. The grove runs a half-mile south, 165 acres; it's sour orange root stock, set fifteen years ago."

Will stroked his chin. "Who owns it?"

"Tim Barron."

"I thought so. Broke, isn't he?"

"Yes, sir."

"Tim's a good man and he's taken care of his grove. What do his production records show?"

"Three hundred boxes an acre average for the past three years."

"What does he want?"

"Thousand an acre."

"It's a perfect fit for us, and priced right, but we just recently paid off our notes. We'll acquire new groves when we can pay cash."

"Yes, sir."

Will looked directly into Andrew's eyes. "Debt, my boy, is an ugly word to me."

The home Papa had built for the Charlotte and Tommy was a much smaller version of Rachel's home. It faced the lake and stood adjacent, like a guest house, to Bellemere. Rachel had selected every stick of the furnishings right down to the color of bathroom mats, but Charlotte had said nothing as long as Mama paid the bills.

Two weeks before Thanksgiving, Charlotte invited Alice and Adam to their home for dinner. It had all the trappings of a Rachel Taylor affair with candlelight, roses, and fine china. She served imported Chardonnay, quail, asparagus, wild rice, and baked custard. During the evening Adam whispered to Alice. "She's up to something."

"Hush. She's just being sweet."

Adam chuckled. "I know my sister."

Charlotte looked at Adam. Her voice flowed like warm honey. "You're just like Papa, smart and hard-working. I just hope you don't kill yourself trying to manage everything alone."

Adam closed his eyes. Here it comes, he thought.

"Why don't you let Tommy help you? He could manage the sales side."

Adam nodded. "Tommy's very capable. He could be an enormous help in sales, but that's Papa's call, not mine."

Charlotte snapped. "Oh, come on, Adam. You know perfectly well who's running the company. Papa will do anything you say."

"Charlotte! broke in Tommy. "Why don't you bring in the coffee tray."

Charlotte forced a smile. "Of course. Now, who would like coffee?"

After the party ended, Charlotte sat before her mirror brushing her hair. In his pajamas, Tommy stood behind her. "I had no idea you would embarrass me like that."

She saw his reflection in her mirror. "One of us had better have the backbone to stand up to the Taylor men. Left alone, they'll keep you in the field, like a picker, for the rest of your life."

"You're talking about your brother and father, the men who took me in when I needed a job."

"Don't get melodramatic. You and I are earning our way in the business and I won't let them keep you down."

"I may not be the smartest person in the world, but take a good look at my feet. I stand very well on them. I want you to remember that, my dear."

May 1939. As Will had predicted, demand for citrus had greatly strengthened for three years running, and prices increased correspondingly. Tim Barron's grove was still for sale, and even though Will paid twelve hundred an acre, cash, he had repaid his notes and still had money in the bank. Now, Will owned 765 acres of bearing grove, and the cash was pouring in.

It was Saturday evening. Rachel and Will walked out of Morrison's cafeteria, turned right on Orange Avenue, and followed the crowd to the corner of Church Street. Salvation Army band members stood on the sidewalk playing *Onward Christian Soldiers.* The "Army," was always there on Saturdays, men and women dressed in dark uniforms, speaking out for Jesus Christ, encouraging the lowly and the downtrodden.

When the band had stopped playing, a white-haired Salvation Army major laid aside his trumpet, stood on a wooden box, and began reading from the Holy Bible. "Blessed are the poor in spirit, for theirs is the kingdom of heaven ..."

Will's mind churned. Many people in this town are poor, but their heads are held high. All they need is the opportunity to work, and money to pay bills. He listened as the major continued. "You are the light of the world. A city set on a hill cannot be hid. Nor do men light a lamp and put it under a bushel, but on a stand, and it gives light to all in the house. Let your light so shine before men, that they may see your good works and give glory to your Father who is in heaven."

That night, Will lay in bed beside Rachel. She was almost asleep when he touched her shoulder. "I want to do something beyond tithing."

Rachel sat up. "What are you talking about?"

"Consider how little we had when we started out, and think about the challenges we faced. We began on faith, a belief that we could make it. Now, with the good Lord's help, we have overcome everything the world has thrown at us."

Rachel turned on the bed lamp. "What do you want to do?"

He sat on the edge of the bed and folded his hands together. "I want to help people get back on their feet, deserving people who cannot afford decent housing, medical care, or educational opportunities for their children." He stood beside the bed and held out his hands. "After we're gone, what will we say when we arrive at wherever we're going? Gee, we were some of the most successful people in Greenwood Cemetery."

Rachel rubbed her eyes. "What do you have in mind, darling?"

"We could set up a foundation. I'm thinking about fifty thousand dollars, to start."

Her eyes opened wide. "What in the world are you talking about? We can't afford that."

He looked straight into her blue eyes. "It's not a matter of what we can afford."

On Monday, Will sat in the office of his attorney, Paul Knight, Jr. "I understand your wishes," said Knight. "We will be happy to draw a charitable trust agreement. If you wish, we can name the entity The Taylor Foundation. Which bank shall we use?"

"First National Bank. I'll be sole trustee. You handle the details."

Paul Knight nodded. "Thank you, Mr. Taylor. This is a fine thing you are doing."

Will stood and made his way to the door, his right hand shaking uncontrollably. Doctor Early had prescribed a sedative, but the shaking continued.

At Bellemere, Adam sat across the breakfast table from his father and watched Will's hand shake. "What does the doctor say, Papa?"

Will didn't look up. "You know how doctors are. They feel obligated to find something wrong. I'm fine."

"Papa, listen, we want you to go to the Mayo Clinic. You owe it to your family."

"I'm not going to Minnesota and have a bunch of Yankee doctors pawing over me."

"The family's worried. Don't you care about that?"

"Now you sound like Mama, shifting it to me."

Adam's voice edged. "Either you go, or we bring one of their doctors here. It's up to you."

"I'll think about it. Now, what about the groves? How did the year end up?"

"We picked 210,000 boxes of fruit; all sold at an average price of $1.40 a box. Gross income is $294,000. All expenses are not yet in, but cash flow is $147,000."

Will adjusted his steel-rimmed glasses. "I just wish Billy Pastin could have heard that report. I'm proud of you."

Adam smiled. "Course, Uncle Billy would have said, 'Should'a gotten another dime a box, son.'"

Will laughed, and rose to leave the table.

"Wait, Papa. I want to talk about something else. Our business is growing. The little joke about getting another dime a box for our fruit may not be funny. I'm working ten-hour days trying to cover all the bases. I need help, particularly in the area of marketing, and I'd like to bring Tommy in to manage sales. With extra effort, I believe we could get better prices."

Will looked puzzled. "I'm sure Tommy's qualified, but what about Andrew? He should be your number one man."

"He is, Papa, he's doing an outstanding job, but he's young. If Tommy were managing sales, Andrew could run all field operations."

Will nodded. "Sounds like a good plan. You three boys running the business."

Late that afternoon, Adam called Tommy to his office, offered him a smoke, and said, "The business is getting large. The way I figure it, if you can sell suits of clothing, you can also sell oranges. Now, seriously, Papa and I want you to take over sales; it's a big job and it means travel, but we know you can handle it. What do you say?"

Tommy took a long draw on his cigarette. "Hope this isn't a response to Charlotte's overtures."

"Tommy, you and I go back too far for me to make up a job for you. I can't do it all. I need help."

Tommy nodded as he snuffed out his cigarette. "When do I go to work?"

That night, when Charlotte learned of Tommy's promotion, she smiled and said: "We're finally on our way. Let's drink to that." Tommy's gaze followed her as she crossed the room and poured bourbon.

"I still feel funny about it," he said. "Whatever position I hold in the business, I want to know it's one I've earned."

"Of course, darling, you've earned it."

In mid-morning sunlight, Will stood on the loading dock of Taylor Groves' new packing house in Winter Garden. Employees and friends listened as he dedicated the facility. "We'll ship fruit under the "Bellemere" label to every state east of the Mississippi. Come up here Adam, Andrew, and Tommy. Folks, you're looking at the management of the company. These boys are running the business, and I'm proud of them." Everyone applauded. Everyone, except Charlotte. Her face turned crimson. How could Papa say that? she thought. He says he loves me, then he slams a door in my face. It'll always be that way. Tommy third and not a word about me.

Charlotte closed the door to Adam's office and sat in a chair by her brother's desk. "I'm surprised," she said, "that you haven't talked to Papa about dividing his estate. Taxes will take most of it unless he does something before he dies."

Adam frowned. "I have no intention of discussing that subject with our father."

"Are you blind?" she snapped. "If he forms a corporation now and makes gifts of stock to his children, we avoid taxes. He is going to die someday, isn't he?"

Lines in Adam's forehead deepened as he listened. "I don't want to talk about it."

Charlotte stood abruptly, walked to the door, and grasped the brass doorknob. "Well, I'm not calling you a fool. Let's just say it's not smart to watch Papa's estate go down the tax drain." Before he could answer, she walked out and slammed the door.

Over lunch at the country club, Rachel watched her daughter pick at a tuna and avocado salad. "Something's bothering you, honey."

Charlotte blinked. "Am I that obvious?"

"Yes, darling."

"Mama, I'm worried about Papa. He's not well."

"I know. The doctor from Mayo Clinic will be here next week."

"Good. Tell me, have you and Papa talked about his estate?"
Rachel looked surprised. "No."

"Part of my job involves tax matters. Unless Papa makes preparations now, his estate will be greatly reduced when he passes away. I'm concerned for you, Mama."

Rachel stirred her tea. "Why don't you talk to your father?"

Charlotte sighed. "He listens only to you and Adam. I'm just his little girl — always will be."

Rachel touched her daughter's hand. "You're always concerned with the family's welfare. I'll look into it."

"I love you, Mama."

Rachel smiled. "Save me a day next week. I want to take you shopping for some pretty things."

Dr. Howard Abbott of the Mayo Clinic had arrived on the noon train. After examining Will, he sat in the parlor with Rachel and Adam while Will napped. The doctor's sagging, pale cheeks hung deeply over his stiff white collar. "It's Parkinson's disease," he said." Involuntary tremors will continue as paralysis of the muscles increases. In the final stages, Mr. Taylor will be bedridden, unable to move."

Rachel cleared her throat. "How much time does he have?"

Doctor Abbott shrugged. "Very difficult to say. He may live for years."

Adam stood. "Wait a minute. What can be done for him? What's the cure?"

The rotund doctor sniffed. "There is no cure."

Adam breathed deeply. No cure, he thought. Now, reality struck. He had taken for granted that Papa would always be present. Managing the groves presented no problem, he had done that for years. But Papa's light had been his North Star, the tap root of the family. He took his mother's hand and gently squeezed. Rachel nodded as she looked at her son. "I'll talk to your father about dividing his estate."

Paul Knight, Jr. sat at the head of the highly polished, mahogany conference table in his law offices. Harvard crimson draperies hung at the windows, touching a deep-piled gray carpet. After everyone had refused coffee, Will, Rachel, Adam, Charlotte, and Andrew listened as Knight began. "Mr. Taylor instructed me to form a Florida Corporation entitled Taylor Groves, Incorporated. He has named the following persons as directors: William Silas Taylor, Rachel Adamson Taylor, John Adamson Taylor, Charlotte Taylor Lane, and Andrew Cummings Taylor. He has authorized 200 shares of capital stock. Mr. Taylor retains 104 shares. The four other directors will receive 24 shares each. Mr. Taylor suggests the following slate of officers: Chairman, William S. Taylor, salary, $75,000; President, John Adamson Taylor, salary, $60,000; Vice President, Andrew C. Taylor, salary, $30,000; Vice President, Thomas C. Lane, salary, $30,000; Charlotte Taylor Lane, Secretary and Treasurer, salary, $20,000. Is there a motion?"

Adam moved the motion and Andrew seconded. The motion carried and the meeting ended.

Charlotte left the table and walked with Tommy to their car. Her temples throbbed as she spoke. "Papa's always favored Andrew, our little bastard, and he wants me to work for field hand pay. Well, we'll see."

Will's C.P.A., bald old Jesse Murdoch, strolled into the Pine Street office and plopped down in a captain's chair.

"Morning, Jesse, must be tax time," said Will.

"That's right. Ernst & Ernst is on the job. Hope you're ready for me."

"I've been getting the books ready for too many years. Charlotte's taking over. Talk to her."

Jesse grinned. "Getting old, are you? Well, I've been hoping to spend more time with your little girl."

Charlotte patted the pink skin on top of Murdoch's head. "Come on, Jesse, Papa doesn't allow romance in the office."

By Wednesday, Murdoch's audit team had plowed through ledgers, journals, files, bank statements, and canceled checks. Jesse sat across from Will. "Going to Rotary?"

"Yeah."

"Let's walk over together."

Murdoch looked straight ahead as they moved along Pine Street. "Are you aware that Andrew's expense account is eighteen thousand dollars out of balance?"

Will kept walking. "No."

When they returned to the office, Jesse pointed to journal entries and cash receipts. "It goes back at least eleven months."

Will nodded as Murdoch closed the journal.

That night, long after dark, crickets played their symphony as Will sat alone on his porch. He had called Andrew, asking him to come to the office in the morning. There is a logical explanation, he thought. There is no way the boy would do the wrong thing. He rose, walked inside, and climbed the stairs, wondering what Andrew would say.

At 8:00 a.m., Andrew tossed his cap on the office coat rack and flashed a smile as he passed Charlotte's desk. "How's my big sister?" Charlotte didn't look up.

Andrew entered Will's office. "Close the door and have a seat," said Will. "The auditors are finishing up and they say your expense account is out of balance. How did it happen?"

Andrew's jaw fell. "I have no idea. I settle up every month."

Will nodded. "That's what I thought. Get with Jesse and Charlotte."

Andrew and Charlotte sat beside Jesse Murdoch. "You see, Andrew, you're eighteen thousand short," said Murdoch.

Andrew frowned as he looked at Charlotte. "What's this all about? You know perfectly well I balance every month."

She gazed at Murdoch. "The numbers are there. I merely make a record of transactions."

"Look at me," Andrew blurted. "I'm not behind and you know it."

She slowly turned. Cold indifference imprinted across her face.

Why? Andrew wondered. Why? "Come with me to Papa's office," he said.

Will removed his glasses and pinched his nose as Charlotte and Andrew sat before him. He focused on Charlotte. "Andrew says he settles up every month. Can you explain the cash shortage?"

She spoke softly. "It's been going on for a long time. I assumed you knew it."

Will rubbed his chin. "Thank you, Charlotte."

She closed the door behind her, but Andrew remained. "Do you believe her, Papa?"

Will placed his hand on Andrew's shoulder. "I believe you. We're putting this thing behind us — right now."

"No, Papa. You can't bury it; it's got to be settled."

"I'll deal with it, Andrew."

Andrew stood silently, focusing on Will's eyes. He slowly shook his head, then turned and left the room.

Long after dark, Will lay restlessly in bed as he told Rachel what had happened. She squeezed his arm. "Andrew could have taken the money. Jeffery Quinn blood may be surfacing."

Will exhaled a deep breath. "She's lying, Rachel. If Andrew had taken the money, he wouldn't demand a face off."

Rachel's lips quivered. "I don't care who took the money. You must not accuse Charlotte of lying. She's been through too much."

During lunch, on the following day, Andrew gave Adam a full account of his story. He smothered his half-smoked Camel and sat back in his chair. "That's all there is to it, she's lying. Only thing I can't figure out is why? I've done nothing to deserve this."

Adam repeatedly nodded. "You know I'm with you, Andrew. You know that."

"Will you stand up to Papa against her?"

Adam shook his head. "Leave it alone. Spare Papa and Mama the agony of seeing the family divided."

Andrew smiled as he stood. "Well, that's it. I'll be seeing you."

"Wait a minute. Don't leave."

"Can't stay."

Andrew packed a bag, wrote a note, and left Orlando on a bus bound for Camp Blanding.

March 12, 1941

Dear Mama and Papa,

You are wonderful parents and I know you love me,
just as I love you. But you see, I cannot continue in
the business under the shadow of doubt that exists.
It's a matter of honor.

When you receive this note, I will be inducted in the
army, and on my way to Camp Blanding.

My love,

Andrew

∞ 23 ∞

July 1941. It was the last two weeks of Andrew's infantry basic training. Long marches on Camp Blanding's hot sandy trails convinced him that years of grove work had prepared him for basic training; but unlike the relative isolation of Taylor Groves, army life offered no privacy, no space, and so, like soldiers of every generation, Andrew blocked out the present and thought of home. He believed Charlotte sought control of Taylor Groves. Divide the family and conquer, a proven strategy. Neither Papa nor Adam had faced the truth, and Mama would stand by Charlotte, no matter what. But if the family believed he had been dishonest, it was best to make a clean break of it.

Training Company "A" halted for rest in the shade of pine trees. Andrew dropped his pack, wiped beads of sweat from his face, and drank heavily from his canteen. He drew on his cigarette and blew a long trail of smoke in hot, humid air, believing that in a world at war, his feelings really didn't matter much.

Newspaper headlines had screamed of Germany's invasion of the Soviet Union. Attacking across a thousand-mile front, German Panzer groups had penetrated four hundred miles into Russia, capturing 280,000 Red Army troops. In Western Europe, England stood alone facing Adolph Hitler. All other countries, except Switzerland, were occupied by Germany.

In the far east, Japan's powerful navy prowled the Pacific, raising questions around the world of their intent. The issue wasn't whether or not the United States would stay out of war, it was, how long she would stay out.

"On your feet," yelled the drill sergeant. "Only seven miles to go." Andrew field stripped his cigarette, adjusted his pack, slung his rifle over his shoulder, and found his place in the column.

The battalion returned from the field, and Andrew entered the barracks, placed his rifle in the rack, dropped his pack, stripped, and headed for the shower. A loud voice yelled, "mail call." When Andrew returned, he found a letter lying on his bunk.

Andrew,

Papa says your furlough begins on Saturday, July 14. How about meeting me at the Roosevelt Hotel in Jacksonville on the fifteenth? Call me as soon as you can.

Sincerely,

Adam

Adam watched a parade of life go by as he waited for Andrew in the lobby of the Roosevelt: a second lieutenant holding a girl in his arms, oblivious to the world around him; two smooth-faced enlisted men, clearly ready for a party weekend; a gray-haired mother saying goodbye to her uniformed son; busy bellmen carrying bags, ushering guests in and out of the hotel. Adam remembered a scene in the Atlanta depot, long ago: noisy soldiers, pretty girls, busy porters, and Alice. The whistle blew and the train had departed.

"Adam."

A familiar voice came out of the crowd. Adam turned and extended his left hand, palm down. Andrew's bronze glow, punctuated by little lines at the corners of his eyes reflected the face of a soldier. "Man," said Adam. "Where's my kid brother?"

Andrew laughed. "Right here, dying for something good to eat."

During lunch, in the dining room of the Roosevelt, Andrew placed his fork on his plate and shook his head. "You would not believe how poorly equipped the army is. Where are our rifles, ammunition, guns, and tanks? Lord, help us if we get drawn into war."

Adam took the last bite of his steak, lit a cigarette, and rubbed his chin with his thumb. "Now, I want to make my little speech. Like the rest of the Taylors, you're headstrong. You should have looked at my sleeve for a reason to stay out of the army, but it's too late now. I'm convinced we're going to war and when it starts, promise me you won't try to win it all by yourself. French soil is filled with dead American heroes." His voice almost became a whisper. "And besides, you're a Taylor, the future of the family."

Andrew swallowed. "Thanks Adam. I've been accepted for Officer Candidate School at Ft. Benning. Don't know when I'll see you again, but I want you to know I never took a cent I didn't earn."

Adam looked into Andrew's eyes. "I never questioned your integrity. I would trust you with my life."

Andrew nodded. "Let's get out of here and have some fun."

August 2, 1941. Andrew and two hundred other candidates reported to Fort Benning, Georgia to begin OCS training. To Andrew, the main post of Benning seemed more like an exclusive small town than an army fort. Beginning at the main gate, a wide, tree-lined boulevard, named First Division Road, wound past neatly landscaped homes leading to a "downtown" area. There, a library, theater, cafeteria, officers club, NCO club, and a large post exchange served the needs of the military establishment. Nearby, a large brick building with the words "Follow Me" inscribed over the entrance housed headquarters of The Infantry School. Additional buildings on the main post were Collins and Lewis Halls, quarters for bachelor officers. Six miles deeper into the reservation was Harmony Church Area, the training ground and housing area for officer candidates.

After the initial indoctrination, Andrew ate lunch in the mess hall with Sam Pilcher, a gangly red-headed boy from Jackson, Mississippi whose accent flowed like cane syrup on a cold morning.

"I hate the army," said Pilcher, as he ground out his cigarette in a butter dish. "The depression wiped out my family's savings, leaving nothing for my college tuition, so, here I am. Guess it's a better option than peanut farming. Why you here, Taylor?"

Andrew grinned. "Well, my option was orange growing; the rest is a long story."

After three weeks of training, candidates Pilcher and Taylor stood in ranks at attention, on a red clay parade ground beneath the scorching Georgia sun. "Good Lord," Pilcher whispered, "this is nothing but basic training all over again with a little tactics, military courtesy, and leadership thrown in. The only real difference between enlisted men and second lieutenants is an extra thirteen weeks of basic training."

Andrew grinned. "Perhaps, but I understand that before we graduate, one-third of us will wash out and return to the ranks. Nobody gets thrown out of basic training."

"You right about that, Taylor."

OCS was a test of endurance for potential leaders of better than average intelligence. But it was more than that, it was also a process of testing a candidate's performance under pressure. Against time, they solved map problems and translated codes transmitted by wire and radio. They delivered two-minute talks to imaginary platoons going into battle for the first time. Each week they took graded tests on their exercise.

Andrew had heard it right. By the end of October, only one hundred thirty of the two hundred candidates successfully finished the course. Sixty-eight men, including Sam Pilcher, were returned to the ranks.

Adam had driven his father to Fort Benning to watch Andrew stand with his class as the Commandant of The Infantry School commissioned him a 2nd lieutenant. With quivering fingers, Will pinned gold bars to Andrew's shoulders. "I'm proud of you, son. Forgive me for allowing you to think I do not trust you. When your time is up, come home. I want you in the business."

Andrew held his father in his arms and said, "I love you, Papa."

During lunch, Andrew asked about the groves. Adam beamed. "We bought two hundred acres of Hamlins east of Winter Garden. If we keep buying, we'll own everything between Orlando and Clermont. We're shipping lots of fruit. Packing plant's running night and day; only problem is, we need our field manager, but he's in the army."

Andrew grinned. "How are Alice and little Kathleen?"

Adam smiled. "Fine, they send their love."

Andrew looked at Will. "Is Mama well?"

Will's hand shook as he reached for a box. "Mama's fine. She knitted this for you."

Andrew opened the box and withdrew an olive drab wool scarf. Andrew took his father's hands, squeezed them and said, "Tell Mama, I love her." He turned to Adam, "and you too, brother."

December 1, 1941. A cold rain greeted Andrew on the day he reported to 1st Infantry Division Headquarters, Indiantown Gap, Pennsylvania. Captain Austin Kelly welcomed Andrew to "E" Company, 26th Infantry Regiment and assigned him to First Platoon. He met other officers and non-commissioned officers of his company, including 1st Lieutenant Jack Merrick, Staff Sergeant Ivan Gabrielski, and Sergeants, Palmer, Baker, and Valdez.

After retreat, Jack Merrick lay on his bunk at Bachelor Officer Quarters, clad only in olive drab shorts. His blond crewcut hair, sleek tanned body, and boyish face reminded Andrew of a country club lifeguard.

"Hey, Taylor," Merrick said, "what do you think of Captain Kelly? Kinda' fat for infantry, isn't he?"

Andrew smiled. "Yeah. Tell me about Sergeant Gabrielski."

"You're lucky, son. He's the best non-com in the division. By the way, you married?"

"No."

"Good. I'll round us up some girls this weekend."

Andrew chuckled. "Thanks. I'll manage my own love life. Now, I believe we were talking about Sergeant Gabrielski."

Merrick snickered. "Yeah. He's an old soldier — eats new second lieutenants for breakfast, but as I said, he's the best. I'd want him with me in a fire fight."

The following morning, Andrew knocked at Gabrielski's room in the barracks. "It ain't locked," came a deep voice from within. Andrew walked in and saw a short, stocky man with a huge neck and muscular shoulders. A wisp of gray brushed his temples, and thick dark eyebrows hooded steely eyes.

The sergeant rose from his bunk. "Come in Lieutenant. I'm always glad to have a new officer of my platoon. What can I do for you?"

Andrew gazed about the room. A case of Four Roses whiskey sat in the corner. A box of Perfecto Garcia cigars lay on a small table. "I understand you're regular army," said Andrew.

"That's right. Sixteen years in — been all over the world."

"Do you believe 1st Platoon is in good physical condition?"

Gabrielski smiled. "No question about it, Lieutenant. I take care of that, myself."

Andrew sniffed. "Glad to hear that. We're going on a march with full field pack. Have the platoon in formation at 0600, tomorrow, and Sergeant, get that liquor out of the barracks at once."

A little smile crept over Gabrielski's lips. "Lieutenant, sir. Please have a seat." The sergeant reached for a box of cigars. "Would you have a cigar, sir?"

"Thank you, sergeant." Andrew unwrapped the cigar and held it in his mouth as Gabrielski lit a match.

Gabrielski scratched his ear. "I've been in this outfit seven years, and I know and respect every man and every officer. I do my job and stay out of trouble. I can make life real easy for you, sir."

Andrew blew a long trail of smoke, then looked deeply into the sergeant's eyes. "Sergeant Gabrielski. Any day now, this army is going to war. When we do, our platoon will be ready. I'll see to that. Any questions?"

"No, sir."

"All right. Draw rations, we'll be in the field until dark, and sergeant, shave that stubble before you leave the barracks."

Rain began falling shortly after midnight, and by dawn, "E" Company area became a sea of cold mud. Led by Andrew, First Platoon formed and moved out along a road leading to a bivouac area, ten miles away. Nine miles out, Gabrielski came alongside Andrew. "We've got stragglers, sir. Better slow down the pace."

Andrew looked straight ahead. "Thought you said they were in good condition."

"Not for this kind of punishment."

"This little march is just for openers. We're going twice this distance tomorrow. Bring up the stragglers, sergeant."

On Friday, 1ˢᵗ Platoon took calisthenics before dawn, and after mess, they marched smartly to the field for combat simulated fire and movement drills. Map reading exercises followed, and after that, they moved in quick time back to the barracks just as the sun dropped below the horizon. The platoon stood at attention until Andrew left the area. "Listen up," said Gabrielski. "Barracks inspection at 0800, tomorrow. First Squad scrub the floors, Second Squad clean the latrine, Third Squad clean the windows. We'll do it tonight."

On inspection day, each soldier of 1st Platoon stood at the foot of his bunk. The barracks room door opened and Sergeant Valdez shouted, "Attention!"

Andrew entered with Gabrielski at his side. Carefully, he checked rifles, footlockers, field packs, shoes, and uniforms. He looked at scrubbed floors and clean windows. In the latrine, urinals, basins, and stools shined brightly. He entered Gabrielski's room. It was clean and orderly, no case of whiskey in the corner, no cigar box in view. Andrew turned and looked squarely at Gabrielski. "Sergeant. This barracks passes inspection. I'll arrange with the captain to issue passes to every man in the platoon. Congratulations."

Gabrielski saluted smartly. "Thank you, sir."

Andrew returned the salute. "Good work, sergeant. We're getting there."

Andrew and Jack Merrick had just finished Sunday lunch in the officers' mess. Merrick grinned as he pushed his plate away and said, "You're getting a reputation as one tough shavetail, boy. What you bucking for?"

Andrew grinned. "When I arrived, you said Gabreilski was the best non-com in the division, but that he eats second lieutenants for breakfast. You were partially right. He is the best, but he needed to know that eating this lieutenant would give him a terrible stomachache. Now, Gabreilski and I have a very good relationship." Merrick chuckled, then glanced over Andrew's shoulder. "Uh-oh, here comes old fatty."

Captain Austin Kelly hurried over and blurted, "Pearl Harbor has been bombed. All leaves and furloughs are canceled."

༄ 24 ༄

ugust 1942. 1st Infantry Division sailed from New York on the *Queen Mary*. The ship's paneled state rooms, crystal chandeliers, gold-framed mirrors, and plush furniture made the crossing seem like a summer cruise for officers, but not for enlisted men; they were herded below decks in poorly ventilated quarters and slept in hammocks four-deep from bottom to top.

On deck, Gabrielski chewed his cigar as he approached Andrew. "Don't know how much clout you have around here, Lieutenant, but the food stinks, and the men ain't getting enough time on deck."

Andrew sniffed the salty air. "On this ship, second lieutenants have less influence than cooks, but I'll speak to Captain Kelly." Andrew studied the sergeant's beard. "Shave the whiskers, sergeant. We aren't in the navy."

After five days at sea, the *Queen Mary* entered the Firth of Clyde on the western side of Scotland and sailed on to the Clyde Estuary. Docking at Gourock, the division disembarked and immediately boarded trains headed south for Tidworth Barracks near Salisbury in southern England. The "Barracks," a military training headquarters built in the early 1800s, stood at the center of the verdant pastures and clear streams of Salisbury Plain. With its ivy-covered walls, cobblestone courtyards, and arched gates, the Barracks looked like a medieval castle, from which, Andrew thought, mounted knights might appear.

At mid-afternoon, post commander Colonel Stephen Mallard, a robust man wearing a thick mustache, stood on a raised platform at the center of the Great Hall. "Greetings, gentlemen of 1st Infantry Division, and welcome to wartime England. You will experience shortages of just about everything to which you Yanks are accustomed, but we will do our best to accommodate you. The mission of the British Army is not to lead you, but rather to impart lessons we learned on the battlefield. Training begins tomorrow at 0700. Immediately after this meeting, regimental and battalion commanders will be briefed by Major Harrington in conference room 'A'. This evening at 1800, you are invited to a reception here in the Great Hall. Thank you, gentlemen."

Merrick sneered. "Sure hope they serve something more than tea at the colonel's reception."

Andrew chuckled. "Lieutenant, this place looks rather formal. If they serve whiskey, try not to fall in the punch bowl."

Merrick laughed. "I know you don't like girls, old boy, but are you saying you disapprove of booze?"

Weeks of intensive training went by, leaving Andrew with little time to become familiar with Southern England. In a letter to his parents he wrote ... *"I finally managed a weekend off and bicycled many miles through the countryside. We think we have seen green grass and rich milk at home. Believe me, there is no greener grass or richer milk than that of Salisbury Plain. And I always thought our Presbyterian sanctuary was old. What a laugh. The "New" Salisbury Cathedral was finished in 1220. Everything here is old and formal. I like that ..."*

An early October, dinner dance was scheduled for officers of 1st Infantry. Thirty girls plainly dressed, but wearing bright ribbons in their hair, arrived on buses from London. As the young ladies entered the Great Hall, Merrick outflanked all officers and moved to the side of a brunette beauty. He guided her to a table for two, hurried to the bar, and returned with a pitcher of Shantygaff.

Merrick studied her features. Bobbed ebony hair, dark bright eyes, and sensuous lips. "I knew from the moment you arrived, you weren't English," he said.

She looked surprised, then turned up her nose. "You Yanks are all alike. The Tommies say you're overpaid, oversexed, and overhere."

He shrugged. "You're beautiful and from Ireland, I'll bet."

Her eyes sparkled. "Yes. How did you know?"

He smiled. "I'm Jack Merrick — Savannah, Georgia."

"Patty McMichael — Dublin."

"Would you like to dance?"

From his table, Andrew watched and wondered as Merrick confidently whirled the brunette beauty around the floor, never missing a step. Was he a dance instructor before the war? And why do some men just know how to talk to women? He wondered as he shook his head and finished his beer.

Merrick was in London every weekend with Patty McMichael, and Andrew heard it all: where they went, how she looked, what she said. "Sounds like love to me," said Andrew.

Merrick chuckled. "You got a girl, old boy?"

Andrew smiled. "Don't worry about me."

"Better hurry, winked Merrick. I hear we leave in two weeks."

Two weeks, thought Andrew. He'd never had a girl, never slept with one, would probably die a virgin, but then, he wasn't Jack Merrick.

As autumn winds whipped across Southern England turning leaves red and gold, 1st Division boarded trains for transport to Inveraray, there they boarded the *Monarch Of Bermuda* and sailed in the Atlantic to join a convoy moving south. "Any guess where we're going?" asked Merrick.

"Not a clue," answered Andrew. "Maybe we're going home."

"Yeah. What we have here is a lad who for the lack of a woman has lost his direction. I tried to cure you. Remember that."

During the third night at sea, the convoy passed through the Straits of Gibraltar. They steamed on, past the coast of Morocco, to their objective, the port city of Oran.

Andrew and Gabrielski studied a map. "We land here, just west of Aine el Turk," said Andrew. "From there we move to Mers-el-Kebir. It's a night landing, so be sure the men are checked out before dark."

The *Monarch* crept within 1500 yards of the Algerian coast. Andrew remembered Adam's warning: "French soil is filled with dead American heroes." But, Adam had distinguished himself in combat and brought honor to the family as he faced enemy fire without regard for his own safety.

All engines stopped as landing craft prepared to receive troops.

"Over the side, let's go," said Captain Kelly.

Andrew glanced at his watch. The order came at exactly 0100 hour. First Platoon climbed down debarkation nets to a landing craft that was pitching and rolling in the sea. As the shallow boat sped toward the beach, Andrew expected that an exchange of fire with French Colonials would occur any minute.

What a crazy world we live in, he thought. In World War I, the French were our allies, now they're enemies.

"Two hundred yards," shouted the coxswain.

A soldier vomited all over the hull of the boat. "Lean him over the side. Right now!" said Gabrielski.

With a thud, the landing craft hit the beach. The steel gate dropped and First Platoon raced across the sand to take cover in a shallow ditch.

"Gabrielski," yelled Andrew, "get your scouts out. Form the platoon and move out, up that road."

Two riflemen spearheaded the column as the platoon moved silently down a twisting asphalt road. Hours had passed, and at first light, Andrew breathed a sigh of relief. At least, he thought, we can see. Suddenly, ear-splitting machine gun fire raked the platoon. Soldiers took cover as bullets peppered the road and ricocheted off gnarled trunks of olive trees. After ten minutes, the gunfire ceased. Andrew crawled to Gabrielski's position. "Get 'em up and move forward."

Grabelski waved his arm. "Move out!" Then, before them, in the mist of early light, appeared a small, bearded man, riding a bicycle on the narrow road. "What's this?" screamed Gabrielski. "Get him out of here."

Scouts lifted the man from the bicycle and rushed him to Andrew. Straining to communicate, the little man said he was a French doctor making his rounds. He was astonished to learn an American army had landed.

"Doctor," said Andrew, "you're in the middle of a combat zone. Please go to your home and stay there." The doctor shrugged, turned his bicycle around, and peddled back over the hill.

First Platoon advanced along a road lined with palm trees to the outskirts of the seaside village of Aine el Turk and forced entry to a small white cottage. There stood the trembling physician who had appeared earlier on a bicycle.

Without a shot being fired, Aine el Turk was taken and a command post was established in the back room of a clothing store that

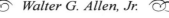

stood at the center of the village. Andrew studied his map as Gabrielski entered the room. "Lieutenant, the doctor wants to see you."

Andrew grinned. "Let him in."

Dressed in a baggy black suit and white bow tie, the doctor resembled a character from a nineteenth century French novel. He removed his bowler, bowed, presented Andrew with a magnum of champagne, and said: "Monsieur. This is for you and your men."

Andrew shook his head. "I'm sorry, sir, but we cannot accept your gift."

The little man's head dropped as Sergeant Gabrielski hopped forward and took the bottle. "Sir, what the Lieutenant means is that we cannot accept your gift without saying thank you, for your generosity. Isn't that right, Lieutenant?"

Andrew looked out of the corner of his eyes at his platoon sergeant. "Well, yes. Thank you for the gift."

The doctor bowed several times as he backed out of the room. Gabrielski smiled. "Is that all, sir?"

"Plenty for one day."

After two days fighting, Algeria was secure. Now, the long trek across the desert to the Tunisian border began. The final battles for North Africa would soon begin.

January 1943. Just inside the western boundary of Tunisia, lay the Ousselta Valley. On the west, a steep ridge guarded the valley extending fifty miles from north to south. In staggered formation, 1st Infantry Division advanced to the ridge, with "E" and "F" Companies of the 26th Regiment occupying elevated positions on the northernmost slope.

At the eastern side of the valley, the ground rose to form a second high ridge; there, entrenched German and Italian forces waited for the Americans.

In drizzling rain, Captain Kelly led "E" Company in a probing action across the wind-swept valley, to the foot of a barren ridge on the far side. Meeting no resistance, they began climbing toward the summit, but within minutes, three mortar rounds exploded in their midst. From high ground the enemy enjoyed an unobstructed field of fire as machine guns caught "E" Company in deadly crossfire. Kelly ordered a withdrawal, but it was too late; eleven men fell as the company scrambled down the ridge and stumbled back across the valley, carrying their dead and wounded.

Merrick threw his helmet in the mud. "Too bad Kelly didn't catch a piece of lead in his butt. He shoved us right into a fortified position. No reconnaissance, no nothing. We just marched right into it. Hell, Andrew, you ain't even mad."

Standing in drizzling rain, Andrew buttoned the top button of his field jacket, "Pretty silly to get upset. If I get mad every time a superior officer makes a mistake, I'd stay mad the whole war. Tell you what I'm gonna' do; I'm gonna' concentrate on my performance." He grinned. "You see, I can't do anything about the performance of people above me. Let's get some chow."

Merrick grinned. "You never overreact, Taylor. That's what I like about you."

Second battalion moved in convoy on the road to Beja. Sergeant Plummer smoked a cigarette as he drove Andrew's Jeep. Angrily, he asked, "How did the brass let First and Third Battalions get slaughtered at Kasserine, Lieutenant?"

Andrew wondered the same thing. II Corp's first big engagement. He shook his head, "It was a wake up call, Plummer. We better be ready the next time we fight Rommel."

The convoy pulled into a bivouac area fifteen miles from the front. Captain Kelly spread his map before platoon leaders and pointed a pudgy finger to a place marked Hill 575.

"That's the objective," he droned. "Trucks will deliver us to a field two miles from the hill. Merrick, take right flank; Taylor, left flank. I'll support with Third Platoon."

Merrick cleared his throat. "What's on the ridge?"

"I have no idea," Kelly growled. "Artillery says they'll saturate the area before we go in. Any more questions?"

Andrew explained the plan of attack to Gabrielski. The sergeant scratched his ear. "Looks like a duck shoot for the Krauts. Well, tomorrow's Good Friday. If we get it, at least we'll be in good company."

Andrew didn't smile. "Get the men together."

As the trucks moved out of the bivouac area, Andrew rubbed his eyes. Brilliant, blood-red poppies grew everywhere along the sides of the road.

"E" and "F" Companies unloaded in a field of green grass dubbed "Pea Patch," by the men. Gabrielski laughed. "Guess scared soldiers keep it green."

American 155 howitzers opened fire at 1000 hours. The sound was familiar. Boom! Whew, whew, whew — ba-lam! Over and over the macabre sound repeated as "E" Company moved into position. The barrage lifted, and Captain Kelly's arm motioned forward, signaling the attack. As the company crossed open ground, the memory of Ousselta Valley flashed through Andrew's mind. At that moment, enemy mortars and machine guns opened fire, catching the company in crossfire. Within minutes, seventeen men dropped, including Lieutenant Merrick, who died instantly from head wounds. Captain Kelly died in the field from mangling shrapnel wounds as he brought up Third Platoon. Andrew assumed command of the company and immediately ordered artillery fire, blanketing enemy gun placements for an hour. When the barrage lifted, the enemy withdrew and "E" Company occupied Hill 575.

Andrew reported to battalion headquarters. Big-boned Captain Rupert Walton, a man with thick eyebrows and a large, bent nose, handed him an envelope. "Get your stuff and take a Jeep over to regiment. I don't know what it's all about."

"Yes, sir."

Andrew parked near the command post of regimental headquarters and walked quickly to Major Paul Markel's desk. "Congratulations, Taylor. You're promoted to captain, and temporarily assigned to British V Corps. Be at Mateur in two days."

When Andrew returned to his unit, Gabrielski looked as disappointed as a man who had dropped a quart of Canadian Club. "So, Captain, you're going over to the Limeys."

"Nobody knows why. Guess my name got pulled out of the hat."

"Sir, I hear your replacement majored in music at Princeton. What am I gonna do with him?"

Andrew chuckled. "Maybe he'll teach you to sing. Now listen, have a driver and my Jeep ready at 0700 tomorrow."

"Yes, sir."

Andrew smiled as he offered Gabrielski a cigar.

At dawn, Andrew threw his bag in the back of the Jeep and jumped in next to the driver. "Gabrielski! What are you doing?"

"Tell you about it in a minute, sir." He threw the Jeep in gear and roared off, leaving a long trail of gray dust behind. "You need a driver and an aide. I don't need a singing lieutenant so I fixed the paperwork and signed your name. Any other questions, sir?"

Andrew paused. "Yeah. Did you bring anything to eat?"

"Hot coffee and fresh sandwiches in the back, sir."

Silently, they drove on as the bleak North African desert stretched endlessly ahead.

At noon, they pulled into British V Corps Headquarters, parked, and found barrel-chested Colonel David Whitaker. "Welcome Captain Taylor. You and thirty other handpicked junior officers of First Army are here for special training. The Assistant Corps Commander will meet you at 0800 tomorrow." He nodded to his aide. "Lt. Campbell will show you to your quarters."

Special training, thought Andrew. The Brits are going to show us how to fight. More than once he had heard stories of British Army officers referring to American soldiers as overpaid, undisciplined muttonheads. No doubt the battle at Yorktown had been omitted from their history lessons.

On the following morning, thirty American junior officers waited outside the trailer of the Assistant Corps Commander. The door opened and a ramrod of a man emerged, tall, trim, and alert for a person looking over fifty. He wore a tie, battle jacket, khaki breeches, and brown cavalry boots. He walked between ranks, studying each man's face with the eyes of a jungle predator. "I am Major General Jeffery Quinn," he trumpeted.

Andrew's head spun as he tried to regain control of himself. Jeffery Quinn — it can't be, but he's the right age.

Quinn continued. "You will be trained to command infantry companies in the U.S. First Army, and our job is to ensure there will be no more panic-stricken collapses like Kasserine Pass. You will lead your units to victory on the battlefield, or die fighting." He paused. "I'm told that each of you has distinguished yourself in combat, a good beginning for the kind of leadership we demand here." He turned to his aide. "Colonel Whitaker will brief you."

Colonel Whitaker had fought the Afrika Korps across two thousand miles of desert since 1941. "Discipline! Discipline! Discipline!" he barked. "Battles are won by disciplined officers and men in forward echelons. We see too much familiarity between American officers and their men. Platoon leaders and company commanders must gain respect and complete control. Tighten it up, and you win battles. Each of you will be assigned to a combat-tested company commander in V Corps. Listen and learn. Questions? All right — 0700, tomorrow. Right here."

Andrew ate tough beef, red beans, and hard bread as a Lance Corporal approached. "Sir. General Quinn will see you now."

"What? Now?"

"Yes, sir."

Andrew's pulse quickened as he entered the general's trailer. "Captain Taylor reporting, sir."

"Sit down Captain. I am personally interviewing each American officer. Smoke?"

"No thank you, sir."

Quinn scanned Andrew's file. "2nd battalion, 26th Regiment, 1st Division. Were you at Kassarine?"

"No, sir. My battalion was at Le Kef."

"I see. At Kasserine, the Germans almost ran you Yanks back to Algeria. What do you say about that?"

Andrew stiffened. "Sir, I wasn't in that fight."

Quinn, smiled. "Where is your home?"

"Orlando, Florida."

The general paused. He rose and walked to a table. "Tea?"

"No thank you, sir."

Quinn focused on Andrew's face. "Our training is simulated battlefield exercises — battalion in attack of a fortified position, that sort of thing. We'll go at it night and day."

"We're ready, sir."

They talked about the war for half an hour. Then Quinn stood, and in a friendly tone said: "Welcome to my headquarters, Captain."

As he left, Andrew shook his head. He had talked with the man who fathered him, the man who deserted his mother. He wanted to erase the meeting from his mind, but he couldn't.

After Andrew left, General Quinn studied Taylor's file. There it was. CLOSEST OF KIN — WILLIAM S. TAYLOR and RACHEL A. TAYLOR. Ann's brother, he thought. He lit a cigarette, drew heavily, and exhaled a plume of smoke. He remembered Ann's letters, pleading to join him, but army life in India was no place for a teenage wife. And then his mother's letter, telling of Ann's death, a victim of pneumonia. So long ago — so far away.

Fourteen days of maneuvers in desert wind and sun came to an end as British lorries transported 1st Division officers from training sites to V Corps Headquarters.

Soap and water stung Andrew's face as he shaved his beard. He dressed and as he walked to officers mess, Gabrielski handed him an envelope.

Captain Taylor,

Please join me for dinner in my trailer at 1900, today.

General Jeffery Quinn

"Who gave you the note?" said Andrew.

"The general, himself. You ain't staying here, are you?"

"No. Pack your gear, we leave tomorrow."

No others were present as Andrew entered the general's headquarters. "Good evening, Captain Taylor. Thank you for joining me. Drink?"

"No thank you, sir."

Quinn poured a double whiskey for himself as he spoke. "Give me your opinion of the training."

The general listened as Andrew detailed every aspect of the past three weeks. "In conclusion," Andrew said, "the training was excellent. I'm fortunate to have been included in these exercises."

"Very good, Captain." Quinn summoned an orderly who appeared with a tray of food. An awkward silence followed as they ate canned ham, roast potatoes, and biscuits.

"Well," said Quinn, "you're from Orlando, Florida. Tell me about your parents."

"My mother died when I was an infant. My grandparents adopted me."

"Your father is Adam Taylor?"

"No, sir. My mother was Ann Taylor."

Suddenly, Jeffery Quinn saw himself in the face of Andrew. Same eyes, jaw, and nose. Under the table, he clinched his fists. Like specks of matter from different worlds, blown together by war, he sat facing his son. What could he say? Hello, I'm your father, the man who deserted your mother. Nice to know you. Quinn stood, walked to a table and poured another drink. "My parents were your grandparents' neighbors in Orlando, years ago."

Andrew glared. "Yes, sir. I know."

Softly, Quinn placed his glass on the table. "I knew Ann, a lovely person — died of pneumonia."

Andrew stiffened as he carefully measured his words. "No, sir. She died in childbirth."

Color drained from the general's rugged face. *"Childbirth?"* Slowly, he shook his head and whispered: "Andrew."

As truth swept through a broken dam, Andrew maintained a mask of composure. He stood rigidly. "Sir, if there is no other matter, I request permission to leave. Thank you for your hospitality."

The general nodded. "Of course. Of course. I understand. Thank you for joining me."

Wind howled through the African night, blowing stinging sand against Andrew's face as he walked swiftly to his tent.

*L*ondon 1944. Andrew and Lieutenant Mark White sat at a small table in the ballroom of the Grosvenor Hotel, watching officers of 1ˢᵗ Infantry dance with English girls to strains of *"I'll Be Seeing You."* White finished his cigarette. "Excuse me, Andrew, just spotted a good friend." Andrew turned and saw a pretty American Army nurse making her way to their table. White kissed her on the cheek, then hurried her away, vanishing in the crowd.

Andrew lifted his glass taking the last swallow of beer, then reached for his coat.

"Hello, Andrew." He looked up at soft brown eyes and a beautiful face.

Andrew rose. "Patty! Patty McMichael. Where did you come from? Please sit down."

"Been right here, all along." Straining, she asked, "Can you tell me anything about Jack?"

Andrew hesitated, then shook his head. "Sorry Patty, Merrick didn't make it ... killed in Tunisia."

She closed her eyes. "I thought so. His letters stopped coming."

"I didn't have your address — couldn't let you know."

She looked at his silver bars. "You've come a long way, Captain."

"Yeah. More people to worry about. Tell me what you're doing?"

"War office dispatcher. First night I've been off in a month."

"Hungry?"

"Starved."

"Let's get out of this place before they make us dance." As he helped with her coat, he detected the fresh scent of cologne.

While they drank ale and ate sandwiches at a pub near Grosvenor Square, he told of his promotion to company commander. "After Jack and Captain Kelly were killed, and the Sicilian Campaign ended, the division sailed for England. Now, we're training in Dorset, preparing for the invasion." He smiled. "What's a pretty girl like you doing all alone at the Grosvenor?"

"First time I've been there in months."

"Come on, I thought you were into entertaining the troops."

"Not since Jack. He was special."

Her dark eyes accentuated the texture of milk-white skin. But it was her voice that set her apart. Low, soft, a musical quality to her Irish accent.

It was nearly one o'clock when they left the pub and walked through numbing air to the tube. As they waited on the platform for her train, she looked up. "Will I see you again?"

"Should be back in three weeks," he whispered. "I'll call."

When the train pulled in, she boarded and vanished in a crowd of uniforms. For the first time in his life he felt a sense of emptiness.

At 1st Infantry Division Headquarters, Andrew sensed the enormity of an engagement that would commit allied troops to the beaches of the European continent. Sitting in a planning meeting with General Huebner's executive officer, he learned that infantry, artillery, and armor in army group strength were in place throughout southern England.

American bombers flew overhead by day, and RAF bombers by night, relentlessly attacking German airfields, troop concentrations, storage tanks, rail heads, and coastal gun emplacements. As the world waited, the only questions were where and when the invasion would take place.

Weeks later, at the British War Office in London, Patty's telephone jingled. "Patty. It's Andrew. I'm in town for two days. Can you meet me at the Savoy for dinner?"

"Yes. Make it nine o'clock, in the lounge."

Wind-driven rain sprayed Andrew's face as he made his way past fire-gutted buildings to the Savoy. This is crazy, he thought. I really know nothing about her. For all I know, she could have slept with the whole army. He found a table in the lounge, lit a cigarette, and waited. He knew it was no time to become involved. There was no reason to share more than friendly conversation. He glanced at the doorway and saw Patty. She had removed her coat and stood in the dark entrance to the lounge. Her blue wool uniform couldn't hide a shapely figure silhouetted by light from the foyer. Andrew stood and stared, wondering what he would say. She came to his side and kissed his cheek; then he held her. She clung to him and whispered, *"Andrew."* Nothing had prepared him for what he felt. The only women in his life had been Rachel and Charlotte. Now, for the first time, he held a warm, beautiful woman who needed him.

During dinner, in candlelight, she told of her family's poverty in Dublin, and the death of her father, killed in a riot when she was only eight. Her mother had died of tuberculosis in 1936. Orphaned at fifteen and destitute, she had sailed for England where she sewed clothing in a linen sweatshop. When war came, she volunteered and had been at the war office ever since.

Andrew lit a cigarette. "Tell me about Jack."

She paused as she stared at the flame of the candle. "Jack was full of life and very kind to me. I loved him and would have married him if he had asked."

Andrew smiled. "Soldiers go into battle and their women wait."

She reached for his hand and held it tightly.

From the farthest corner of his mind came the image of the mother he never knew. She had watched Jeffery Quinn sail away to join his regiment in India.

Andrew touched Patty's cheek then rose. "We go to a marshaling area next week. Wish me luck."

Patty studied his eyes and lips. "Good luck Andrew. Goodbye."

June 3, 1944. In blowing rain, First Sergeant Ivan Gabrielski chewed a wet cigar as he waited to board the *Samuel Chase*, headquarters ship of the 16th Regimental Combat Team. "Well, here we go, folks, off to liberate the 'Frogs.' We kicked their butts in Algeria, but now we go to rescue 'em. But, hey, think of all the girls we gonna get."

The men yelled with laughter.

Andrew listened and shook his head as he glanced at Mark White. "If Ivan wasn't the best soldier in the army, I'd bust him to private."

"You should anyway. He gets away with murder."

"Yeah, I know, but it's the enemy he murders."

Andrew quickly changed the subject. "Can you believe this weather? We could stay at anchor for a week waiting it out."

Waiting, that was the hard part. Little things became increasingly distracting: a Zippo lighter that didn't light, a hole in the heel of a sock, a hangnail, a lost photograph, a letter that didn't come. There was conversation — simple stuff, but nothing personal, no mention of what would come, no show of fear imbedded below the surface.

June 5, 1944. In the wardroom of the ship, Andrew and other unit commanders stood over a large relief map of the Normandy Beaches. As he spoke, Colonel Ryan Boyd's eyes scanned each officer's face. "Our Division has been given the honor of spearheading the invasion. Bombers and warships will provide cover for the landing of tanks; then, we will make the initial assault, right here." Using his pointer he touched an area labeled OMAHA BEACH. "The landing area is guarded by stakes, hedgehogs, curved rails, wire, and, of course, mines." Laying his pointer aside he stroked his chin. "The weather is terrible. I cannot tell you when we go in, that's up to the big brass; whenever it is, the going will be rough, but this is the largest invasion force the world has ever known," he nodded his head. "We will succeed."

Andrew focused on "Easy Red," his company's assigned sector. The map showed at least 200 yards of open beach from water's edge to a steep bluff. Easy Company would fight from the beach to a draw in the bluff, code named Exit-1, then reform with the remainder of the battalion and fight inland.

In the hold of the ship, Andrew covered every detail of the battle plan with his platoon leaders and sergeants. There were no questions. Most "E" Company officers and non-coms had seen combat in North Africa and Sicily; they knew what was ahead. There would be casualties, many casualties. Silently they returned to their platoons and briefed their men.

In late afternoon, the *Samuel Chase* cleared Portland Harbor and joined the armada sailing toward the French coast. Throughout the ship the roar of bombers was heard as wave after wave flew to Normandy.

Knowing that Mark White had not seen combat, Andrew began a conversation. "The pretty nurse. You planning to see her again?"

White leaned back against the gray bulkhead and smiled. "I met her at Christmas. We became very close and tried to squeeze every minute. Yeah. I'm going to see her again. All I have to do is get out alive."

Andrew made a fist and lightly punched White's shoulder. "Don't worry about that. We'll be drinking beer in Berlin before you know it."

"Listen, Andrew. If I don't make it, call her. Will you? Here's her name and number."

"Sure. Get some rest. Long day at the office tomorrow."

At first light, "E" Company soldiers waited on deck as the *Chase* thrashed in a turbulent sea. Andrew looked to the horizon. White flashes against gray skies and muffled explosions provided the opening scene of an invasion where thousands would die to benefit millions of others. He wondered how many future generations of soldiers would fight to maintain a balance of power in the world.

Through a megaphone, a voice blared. "Easy Company, boats 12, 13, and 14. Begin boarding."

Loaded landing craft circled until the last boat in the battalion joined; then, as six-foot waves drenched soldiers with cold sea water, the boats moved in staggered formation toward Easy Red Beach.

Five hundred yards from shore, Andrew flinched as a shell hit an assault boat on his right flank, igniting fuel tanks and enveloping men in a whirlpool of yellow flame. Now in range, and under attack, assault boats sped forward as shells exploded in the surf, sending geysers in the air. Through the haze of morning mist stood an endless web of barbed wire crowned obstacles, half-submerged. Some boats raced through openings unloading men in shallow water; other craft, caught in steel entanglements, discharged soldiers far from shore, many men sinking in the surf.

From bunkers on high bluffs above the beach, the enemy's well-laid fields of machine gun fire savaged 16th Infantry's first landing wave. Bleeding bodies wallowed in breakers near the shore. Soldiers dug sand with fingers, scratching for whatever protection they could find. New waves of assault troops followed, crowding the beach with huddled masses and hundreds of casualties. The smell of blood- soaked sand settled over the beach.

Above the roar of explosions, gunfire, and screaming men, Andrew crawled to Gabrielski's side, yelling: "We're not staying on this beach. Get 'em up!"

Soaked and cold, Gabrielski looked at Andrew in dismay. "Where we going?"

"To the draw. Now!"

The two men moved along the beach, pulling soldiers to their feet. "Get up! Move out!" screamed Gabrielski, as he feverishly waved his arm. "Go! Go! Follow the captain."

Mark White remained in a fetal position as Gabrielski approached. "Lieutenant. Get on your feet! Get up!" He lifted White and saw a charred mass of red flesh where White's face had been.

Gabrielski dropped the lieutenant on the sand and waved the platoon on. Ten men rose, then one hundred others followed, running with Andrew and Gabrielski, moving toward the bluff. As they neared the draw, an American destroyer opened fire, scoring a direct hit on a pillbox guarding Exit-1. Through smoke and gunfire the battalion fought its way to the draw and swept inland, joining other units of 1st Division.

At 1400, Gabrielski reported to Andrew. "Fifty-two casualties, Captain." He pointed to Andrew's steel helmet. An enemy round had made a deep crease in one side. "Somebody upstairs is looking out for you."

Andrew nodded.

↶ *26* ↷

May 1945. Will Taylor, pale and bent, sat in his rocker at Bellemere, overlooking Lake Ivanhoe. Azalea and camellia blossoms had long since dropped; now, pink roses bloomed in Rachel's garden, and red begonias lined the walkway to the dock.

Adam burst on to the porch. "Papa! Papa! Germany surrenders."

A distant look appeared on Will's face, as if it were a different time, a different place. "Adam, you're home and safe." He raised his head and held out his arms.

"No, Papa. Andrew's coming home."

Will managed a crinkled smile. "Yes. Good. Andrew's coming home. Tell Mama and everyone."

Adam came to Will's side, held his father's bony hands, and said, "Now I know what you and Mama went through when I was overseas. The ones left behind do the suffering."

October. The Taylors waited at Orlando Municipal Airport for Andrew's flight. Will sat in his wheelchair near a broad window in full view of arriving flights. He looked up at drifting clouds, remembering Ann's final words: *Don't give my baby away.* Will's lips moved, but no one heard. "Another war, another son spared. Thank you, God. Thank you."

At noon, an Eastern DC-3 made a perfect landing and taxied to the ramp. In single file, passengers entered the terminal clasping hands and hugging friends and relatives. "There he is," cried Adam.

In uniform, Andrew looked older and worn by the weight of war. He grasped Adam's hand, hugged Will, and kissed Rachel and Alice. He turned and reached for the girl behind him. "Papa, Mama, family - meet my wife, Patty McMichael Taylor."

In awkward silence, the family gawked. Then Alice held out her arms. "Patty. I'm Alice, Adam's wife. Welcome, my dear." Everyone crowded in, hugging and kissing the bride.

As they drove to Bellemere, Rachel touched a gold leaf on Andrew's shoulder. "If I had known you were promoted to major, I could have told everyone in my bridge club."

After dinner at Bellemere, Andrew and Adam sat on the dock. Deep gold and purple painted the western sky. A flight of ducks landed just off shore as Adam spoke. "The business has grown so much during the war. Thank heavens you're back. When can you start?"

Andrew nodded. "Thank you, brother. I appreciate that, but I can't come in. My back pay will stake me to a small grove. Patty and I will live in Clermont. It's better that way."

"It's going to kill Papa."

"No. I'll stay in close touch with the family."

"Papa will give you a grove."

"Couldn't do that. We'll be fine."

"I need you, Andrew."

Andrew touched Adam's shoulder. "Thanks. I'll stay close."

They stayed and smoked until the last glimmer of light faded away.

Andrew entered the Pine Street office and came to Charlotte's desk. "Good to see you, sister. How's Tommy?"

She stared at her nails, then looked up. "He's all right."

"Is Papa in his office?"

"He's waiting for you."

Andrew closed the door and sat by his father's desk. Will wheeled his chair close to his son's side. "I'm so glad you're back home. Adam needs you, but he tells me you want to strike out on your own. Don't do that, Andrew. Oh, I know how you feel. The thing with Charlotte nearly killed me, but I couldn't send her away — couldn't do that. She's our blood. Time will heal it." Will's hands shook as he removed his glasses and pinched the bridge of his nose. "Son, the groves are partly yours and you're a part of me."

Andrew understood. It wasn't a question of honor. Everyone knew what Charlotte was. The wolf that had eaten his heart was pride. He looked at Papa with eyes full of love. "When do you want me to start?"

Will's wintry face brightened. "Just as soon as you and your bride select a building site for your new home. You can cut out two hundred feet on the lake next to Adam."

"Oh, no, Papa."

"Oh, yes, son."

In his office, Adam stood before a large wall map, pinpointing Taylor Groves holdings, then he looked at Andrew. "Tommy's responsible for sales. I'm responsible for field operations, and I set prices. Charlotte runs the office." He pointed to Andrew. "You take over field operations, that will free me to seek out buying opportunities." Adam ran his fingers through his graying hair, then rubbed the back of his neck. "Think of all the men returning from overseas, ready to start families who we dearly hope will eat our oranges and drink our juice."

Andrew sniffed. "Sounds like we're ready to expand. What's our cash position?"

Charlotte read from a ledger. "Thanks to Papa, we have more than a million in the bank, and no debt."

Strumming his fingers on the table, Andrew asked, "There's got to be some problems. What are they, Tommy?"

Tommy chuckled as he ground out his cigarette butt. "I don't know. Prices are low, but we're making money. It's too good to be true."

Andrew nodded. "Well, I'll do my best to keep the trees growing."

Adam laughed. "Good. Well, that's it. See all of you at Bellemere tomorrow. I hear Mama's party will overtake any Mrs. Rockefeller ever planned."

Andrew had warned her, but no one could have prepared Patty for a Rachel Taylor party. Brightly colored Japanese lanterns lined the driveway and hung in live oak trees throughout the landscape of Bellemere. On the lawn, a five-piece orchestra played soft music as guests dined on crab dip, boiled shrimp, and beef tenderloin. Rachel had said the occasion was planned to introduce Patty to Orlando, but Andrew knew better. Wearing yellow chiffon, Rachel was queen of the receiving line as she kissed and hugged every guest of any importance. Patty's introduction had become a passing thought.

"I tried to tell you," whispered Andrew.

Patty flashed a nervous smile as she held out her hand to another guest.

Alice came up behind them carrying two cups of punch. "You two must be dehydrated. Sorry, no kick in Rachel's punch."

"Thank you," said Patty. Could we have lunch sometime?" Her eyes were pleading.

"Tuesday, at the club. I'll pick you up at eleven."

Alice had requested a corner table for two. When they were seated, she placed her hand on Patty's. "Thank you for wanting to talk. We're Taylors — now sisters."

This was the kindness Patty craved, the female companionship she had hoped for but never found, in either Ireland or England. Sister. What a beautiful sound, she thought. She smiled, then asked, "I want to know so many things, but first, tell me about Mrs. Taylor."

Alice giggled. "Of course she's queen, and always gets her way, but she doesn't interfere — huge concession. She has a dual personality: one is charmingly elitist, the other, brutally frank; those who cross her feel her sting. Never underestimate her, she's very bright. She has endured much, and to her credit, she is a first lady of Orlando."

Patty shrugged. "She intimidates me."

Alice laughed. "Of course. She intimidates everyone."

Patty joined in the laughter. "Thank you. I really appreciate you."

Alice glowed. "Our soup is getting cold."

Patty touched her spoon. "Could we go shopping? Practically everything I own is on my back."

"We must. So many new things are arriving at our stores, and you're much too pretty not to be wearing them."

July 1946. "Papa, it's a boy!" cried Andrew, as he called from Orlando Memorial Hospital. "Seven pounds, four ounces. Yes, Patty's doing fine. We named him William Silas Taylor II, we'll call him Billy."

A new generation, thought Will. The name might have ended, but now, a boy — Billy Taylor. His hand shook as he held the telephone. "Good. Good. Bring him to me when he comes home."

"I will, Papa. Tell Mama and the family."

"Yes. Yes."

Will replaced the telephone in its cradle, held his hands together, closed his eyes, and whispered, "Thank you."

On his fifth day, Billy came home to Bellemere. Rachel had converted Adam's old room to a nursery. New, ocean blue carpeting covered the floor. Pastel blue curtains draped the windows, and fresh cream paint covered the walls. Patty and Andrew laughed as Ada and Elizabeth argued over who would prepare the baby's bottle. A prince had come to Bellemere.

That night, Patty lay her head on Andrew's shoulder and said, "Remember the night at the Savoy, before the invasion? It was late in the evening when you rose and asked me to wish you luck. You'll never know how much I wanted you that night, but you were so much the gentleman; that made me want you all the more. When war ended and you called, I knew I'd never let you go." She turned her head and kissed his cheek. "And here we are, my love, in your Mama's bed."

Andrew chuckled. "Yeah, in Mama's bed, but not for long. Our home will be finished soon."

"I hope so."

He smiled. "Rachel getting to you?"

"I think she looks down on me. I see it in her eyes and hear it in her voice. She talks about the Rands of Richmond and the Nelsons of Atlanta. She sees me as a seamstress, an orphan." Patty sighed. "I want to be a Taylor, a real Taylor, but it's all so new to me. If it weren't for Alice, I don't know what I'd do."

Andrew held her. "Stay close to Alice, she's sweet and fine."

Patty's brown eyes brightened. "She is that, and so are the Taylor men; besides, I like the men. Irish girls always like the men." She laughed and kissed her husband's chest.

At the office, Tommy Lane dropped a copy of the *Orlando Sentinel* on Adam's desk. "Did you see this?"

MINUTE MAID TO PRODUCE FROZEN
ORANGE CONCENTRATE

Minute Maid President, Jack Fox, announces plans to produce frozen concentrated orange juice at Plymouth, Fla.
Calling it the "Cinderella' product, Fox claims concentrate
tastes like fresh juice. Predicting an enormous new market
for Florida growers, Mr. Fox sees frozen concentrate as
the "wave of the future."

Adam looked up. "Yeah, I understand they take most of the fluid
out of the juice and freeze what's left. You add water to bring it back to
single strength. Interesting, but I wonder if food stores will stock it?
Hope so, I'm for anything that stirs up demand. Why don't you run
over to Plymouth and see what's going on? I'll ask around at the bank."

Adam met Vice President Paul Hutton in the lobby of The First
National Bank and followed him to his desk. Responding to Adam's
questions, Mr. Hutton began, "Originally, the name was National Re-
search Company. They were successful in developing a variety of hi-
vacuum products, including powdered blood plasma, but when the war
ended, Fox looked for a consumer product he could advertise and market nationally. He found it in frozen orange concentrate. Now he plans
to take the company public under the name Minute Maid. They're using a plant next to Plymouth Citrus Growers." Mr. Hutton touched his
chin with his index finger and tilted his head. "We're impressed with
Jack Fox and pleased to be his banker."

Early Monday morning, Adam sat at the head of the conference
table in the Pine Street office. "I have the feeling we're at the beginning of the most exciting time in the history of our industry. Concentrate is coming. Minute Maid will build a plant at Plymouth and, if
they're successful, there won't be enough fruit to fill the demand. Prices
will skyrocket." He folded his hands together. "I have an option on a
six-hundred acre Valencia grove near Haines City, sixteen hundred an
acre; that's cheap compared to what they'll be selling for in a few
years." He looked at Charlotte. "We have the cash, so what do you
say?"

"Absolutely," said Andrew. "This is the time."

Charlotte and Tommy nodded.

"All right," said Adam, "I'll meet the owner in Haines City tomorrow and sign the contract."

On Tuesday, Adam drove his blue Pontiac past Kissimmee. He thought of Billy Pastin. Uncle Billy had taught him many things: how to shovel fertilizer and care for trees, how to fish, and how to drink beer. He had asked Ben if he had talked too much, and Ben had answered, "Yassah."

Adam entered Polk County, passing miles of groves flanking each side of the road. Gold, pure gold, he thought, and we're right in the middle of it. There had been dark days: a killing freeze, the loss of Ann, Charlotte's behavior, the depression; but we're a family and the Lord's been good to us. He drove on, counting his blessings. Without warning, a black dump truck pulled out of a side road into his path. He swerved left and met an oncoming car. For an instant, before impact, he lay in mud at Cote-de Chatillon. He reached for his scarf, but he had no arm. Brakes squealed as metal, glass, and rubber shattered on impact, pinning him to the dash. Gas gushed from his ruptured tank and ignited, enveloping both vehicles in a swirl of blue and yellow flame.

After the funeral. Alice and Kathleen had returned to Atlanta with the Nelsons for an extended stay. Rachel, Andrew, Charlotte, and Tommy sat in the parlor at Bellemere. Rachel's hair was snow white and deep lines appeared around her eyes and neck. She cleared her throat as she looked at Charlotte. "Papa's very weak, so I'll speak for him. Until we've had time to sort things out, I think it best that you and Andrew share responsibility for running the company. You know what to do, so that's all I'll say. I'll go up and rest now."

The family stood as Rachel left the room, then Andrew moved to Charlotte's side. "Please stay for a few minutes."

"Very well," she said, her tone was noncommittal.

"You and I must work closely together. I don't want a wall between us. Let's work it out."

She looked detached, as if she were a stranger, far removed. "I'll do my work," she said, "You do yours."

Tommy stared at his wife, shook his head, then slowly followed her out of the house.

∽27∾

At the edge of the half-century mark, everything in Orlando had changed. Judge Cornelius White's home on Pine Street gave way to an attorney's office, the old Pendelton home on Central Avenue was torn down, and McElroy's Drug Store closed.

It was typical winter weather for Orlando, cool mornings and warm afternoons. Andrew turned his Buick past the white picket fence and onto the private driveway of Bellemere. The grove was now gone, replaced by fine homes near the shore of Lake Ivanhoe.

Papa was dying and, more than ever, Andrew felt his presence in a deep place in his mind. He would not permit sad thoughts to replace cherished memories. Like Adam, he too had fished with Papa on the lake. His grandfather's old stories had come to life again and again as they had drifted aimlessly in the water, talking, joking, laughing. He remembered the warmth of Christmas at home and the family gathered around the dining room table, and Mama, beautiful Mother, how fitting it was to name the home for her.

Andrew stepped out of his car and walked around the house, past tall palms flanking the path leading to the dock. Winter sun warmed his back as he scanned the north horizon. A gnarled orange tree, all that remained of the grove, stood near the lake, heavy with golden fruit. An off-shore breeze bent cattails and made ripples on the lake. Soaring overhead, an eagle searched for dinner. Andrew turned and stared at Bellemere. Time had left its print on everything.

Upstairs in his room, Papa lay motionless, unable to speak. Andrew came to his bedside, remembering Papa's once ruddy complexion; now a cadaverous pallor encased his face. He glanced at his grandfather's desk; there, a thousand things had been locked away from children's prying fingers. A family picture of Adam, Ann, and Charlotte stood beside his reading lamp; by its light, Papa had documented every cent he had earned or spent since 1887. A worn Bible, a blotter, and a ring of brass keys lay on his desk. His wooden chair that creaked was silent now. Andrew's gaze shifted to a white enamel bed pan, and a wash basin. The acrid odor of disinfectant soap permeated the air.

Dr. Early turned to Rachel. "There is nothing more I can do."

She pulled at the hem of her handkerchief and said, "I know. I know."

The vigil began, and the family sat in a half-circle, in silence, around the bed. Shortly after midnight, the doctor drew a sheet over Papa's head.

Relatives and friends filled the First Presbyterian Church, listening as Doctor Marshall Dendy concluded the funeral service: "Will Taylor was the essence of manhood: honorable, devout, and kind; firm in his beliefs, but sensitive to others' needs. He built a fine business in the citrus industry and generously shared his wealth with his church and other institutions. He loved his family, his friends, and his city. He was a Christian gentleman whose name is deeply carved in the annals of Orlando's history. We commit him to his Maker. Let us pray."

The family led a funeral procession to Greenwood Cemetery; there, live oak and pine shaded Ann's, Adam's, and Billy Pastin's headstones. Andrew stood at the grave side watching pallbearers place their boutonnieres on Papa's casket. He gazed at the inscription on the family marker:

TAYLOR

Sunset and evening star,
And one clear call for me!
And may there be no moaning of the bar,
When I put out to sea.

Tennyson

The sun was bright and a gentle breeze blew out of the west, filling Papa's sails, Andrew believed.

The family gathered at Bellemere for the reading of the will. The estate was made up of 104 shares of Taylor Groves, Inc. stock. Assets of the corporation included 1,985 acres of orange groves in Orange, Osceola, Lake, and Polk Counties, and $1,000,000 in cash. Will's personal holdings totaled $850,000 in cash, bonds, Bellemere, and other miscellaneous personal property.

Will Taylor's attorney, Paul Knight, Jr., cleared his throat as he shuffled papers. "Mr. Taylor requested that I read a letter to you before proceeding with the reading of the will."

To my family,

All of you are dear to me. As you learn of the content of my will, I hope you will understand that what I have done is for your ultimate benefit.

Andrew, Alice, and Charlotte shall receive one-hundred thousand dollars each. I bequeath Tommy Lane four shares of stock in Taylor Groves, Inc. Rachel shall receive the remainder of my personal property, title to Bellemere, and all other assets, except one hundred shares of stock in Taylor groves, Inc.

I learned long ago that wealth does not provide fulfillment. Concern for one's fellow man accomplishes that end, and sharing with others is the manifestation of concern, therefore, the remainder of my stock in Taylor Groves (one hundred shares) shall be placed in the Taylor Foundation.

The President of Taylor Groves will serve as sole trustee for the foundation. It is my wish that Andrew serve as President of Taylor Groves.

With love,

Papa

Charlotte rose, her face reflecting fury. Like a rattler, she coiled and struck at Andrew. "Your name is not Taylor! You turned Papa against me. You encouraged him to give it away, to name you president."

Alice trembled as she spoke. "What a terrible thing to say. Andrew is good and fine. Who are you to question your father's decision?"

With a piercing look, Charlotte shrieked, "Shut your mouth!"

Andrew placed his arm around Alice, his voice low and soothing. "It's all right. It's all right."

Charlotte stomped out. Wind blew against her hot cheeks as she roared away in her convertible Buick, Papa's words burning in her mind: "*It is my wish that Andrew serve as president.*" Even from the grave, Papa had tried to keep her down, she believed. She gripped the wheel, her mind filled with poison. Wish. Wish, she thought. Papa can't determine who will be president. With Mama's and Tommy's stock, I have a majority. Andrew's outvoted. She hurried home to share her plan with Tommy.

The Taylor family sat in a circle of chairs at Bellemere, as Paul Knight opened the meeting. "The order of business is to elect directors, who will, in turn, elect officers of Taylor Groves, Inc. Shareholders are as follows: The Taylor Foundation, one hundred shares, to be voted by the Chairman and President of Taylor Groves; Rachel Adamson Taylor, twenty-four shares; Andrew S. Taylor, twenty-four shares; Charlotte Taylor Lane, twenty-four shares; Alice Nelson Taylor, twenty-four shares; Thomas Lane, four shares. The by-laws of the corporation state that shares may not be voted cumulatively, therefore, directors will be elected by a simple majority vote. A motion for the election of directors is in order."

Charlotte's voice was steady. "I move the following names: Rachel Adamson Taylor, Andrew S. Taylor, Charlotte Taylor Lane, Alice Nelson Taylor, and Thomas Lane." Rachel seconded the motion.

Paul Knight cleared his throat. "Are there other nominations? Discussion? All in favor of the motion say aye."

The motion was affirmed.

Before he spoke again, Paul Knight adjusted his tie. "Now, we will elect officers. Is there a motion?"

Charlotte raised her hand. "I move the following slate of officers: For President and Treasurer, Charlotte Taylor Lane."

Stunned in disbelief, Andrew glared at Charlotte. "Papa named me president and trustee. You can't do this."

"You didn't read the fine print," Charlotte sneered. "You must be voted in as president to vote the foundation's stock."

Andrew turned to Paul Knight. "Is she right about that?"

Knight nodded. "Yes. That is in accordance with the by-laws."

Alice placed her hands on her cheeks. "I can't believe this is happening."

"Is there a second?" Knight asked.

Rachel raised her hand. "I second the motion."

Paul Knight gulped water from his glass. "Discussion of the motion?"

Andrew looked at Charlotte and shook his head.

"All right," said Knight, "I'll ask each director to vote. Andrew Taylor."

"No."

"Charlotte Lane."

"Yes."

"Alice Taylor."

"No."

"Rachel Taylor."

"Yes."

"Thomas Lane."

"No."

An expression of confusion crossed Charlotte's face as she turned and looked at her husband. "No — What do you mean? Of course, you meant to say, yes."

Tommy stood. "No, by God. No!" He pointed a finger at his wife. "You squeezed the last drop of loyalty out of me when you turned your mother against Andrew. You made it appear he had defrauded the company. I should have spoken sooner, but didn't have the backbone. And now you go against your father's last wish. He knew Andrew has integrity, a thing you've never known."

Tommy's face was flushed as he dropped back in his chair.

231

Rachel gasped, her face distorted in pain. "Charlotte. You did that to Andrew?"

Without looking at her mother, Charlotte rose and stalked out of the room.

Rachel moved to Andrew's side, placed her hand on his arm, and shook her head. He stood and held her in his arms, her head resting on his shoulder. Finally, she pulled back, stood erect, and said, "I don't cry any more."

Andrew watched his grandmother withdraw and slowly climb the stairs until she was out of sight.

At eleven o'clock, Rachel, Andrew, and Alice sat around the conference table in Paul Knight's office. A fresh breeze blowing through the window stirred sheers bordered by burgundy panels.

"Now," said Knight. "We're here to elect officers of Taylor Groves."

Sitting erect and clad in black, Rachel made a motion, and Andrew was elected chairman and president. Tommy became vice-president.

"Is there a nomination for secretary and treasurer?" asked Paul Knight.

Andrew spoke up. "I suggest we defer the motion until a later date."

Rachel's nod ended the matter.

"Well," said Knight. "If there is no other business, the meeting is closed."

Rachel glanced at Andrew and said, "Stay a moment."

When the others left the room, she spoke with the weariness of old age in her voice. "Of course, you have every reason to object, but will you find a place for Charlotte in the business?"

Andrew hesitated before speaking. "I hold no grudge. The question is, can we trust her?"

Rachel lifted her chin and looked into Andrew's eyes. "I understand. Please take me home."

All the way to Bellemere, Andrew wondered if he and Charlotte could ever work together again. What would Papa have done?

That night Andrew called Tommy, asking him to meet him at the office in the morning. He inquired about Charlotte.

"She's all right," said Tommy, "but she will not leave the house."
"I understand. See you tomorrow."

Andrew had finished his second cup when Tommy walked in and closed the office door. Tommy dropped into a chair, lifted the coffee pot, and poured into his mug. "Can't tell you how badly I feel about things," said Tommy. "My whole world's coming apart. Our marriage may be finished. It all started in Winter Garden on the day our new packing plant opened, the day Papa told the crowd that you, Adam, and I were running the company. Charlotte was furious, felt left out, vowed to get even, and she took it out on you; then when Papa set your salary and mine at thirty thousand, and hers at twenty, she went berserk. Nothing I said did any good. She had to hit somebody, and you were it. I can't live with it any longer. Here's my resignation."

So, that was it, reflected Andrew, pride drove her to retaliation. Would Papa have denied her equal status to the men if he had known how deeply she was wounded? Andrew shook his head. "Tommy, you are vital to the success of our business. I will not accept your resignation. As far as Charlotte is concerned, I'll deal with her right now. Call her and tell her I'm coming to her home."

At twelve-fifteen, Andrew followed Tommy north on Orange Avenue to Lakeview Street, then right on Colombo Circle. They pulled into the driveway of the Lanes' home, entered and found Charlotte sitting by the fireplace in a pink upholstered wing chair. Tommy broke an awkward moment of silence. "Sit here, Andrew. I'll be back in a moment."

An air of chilled composure surrounded Charlotte as she waited for Andrew to speak. What could he possibly want? she wondered. Perhaps he comes to gloat, to finish me. Her voice was low and calm. "Well, Andrew?"

He settled back in his chair, then looked into her eyes, pausing momentarily as he collected his thoughts. "Charlotte, when the war ended, Patty and I came to Orlando with the intention of buying a small grove in Clermont and living out our lives there. It wasn't what I wanted, but under the circumstances, I felt it was for the best. But Papa persuaded me to rejoin the family business. More than anything, he wanted his family united. How many times have we heard him say, 'Family is everything?' He knew you lied about me, but he said you were his blood, and he would never turn you out. He believed that time would heal the matter. Later, when you attempted to vote yourself in as president, Tommy told the ugly truth about you. How simple it would be to smear your name, split the family forever, terminate Taylor Groves." Andrew shook his head. "That's not the way it's going to be. You and I owe Papa and Mama so very much."

Andrew rose and moved to her side. "Tommy offered his resignation, but I refused it. All we need now is the return of our office manager — not many Taylors left." Through her expression he knew that blades rammed through her heart.

"Don't do this. Don't open your arms to me."

A puzzled expression appeared on Andrew's face. "If not this, then what? Revenge? Hatred? In four years of war I saw too much of that. I realized that what I wanted most was the privilege of staying alive and coming home to family. Can't you understand that?

But the sternness in his face departed as tears began to well in her eyes. Assurance replaced agony in her expression. She rose from her chair and dabbed the corners of her eyes with her sleeve. She took a step toward him. "Stay for lunch, Andrew. I'm serving beef stew and biscuits — it's Ada's recipe."